BOURBON LULLABY

A Bourbon Canyon Novella

WALKER ROSE

LE Publishing

upon a time, the boy who read me stories when it stormed. My brothers hate him for the knowledge he took from our family's bourbon company to start his own empire. My sisters have forgotten him. But me? I'm going to be his new assistant.

To him, I'm just a temp with a deep knowledge about the world of spirits. But if I come clean about just where I got that know-how, he'll toss me out before I can find out what happened to the boy who calmed my fears.

How did the angry foster kid with a chip on his shoulder the size of Montana become the owner of a respected distillery? How did he get my adoptive father to show him so much of the family business, only to run away and become a huge competitor?

How could he disappear from our lives and forget me when I could never forget him?

He doesn't trust easily, and I'm only in his office because of a lie. But if that lie will get me all the answers I've been craving for twenty-two years, then that's what I'll do, right up until the moment he finally remembers who I am. And then it'll be my turn to disappear.

CHAPTER ONE

Myles

"Myles, is that how you spell your name?" Wynter asked, pointing at the drawing of a fuzzy bear in the book I was reading to her.

"No, mine is spelled with a *y*." I was perched on the edge of her bed, and she was rolled to her side, her stuffed ox, Bunyan, clutched in her arms and under her chin. I was reading one of her favorite books for the hundredth time since I'd been fostered by Mae and Darin Bailey.

The countdown was on. I would be eighteen and free to do a whole lot more once the clock struck midnight. I would go and take everything that was mine with me.

A few weeks after I first arrived, Darin Bailey had struck a deal with me. I could work for him for a paycheck if I promised to save it. And I had. I'd fucking *saved*. I'd worked my ass off.

by my shit. To own something that was *mine*. The money in my account wasn't a lot, but it'd get me farther than Bourbon Canyon, Montana. I had plans.

Pent-up fear pushed at the seams of my mind. Something bad was going to happen if I stayed too long. I would log in to my account tomorrow, and the money would be gone. Or the Baileys would blame me for something, anything, and I'd be *that kid* once again.

Sure, I'd been safe here for over two years. No one taking my money, no bouncing from home to home with nothing but a trash bag of donated clothing. But that was coming to an end, thanks to a specific birthday message I'd gotten earlier.

You're legal. No more system. I'll bust you out of that labor camp.

I had to go. On my own terms, or as much on my own terms as possible. And before the Baileys had to deal with a pile of shit because of me.

"Keep reading." Wynter nudged the book with her little finger.

"You know every word, Frosty."

She giggled like she did every time I used the nickname with her.

I had graduated in June, but if any of my old classmates could see me now, they wouldn't believe it. I was reading to a six-year-old girl.

Wynter and her three older sisters had been fostered by the Baileys before I'd come to live with them, and while the other girls had been numb and weary from losing their parents in a car accident, Wynter had been loud and inconsolable.

downpour and keep on going, but an old memory had driven me to grab a book and start reading. Recollections of days when I didn't know about death and drugs and foster homes had kept me reading. With each word, a new memory arose. Pleasant ones. Blissfully normal ones. So I had continued.

At first, I'd read to the empty air while she'd cried, and her sisters had fled the room. The Bailey boys had been out working with their father. I'd been wishing I was already eighteen and gone. Mae had been busy in the laundry room. Maybe it was the lack of witnesses that had made me change my voice with the characters, but the effect had been astonishing.

She'd quieted down. When I'd finished another book, she'd gone to the room she shared with one of her sisters and brought out another. I'd read that one. Mae had peeked out, nearly collapsing with relief when she saw what was going on.

From then on, when Wynter had a tantrum, usually when it was storming, I was called in to read. When she couldn't sleep, I read.

I turned the last page. As the final word rolled off my tongue, she blinked and rubbed her eyes.

"One more book?" She yawned.

Normally, I kept the limit to one, otherwise I'd be up to eighty books before I knew it. She asked anyway.

Tonight, I'd read one more. "How about the adoption one Mae got you?"

Her little lips turned down. "That one's boring."

I chuckled. Mae must've read it to her, to all the

"I don't know if I can call her Mommy," she whispered, her brown eyes wide, like she was scared Mae would jump in and announce the adoption was off.

"Mae doesn't care what you call her." As far as foster parents went, Mae and Darin topped the list. Maybe if I'd gone to them first, I wouldn't be the asshole I was now, a cocksucker to everyone but a girl who had cried like she knew my pain. "Go on. Lie back and I'll read it. You can dream about becoming Wynter Bailey."

"Wynter Bailey," she murmured, frown still in place.

I read the book. By the time I was done with the story about a fox I'd read a hundred times, Wynter was asleep, her head turned and Bunyan escaping the crook of her arm.

I pulled her covers up. "Good night, Frosty."

I shut the lamp off. Now that she was asleep, all I had to do was load my grocery bags full of all the clothing I owned in the world into the beater car Darin had given to me, and I'd be off. I'd drive all night until I hit Denver. Bigger city, more options. Easier to get lost.

I took one last look at the little girl who'd kept me from destroying my chances at yet another foster home. She'd made me feel useful. Worthwhile and productive.

Guilt tightened in a band around my chest. I wasn't used to missing people or places, but leaving was harder than I'd expected. I'd never see her or her sisters again, but her life was better without me in it. The Baileys would raise her and her sisters like their own. She'd have three big brothers to protect her. She didn't need me.

"I'll miss you," I muttered to the dark room and

plan to return to Montana, and with a big family like this to grow up in, I doubt she'd ever leave. We'd never see each other again. "Enjoy your new family."

CHAPTER TWO

Wynter

Twenty-two years later . . .

You know what they say about a man with a big building . . .

I giggled to myself and stopped. The top three stories of the four-story building were lined with big windows, and someone might see me laughing to myself alone in the parking lot. My chances would be over before they started.

I stared up at the imposing brick edifice and clutched my leather bag tighter to myself. Foster House Whiskey. The building was at its tallest on one end—the old mine headquarters?—and it was like another, newer building had been constructed right next to it. The place had been purchased, restored, and converted into a distillery by its imposing CEO and owner when the man had been barely old enough to drink.

I had a few minutes before I checked in. I peeked at my phone. Was I looking for a reason to abandon my foolish mission and go home to Bourbon Canyon?

A message from my sister Summer popped up.

Still open.

My mouth quirked. There was a job opening at my family business. A marketing spot that was perfect for me, like it'd been made for me, because it had. But after months—I let out a sigh—years of stalking Myles Foster, I'd finally found my opening. Besides, I couldn't go home. Not yet.

So I'd tracked down Myles. A sensible person would've emailed. Called. Written a message in the sky via plane. Of all my options, the plane would've been the easiest.

Myles Foster did not do people. He apparently didn't care to talk to anyone, he emailed only when absolutely necessary, and he'd probably ignore messages written by planes. The only contact information on Foster House's website went to his PR team. He had no social media, no dating profile that I could find, and no public phone number.

I'd already tried going through his company and hit a wall at customer service.

The boy who'd disappeared one night without telling me was elusive. I shouldn't have been surprised.

I was curious about him. I had questions. But mostly, I wanted to...

I didn't know what.

Time to cater to that curiosity.

I left my sensible Honda hybrid SUV in the parking lot and strode to the entrance. The heels of my ankle boots struck the asphalt in succinct clips, and the mountain breeze kept me from breaking a sweat in the early July sun. One wall of the distillery was nothing but windows, making the stills visible from the outside. Copper stills matched the metal brackets that attached the thick wooden posts to the walls and ceilings.

The entrance was on the office side of the structure. When I stepped inside, I slowed. The interior of the distillery was breathtaking. Wood, metal, and stone were artfully arranged to make the place look like the mountains' centerpiece.

A guy in a sharp yellow polo shirt the same shade as the Foster House label smiled brightly at me. His name tag read *Braxton*. "Hello," he said much too cheerfully for 7:53 in the morning. "How may I help you?"

Did they have that many visitors show up before the typical workday started? The distillery gave tours, but they didn't start earlier than ten.

"I'm here for the temp position with Mr. Foster."

His expression didn't register shock. He'd known who I was before I'd walked in the door. "Yes. Mrs. Crane is expecting you." He glanced at the clock, and dismay flickered in his expression.

"Is something wrong?"

His features snapped to neutral professional. "Absolutely not. You can take the stairs to the fourth floor or use the elevator around the corner."

I eyed the steps. Four flights. The journey would be

"If I cheat and take the elevator, will you hold it against me, Braxton?"

He smiled, revealing a dimple. "*I* won't."

Okay. On that foreboding note, I found the elevator and took it to the top.

An imposing grandfather clock faced the elevator when the doors slid open. More wood- and metal-accented brick made up the exterior walls. The office was posh with a rustic, Aspen-ski-lodge aesthetic that fit right into the whole playboy-bachelor vibe.

Was that what Myles was? Did he go skiing and leave a wake of satisfied snow bunnies behind him?

I'd snooped on the man. Stalked might be a better word, but snooping made my browser history seem less obsessive. The same professional headshot circulated through all the magazines with the exception of a local spread that had one sole picture of him standing in front of a copper still with the impressive view behind him.

He'd oozed power from the page. His piercing blue eyes had been intense and his mouth a flat line. He looked less volatile than when he'd been a teen, but infinitely more powerful and commanding.

Flutters raced through my stomach, zinging from side to side. I left the quiet safety of the elevator and found an older woman behind a desk, reading glasses perched on the end of her nose. The collar of her maroon silk blouse was high, like she chose her wardrobe by the century and not the atmosphere.

She glanced up and a wide smile spread across her face. I'd spoken with Mrs. Crane before, but this was the first time we were meeting in person. We'd gotten along

smoothing her black A-line skirt.

Good thing I'd chosen anything but jeans. My houndstooth leggings and pink cashmere off-the-shoulder blouse were almost too casual compared to Stella Crane. "Good morning, Ms. Kerrigan. Nice to meet you in person."

"Wynn, please." She'd called me Wynn when we'd talked. I extended my hand to shake hers, but she rounded to my side.

She put a firm hand between my shoulder blades and leaned in to speak quietly. "You'll have to go by Ms. Kerrigan around here. Mr. Foster prefers the formality."

I let out a short laugh. "It's a distillery."

She stopped abruptly, her expression guarded. "Why doesn't that mean professional?"

Shit. I was going to get fired before I started. "Sorry. The distilleries I've worked in before preferred a casual environment. The staff was family." Literally.

Stella relaxed and started shuttling me toward an imposing office that was walled off from the rest of the floor. "Yes, well. Mr. Foster is more..." She gave me an almost sympathetic smile as she poised her hand close to the door. "Well, just more." She knocked.

"Enter."

The deep vibration of his voice rippled over my skin, caressing my ear. That wasn't the voice I remembered.

I didn't notice the expansive office. My attention was centered on the man.

Broad shouldered in an ash-gray suit, he had his back to me as he stared out the window. His ink-black hair

The window faced the lot. How long had he been staring out? Had he seen me gazing back? Had he witnessed my giggle?

He looked over his shoulder, not quite seeing me. "You're late."

I recoiled despite the delicious things his voice did to my nerve endings. "It's not even eight."

Mrs. Crane jerked to look at me, her eyes flaring.

Oops. But seriously.

"Early is on time, and—"

"On time is late," I finished, smiling. One of Daddy's favorite mantras. Myles remembered.

"Do you make a habit of interrupting?" He finally turned, and my smart retort stuck in my throat.

The man was *fine*. His suit was cut perfectly, tapering from his wide shoulders to his waist. Those eyes. They hadn't missed a thing years ago, and they were harder now. The clench of his jaw could crush diamonds. Instead of a tie, the collar of his white dress shirt was open. One button only, but enough to expose the strong column of his throat.

He was so tall that I'd be able to nibble along his neck while he—

"Ms. Kerrigan." His voice was a whip crack.

Double shit. I wasn't supposed to have sexual thoughts about Myles. I snapped my gaze up, meeting that flinty stare. "Sorry?" Had I missed something he said?

I leaned forward, unable to pull myself back. I looked deep into his eyes, searching for recognition. I wasn't the little blond child who hated getting her hair

after an even worse breakup—were growing out and tucked behind one ear.

Did he know who I was? People I'd grown up with called me and my sisters the Bailey girls, but the Baileys hadn't adopted us yet when Myles had lived with us. Would he remember my last name?

His unyielding stare remained cold. No hint of recollection. No wish for reconnection.

A spark I'd kept lit for twenty-two years sputtered out, going dark. He didn't know me? At all?

"You didn't answer my question." He almost seemed amused to have startled me into silence.

This couldn't be the same Myles who'd read me stories about a bunny with his name. I'd thought I didn't know what I'd come here for, but that was a lie. I wanted to get to know the guy he'd grown up to be. I wanted him to remember me. I wanted to know if a scared little girl had made as much of an impression on him as he had on me.

"Ms. Kerrigan?" He enunciated each syllable.

Mrs. Crane folded her hands and tipped her head down. She was going to let him be a condescending ass to me. Was this attitude normal, or was it some kind of test? Either way, could I handle it?

I snapped my spine straight. I wasn't leaving. This wasn't the Myles Foster I knew, no. *Mr.* Foster had built Colorado's fastest-growing independent distillery, selling award-winning small-batch whiskey in a highly saturated market before the age of forty—which he'd turned less than a month ago in June. This Mr. Foster employed over fifty people between the distillery, warehouse, and

loyalty, then part of him was still that boy who used to read me stories. The kid who'd even sung when the book called for it. His pitch had been terribly off-key.

My sisters and I might not have changed our last name, but we were still Baileys. We'd grown up learning Bailey principles and Bailey charm. We hadn't been taught to give up. "Sorry, Mr. Foster." I curved my lips into a smile that always infuriated my oldest brother. "I didn't want to interrupt."

He narrowed his eyes.

Mrs. Crane drew in a sharp breath that made her cough. She pressed her fingers to her lips. "Oh my. Excuse me."

Myles wasn't distracted. He kept me in his irate tractor beam. "I find a flippant attitude doesn't work well in this environment, Ms. Kerrigan. You may go."

I needed a moment before his words caught up with me. "Excuse me?" I had to be wrong. I'd come so far. I'd planned this. I couldn't leave now that I had him in front of me. He had no idea the impact he'd had on my life. Or the effect his departure had had on me.

If his eyes had been cold before, they were frigid now. The temperature in the room dropped ten degrees, and goose bumps broke out over my skin.

"You're fired, Ms. Kerrigan."

I sat cross-legged on the floor of my apartment on the southern outskirts of Denver. The complex was teeming with people and surrounded by even more complexes

in the right direction. But soon I'd be returning to the stunning view from Mama's doorstep. I'd been fired.

I seethed over my bottle of wine. I hadn't bothered with a glass. Drinking an entire bottle was better than downing a pint of my family's bourbon. I was pissed, but I didn't want to fuck myself up. Merlot was a safer option for a pity party.

Half-empty packing boxes were piled around me. Yesterday, I was half unpacked. Tonight, I was half packed. Maniacal laughter bubbled out of me.

Myles fucking Foster.

I was jobless. Instead of moving in, I had to move out.

My brothers were right. Myles was a selfish prick. He didn't care about anyone but himself. He'd taken our car and all of Daddy's knowledge and built an operation that competed with us.

Technically, he specialized in whiskey while the Copper Summit brand was built on bourbon, but we had lines of whiskey, too. Daddy's grandpa had started with bourbon, giving our hometown the name Bourbon Canyon, but the family business had expanded. Copper Summit now had whiskey and bourbon distilleries in Bozeman, Billings, and Helena.

Montana made. Montana proud.

The phrase was on our labels.

"Fucking Foster has 'Make every house a Foster House.' Ugh." I huffed out a breath and took a swig from the bottle. Merlot wasn't the best for rage drinking, but the wine had been left by the ex who'd caused my bangs.

A message buzzed on my phone. Summer again.

the Bourbon Canyon office. I had wanted to see the country and experience a life I couldn't find in a small mountain town that had more cattle than people. I hadn't wanted to return to a family who ranched those cattle.

And now I had to do all of that. My plans would have to wait, and it wasn't Myles Foster putting them on hold. Not completely.

HOT GIRL SUMMER

Come on, Wynn. You know he's not going to last long.

The back of my neck grew hot. As if I needed more anger tonight. I punched out a message.

Quiet naggging me.

I hit send and squinted. Shit. I spelled a couple words wrong. She was going to know. I couldn't hide from Summer even two states away.

My phone rang. *Hot Girl Summer* popped up on the screen. I answered with, "You know people our age don't actually make phone calls."

"They have to when their little sister is getting drunk on her own in the city."

"Of all times for autocorrect to fail me," I muttered and took another drink. What I'd give for a good maple-bourbon splash.

"What's the beverage tonight?"

I wrinkled my nose. "Wine."

"Oh, good. Not a guy problem."

boyfriend duties. I didn't care about breakfast in bed or a dozen red roses. Myles looked like he could destroy a girl in all the best ways, and most of them happened between the sheets.

I shivered. I hadn't expected to be so attracted to him. My obsession had started as a little girl's adoration. He was my Prince Charming. He had battled my dragons when I was scared. Then I'd seen his picture as an adult, and the curiosity had smoldered until I'd seen him.

Then he'd opened that wicked mouth.

Could he fuck as hard as he talked?

"What's going on?" she asked.

I couldn't tell her. It was why I'd gotten a place that was solidly in Denver and not closer to the distillery. I couldn't chance any of my siblings figuring out my true goal. If I confessed to Summer, she'd think I was crazy and tell my brothers. They'd tag-team me with their lectures about wasting my time. They'd be even more upset that I was thinking of working for the enemy.

Foster House wasn't direct competition, but they *were* competition, and that was enough for most of my family to feel betrayed. My brothers, really. My sisters rarely mentioned Myles. Daddy didn't seem bothered. He just said, *You gotta be better. Otherwise you're not the best.*

Myles was the harshest. And the hottest. "I got fired. And he was an asshole about it."

"Who?" she asked, indignant.

The beautiful thing about family who were also close friends—they were incensed before knowing the full

She scoffed. "Wynter, you are not going to be an assistant when you can come home and be in charge of the whole marketing department."

My family was holding the position for me. I had even been doing the work before I'd moved away from Bourbon Canyon. Before I'd let my apartment lease go and moved to a town where I knew one man, and he didn't know me. "Just for a little longer." Long enough to learn about the guy who'd gotten me through some of the worst times of my life.

"But Daddy..."

I rolled my eyes to the ceiling, and the room spun. "Daddy's sick. I know." I'd gone home for a few days last month. I'd talked to Daddy, and what he'd said had nudged me over the cliff from cyberstalking to applying for a temp job. *Home is where you land. Fly until you want to go home.*

I needed to fly a little longer, and Stella Crane was supposed to have surgery. She'd never said what type, and it wasn't my business, but it was going to be lengthy, and she needed someone to replace her. But her domineering boss hadn't wanted to hire a replacement, temporary or otherwise. Even if I was *perfect* for the position. I'd been groomed for distillery work. Like Summer said, I could run the show. Any one of us Baileys could—even all the Kerrigans.

"Daddy's not going to last much longer." Her voice cracked and tears burned the backs of my eyes.

"Fucking cancer."

"I know. Every time I get a phone call from Mama or

"Yeah," I whispered. Losing both parents suddenly on a stormy night? That had been a nightmare and had caused bad dreams and a fear of storms for the rest of my life.

"Remember when Mama Starr would buy a ton of toilet paper for people who lost loved ones?" Summer giggled. Mama Starr was our birth mother when we had to differentiate her from Mama Mae, who was Mae Bailey. We'd also called both our fathers Daddy. We'd been lucky enough to have both in our lives, however fleeting. "I was so mortified to be walking up to a house where everyone else was carrying a casserole, and Mama had TP in one hand and paper towels in the other."

I laughed with her, but my memory drew a blank. "I must've been too young to go with you."

"Autumn still gets embarrassed when she thinks about it." Summer sighed. "You sure you're okay?"

"Yeah. I'm giving myself tonight, and then tomorrow I'll figure out what I want to do." Going home to watch Daddy grow weaker and frailer wasn't it.

"What if we found a way for you to work in the Bozeman office with me?"

My heart warmed. Summer could be a pain, but she was always looking out for those she loved. Working next to her would be fun, but I hadn't expected to leave Colorado so soon. "I'll let you know."

A little while later, I hung up and stared at my nearly empty wine bottle. The room was spinning around me, but I scrunched up my face. I missed Bourbon Canyon. I missed waking up and seeing the mountains every

I missed being surrounded by family.

I might not remember a lot about Mama Starr, but I distinctly recalled the fear of having no home. Of my meager belongings being packed in a garbage bag while a stranger spoke to me in slow, overly enunciated words.

My stuffed ox, Bunyan, was on the couch.

"Myles, is that how you spell your name?"

"No, mine is spelled with a y."

Such a simple exchange. So patient with me. He'd argue with Daddy, a little less with Mae, and my brothers had constantly bickered with him. But with me, he'd had all the time in the world.

What had made him such a cold bastard?

Would I be satisfied never knowing?

CHAPTER THREE

Wynter

I could be bullheaded at the worst of times. The imposing distillery towered over me, more intimidating than it had been yesterday.

Instead of my pink sweater and houndstooth leggings, I was in a hot-pink, slouchy top that showed off my black-and-gray sports bra, black yoga pants, and my athletic shoes. My pounding head couldn't be bothered to find something more impressive.

What was I doing here?

I didn't want to leave Denver without Myles knowing who I was. I'd come to reveal myself and see how he reacted. Yet my determination seemed like a bad idea in broad daylight.

The man I'd met yesterday wouldn't care I was Wynter Kerrigan. He probably hadn't ever stepped foot in Montana again and would resent a walking reminder of the childhood he'd left behind.

comments about the various fosters who'd lived with us. Myles had been through several homes, and most of the time his departure had been at the request of his foster family. Then the Baileys had taken him in and made him a deal to help him save money until he turned eighteen.

My heart tugged just like it did every time I thought back to that morning I'd learned he was gone.

Before he'd come to live with us, he'd been shuttled from home to home all over Bozeman. He'd had bruises on his face when he'd first come to the house. A fight at school I'd been told, but I had been scared of him until the lull of his voice had cut through my fears.

I'd never heard how he lost his parents—or if they were still alive and how they'd lost him.

I had a lot of questions, and I probably wouldn't get answers. Yet I'd driven all the way south of Denver to the outskirts of Castle Rock. The view was lovely with white-tipped peaks in the distance, hills and valleys cut by winding roads. The town itself was sprinkled with quaint shops, some giving off an Old West vibe, family housing, and sprawling businesses that pulled the area into the twenty-first century. They were picturesque mountains, but not the ones I'd grown up seeing. A beat of longing echoed behind my sternum. I missed home.

I might as well finish what I'd come to do, or I'd berate myself for being a coward the entire forty-five-minute drive back to my apartment. Then I could get a big breakfast and nurse the dull headache that refused to go away.

Inside, I smiled brightly at Braxton and kept walking. "Good morning."

"I'm here to talk to Mr. Foster." I continued toward the elevator.

He scurried to catch me. Was I going to get hauled out of the building before I hit the elevator? I veered for the stairs. I was wearing workout clothes after all.

Braxton was trying to circle around me like a herding dog. "But Mr.—"

"Let her up."

Both Braxton and I stopped and tipped our heads back. The stairs went one direction and then another, switching back two more times. The very top railing allowed Myles to lord over everything from the foyer on up to the ceiling.

He was doing it now. Glaring down at me, the blue of his eyes deeper than yesterday. Ridiculous that I could tell from here.

"Mr. Foster?" Poor Braxton. He sounded terrified, and it was my fault.

I steeled myself. No. His fear was because of Myles's management style, not me.

Myles only dipped his head to ease Braxton's anxiety. "Ms. Kerrigan. A word?"

"Really?" I muttered. Annoyance pushed at my temples with my hangover. I'd been ready to body-slam the front desk guy—who wasn't much younger than me but seemed infinitely more innocent—and now Myles was *asking* for my time? Yesterday, he couldn't run me out fast enough.

Wait. Did he know who I was? Had it registered, and he planned to chew me out?

His gaze sharpened like he'd heard me, and my heart

From his vantage point, did I look like a field mouse would to a hawk?

A hawk was too mild. Too small. What was more threatening than a hawk? An egret? A falcon? Definitely an eagle.

"Ms. Kerrigan? I seem to have to repeat myself around you."

I tipped my head all the way back, my fear retreating, and irritation taking its place. This motherfucker. He hadn't been this much of a prick as a kid, had he? "Patience is a virtue, Mr. Foster." I adopted a sweet smile. "I'll be right up."

I refused to take the stairs. By the time I reached the top, wine would be leaking out of my pores, and I wouldn't give him the satisfaction of knowing I'd gotten drunk over him. As if he'd care anyway.

My stomach lurched with the elevator. Vomiting on his expensive loafers would be the highlight of my trip.

When the doors dinged open, he was there, hands stuffed in the pockets of his charcoal-gray trousers. He wore a matching suit coat, and again, the faint blue shirt was kept loose at the collar. He was casual yet severely professional.

"Ms. Kerrigan."

The thud in my head dulled at his voice. Because of course it did. His voice had been my balm long ago. The effect had only gotten stronger with time.

"Mr. Foster," I said as if I weren't dressed for Pilates and hadn't cocked off to him minutes ago.

"Come to my office." He strode away.

I had to shoulder past the closing elevator doors and

Inside his office, he didn't bother closing his door. Did that mean he'd chase me right back out after he told me he knew who I was and that he didn't appreciate liars?

I hadn't lied. Technically.

He waved a hand to a plush chair that was more comfortable than any furniture I'd planned to buy for my apartment. I took a seat as he sat behind his desk. The wood matched the beams on the ceiling, and it was filled with neatly piled reports, two binders, and one laptop. A single pen sat atop a stack of papers.

He leveled his stern gaze on me. My body didn't know whether to overheat or ice over. The tension riding in my gut was an uninvited guest.

I folded my hands in front of me, the epitome of calm when my insides were a torrent. "You wanted a word?"

His stare intensified, and he sat back, reclining but nowhere near relaxed. He had an elbow propped on the armrest of his office chair. "Mrs. Crane had to take leave earlier than expected."

"Oh no. I hope everything's okay."

I waited for the accusations. That I was spying on him, or that I was snooping, or that I was being a creep, and if a guy had obsessed about a girl like I had about him, he would get a mugshot and a lawyer. But he only spoke about Mrs. Crane.

Worry formed a lump in my throat. I had wanted to be mad at her for leaving me hanging like a carcass for Myles to berate, but I understood. This was her career.

His lips tightened further, if that was possible. "Nothing serious, but she's out until her ten weeks of sick leave kick in." He sucked in a sharp breath. "Leaving me in need of an assistant."

Glad she was okay, I tapped my index finger against the back of my other hand. Anytime now. I was ready to face my humiliation. Then his meaning sank in, and I froze. "Me?"

"I understand we got off on a bad foot yesterday—"

I barked out a laugh. "You mean how being only two minutes early personally insulted you?"

His expression went arctic. "You seem to have a habit of interrupting."

I didn't miss the power shift between us. I wanted to learn about Myles, but I didn't need this job. He needed an assistant, and he had no clue who I was. "I'm from a big family. It's either talk or get run over."

A ghost, a hint, a mirage of what could someday form a smile played over his lips. He was accepting my explanation? It was the truth, but he came off as a no-excuses kind of guy. "Right. Try to refrain in the office. I don't like repeating myself. The pay and hours would be the same as what Mrs. Crane arranged with you."

I nodded and crossed one leg over the other. His gaze clocked the movement, then rose back to mine. The air sizzled between us and heat seeped into my body, heading south at the worst possible time.

I'd been too into learning about Myles Foster for too long to be unaffected by him. Had he even thought about me? About my family? I opened my mouth to tell him who I really was and find out—but I bit the inside

knew I was Wynn Kerrigan, interested in working in the distilling industry. He didn't know I was also the scared little girl Wynter, one of the Kerrigan sisters from his past. What would happen if I told him?

The Myles who'd fired me for not being early enough would not say *What a coincidence! How have you been?* The Myles who'd sent me packing would think I was a lying liar and want me out of the building as fast as my hangover would allow without vomiting. I wanted to get to know the Myles who was willing to rehire me. The Myles who made my insides zing and gave me very adult sensations.

This man wasn't one to welcome his past with open arms. None of his history had been in any of the society pieces about him, only that he had been a foster kid. People loved a self-made, rags-to-riches success story, but he'd never used it as additional fodder for their articles. Much of what I'd read was nothing but conjecture.

He might be intensely private, or he might hate the Baileys. I didn't know, and I wanted to. I wouldn't let him cut me out of his life again. Not until I knew why first.

When I didn't ask questions, he continued. "You'll miss the training window you would've had with her the next two weeks, but she assured me that you were competent and knowledgeable about the business."

I nodded. Had Mrs. Crane ditched him on purpose? Had she left him hanging because he'd ruined what had likely been a meticulously planned leave?

My respect for her rose several notches. "That's fine. I'm a fast learner."

He didn't know? Was Mrs. Crane the only one with access to my résumé? And she hadn't told him? Perhaps she didn't know about his strained relationship with the Baileys of Copper Summit Bourbon.

I'd use her lack of communication to my advantage. I couldn't tell him I'd worked at Copper Summit in every department since I'd been a teen, but I could give him other truths.

"I've worked with the marketing teams of Leopard Print out of Wyoming and Raging Ears out of Idaho. I was also involved in setting up retail distribution with a few local distilleries in North and South Dakota." All true. Just via Copper Summit. Daddy was generous and believed a rising tide lifted all boats. He liked helping budding distilleries with his experience and guidance.

The back of my throat ached. Thinking about Daddy these days did that.

Myles studied me. "So why aren't you working for them? Why are you interested in a temp position with Foster House?"

Did he always sound so suspicious? "As I told Mrs. Crane, I wanted to know if the Denver area was for me before I got locked into a lease and couldn't move."

"Are you from a small town?" Annoyance pinched his eyes like he couldn't believe he cared enough to ask.

"Very small" was all I said.

One nod was all I got. "Are you interested?"

My attention sharpened. I was so interested. Oh—in the job. "Yes. I'll even strive for five minutes early in the mornings."

His features didn't crack. Did he know how to smile

Crane's workspace. She emailed instructions I can forward you and a link to her procedure manual."

"Thorough," I murmured. I looked down at my clothing. I'd been almost underdressed yesterday. What I was wearing today was ridiculous compared to him. "I'm not exactly ready for a day in the office."

His gaze stroked down my body. "I can be assured you'll dress appropriately tomorrow?"

I needed to fan myself. My internal temperature rose twenty degrees when he looked at me like that. "So appropriately."

A slight narrowing of his eyes was all I got. He might not find me funny, but I was enjoying the small reactions I got. I couldn't wait for the next three months.

&c

Myles

Why was I giving this goddamn tour?

Normally I loved strolling around the old mining headquarters I'd purchased and renovated into a distillery before I was thirty. The location had made sense, an old mine I could purchase for cheap, but more importantly, the mountains had called to me more than some empty warehouse in the city. While the mine was being renovated, I'd planned the rest of the company. I almost wished I could do it again.

I could talk corn varieties, best sources of oak barrels, and evaporation rates all day. I could discuss flavoring with my distillers. But my job was to run this place. To make it the best so all my employees had jobs to support themselves with.

I didn't give the fucking tours.

But I'd be working closely with Ms. Kerrigan, so it made sense.

The excuse rang weak in my head. While Ms. Kerrigan got a tour from another employee, I could work on polishing the most important pitch of my life.

Instead, we wandered past the mashing pots while I explained where we sourced the corn from, then into our fermenting rooms, and past our stills. Finally, I took her to the barrel rooms at the far end of the place.

"Your packaging and distribution take place in the city, correct?"

Every time she asked a question, a thrill zinged through my blood. She didn't ask normal, touristy questions. She probed my relationship with the farmers and how I'd formed those bonds with producers outside of Colorado state lines.

I wasn't a Colorado-only guy. I was a whoever-could-get-me-a-quality-product-reliably guy. When I'd told her that, she'd only nodded, not revealing her real thoughts. Opinions I should care nothing about. I'd met her barely twenty-four hours ago.

"Yes, the process is in the city for now," I answered. "The barrels are transported to a warehouse in town, where they're packaged and loaded for distribution. Currently, I have contracts with local liquor suppliers, but in two months, I'll be pitching to Mainline Grocers."

I dipped my head. "Then we'll expand and move packaging on-site."

She peered at me. "You don't like hauling?"

I shook my head. "The effort and cost are better utilized elsewhere. We're beholden to weather and aging times. I have to make sure we're efficient in every other aspect to optimize profit."

Her stare intensified. "I've heard others say the same."

So had I. One of many insights I'd cataloged over the years.

I'd thought about my exposure to the industry more in the last year than ever, and giving Wynn a tour of the distillery was bringing all sorts of memories back.

The woman next to me was also jumbling my thoughts. I'd seen her yesterday in the parking lot, gazing at the building with rapt appreciation. She'd been stunning by her car, four stories down. Up close, she'd been...disconcerting.

I had no issues controlling my body's reaction around women. I'd met none who were more interesting to me than the tasting room on the second floor. And then Ms. Kerrigan had arrived with her apple ass in tight pants, a sweater that hinted at the dip in her waist—and how her breasts would feel in my palms—and her teasing attitude.

Maybe I'd gotten used to women fawning over me. They vacillated between mild interest and rampant delight aimed toward my pocketbook or my dick. Many ignored me, which was fine. Better, most times. Ms. Kerrigan looked at me like she saw beneath the suit to the age of ten.

Usually when I got that feeling, I wanted to crawl out of my skin, carve the person out of my life. But it wasn't like that around my new assistant. She wasn't digging for weaknesses to hold against me. She just saw me. Then she saw past me. She spoke to me like she was innately interested in the work I did, like she understood it and had a passion for it that wasn't normally found in the people I interviewed.

Leave it to Mrs. Crane to find the perfect temp employee.

Fucking Mrs. Crane. She knew what she was doing when she called to tell me she was sick and had to nurse herself to health in time for the procedure she was having done. I'd upset her carefully laid plans and her detail-oriented procedure manuals, and she'd used the system to teach me a lesson.

"Any further questions?" I asked, my crankiness coming out. I hated change. I'd had enough of it, and Mrs. Crane had been my rock in a windstorm for years.

Ms. Kerrigan was a pretty crystal I wanted to admire. I wanted to hold her in my hands and find out how much she warmed the longer I touched her.

"No further questions." The slight mocking in her tone punched me farther down than my gut. Her voice was a sultry purr, as if she couldn't help it.

When she had first walked in and aimed a shiny smile at Braxton, I'd been tempted to fire him. I'd be a grade A asshole if I did that. Even worse if I blamed the tight black pants and hint of skin around her shoulder for my irritation.

face and the rest fan-tailed behind her in a clip. Casual Wynn was harder on my control than Business Casual Ms. Kerrigan.

I spun on my heel to head back to my office. "I'll get you a passcode for the door. It'll work when I'm in the building only. You'll need an ID, and there's an HR packet waiting for you to fill out on Mrs. Crane's desk."

"Cool." She fell in step next to me, her head tilted away from the sunshine streaming through the floor-to-ceiling windows. Her steps were rushed to keep up with me.

Out of the corner of my eye, I caught a grimace. "Everything okay, Ms. Kerrigan?" Why did I fucking care? I wasn't normally involved in my employees' personal lives.

"I didn't sleep well." She didn't elaborate. As if the reasons behind her slumber were none of my damn business.

"I sincerely hope your calendar is clear. We'll have some work trips to take in the next couple of weeks."

"Mrs. Crane told me. I'm free."

Was she single?

Her left ring finger was empty, but she wore rings on her middle fingers and her right ring finger. No necklaces, but she had three holes in each earlobe. I couldn't say if Mrs. Crane had ever worn so much as a necklace.

I took the stairs, not bothering to see if she'd follow. I hoped she didn't. I needed to get back in my office and remind myself that work and pleasure didn't mix. I didn't need to think about my assistant's toned legs and what it would be like to get between them.

CHAPTER FOUR

Wynter

Working for Myles sucked.

I stifled a yawn and stared at my computer until my eyes straightened out. The first text to clear on my computer was the time.

7:52 a.m.

The constant pings from Myles through the night had disrupted my sleep. He'd said he didn't expect me to drop everything outside of work hours—which surprised me—but when a thought occurred to him, he sent the missive off.

Schedule a time to talk to Ellie about new yeast strain.

Ellie was the master distiller and almost as scary as Myles. She was closer to his age than mine, had five kids, and rattled through timelines of batches so fast my head spun. I couldn't keep up with notes, and Myles would impatiently fill in. I started using dictation in addition to note-taking.

Double-check time with Wes.

Wes Clayton was opening a trendy club in Denver, the second version of one in Colorado Springs. He also had clubs in Oklahoma City and Dallas. Wes had been on Myles's radar since Myles learned Wes's clubs didn't carry Foster House products.

I would triple-check the time and location of the meeting with Wes. It was this afternoon when Wes arrived at the club in Colorado Springs. I was leaving with Myles right after lunch.

I yawned again, grateful my back faced my boss's office.

Myles was at work before seven a.m. but didn't expect me to be there until a quarter to eight. He stayed until at least eight p.m. from what I could tell from the bulk of his messages, but he often dismissed me at six. He only ordered in one meal a day, but those muscles weren't starving. How early did he wake up? Did he collapse from exhaustion as soon as he stepped foot into his downtown loft? Or did he have a mansion in the foothills? A ski lodge all to himself?

When did he have time to hone that body?

A guy with his physique couldn't *not* work out. He was piled with muscle, and he never called a department like IT or HR, he marched there, taking the damn stairs every time.

Thankfully, he let me stay behind at my temporary desk surrounded by pictures of Mrs. Crane's two kids and five grandkids. Our first work trip was coming up soon. We would drive, but he had a private jet when

As for the job itself, it was simple. I got the access code for the main door and an ID card. I learned which files were where, who I had to talk to for what, and the rest was muscle memory. Daddy had made all of us do a term as his assistant when we were old enough to work. He'd paid us and made us save most of the money for college—which he'd then paid for in full and claimed we had a good down payment for a house instead. Since I was the youngest, I had worked as Daddy's assistant the longest.

I'd been in on meetings with suppliers and distributors. Pitch meetings to get our product onto store shelves and into bars. But I'd never been as nervous as I was about flying solo with intimidating Myles and his workaholic ethics.

Had he worked this hard on the ranch? I'd been too young to be a part of chores. He'd helped Daddy in the distillery, too, a fact that inflamed my brothers' hard feelings. Myles had taken family secrets and profited off them. Big-time.

Maybe I'd feel differently if I'd met a man who vacationed in Paris or holed up in a cabin in Aspen with a new snow bunny every night, but looking back on his calendar the last few years, I found no fun time penciled in. Myles worked, and he worked some more.

My brothers would be shocked. Daddy would—

Would Daddy be around for me to talk to him about my experience with Myles? I couldn't tell him yet. I didn't have more to the story than I was working with the man, and he didn't know who I was.

I'd made it through three hours of work when

looked. His cologne was like hiking through the mountains on a bright summer day.

Was that why Myles chose that cologne? Did he miss Montana?

Did he miss us? At all?

"Ready to go, Ms. Kerrigan?"

I swirled my chair and sat straighter. His suit coat was gone, leaving him in only his one-button-undone shirt and heather-gray slacks. His brown loafers gave him a more relaxed air. A trendy businessman in his off state. Even his hair had gone casual, with some strands falling over his forehead.

"Ms. Kerrigan?"

I was staring. Only complete honesty would save me from revealing that I dreamed about being the one to run my hands through his hair. "Sorry, I wasn't expecting pajama day." He was also early for the meeting with Wes.

A small frown tugged at his lips. "Pajama day?"

I waved my hand up and down his frame. "You're practically ready for bed, Mr. Foster."

One corner of his mouth twitched up, and I stopped breathing. Was he going to smile? "My meeting today requires less formality," he explained.

"Stiffness is overrated."

His expression froze for a heartbeat before his gaze intensified. "Stiffness is never overrated, Ms. Kerrigan, under the right circumstances." I sucked in a breath and almost started coughing, but he continued smoothly, "However, Wes Clayton is known for his modern and trendy style. I don't think he'd appreciate a full suit."

I had to be mistaken. That hadn't been innuendo. It

aren't opting for a pair of powder-blue frames, tight brown slacks, a pink polo shirt, and shoes that match the glasses?"

"I still have to be myself." He shoved a hand in his pocket, striking a pose straight from the ad he'd bought the cologne from. "Wes's style is his."

I lifted a shoulder. "It works for him."

His blue eyes turned to ice, and the air between us turned frigid. "Indeed. It's time to go." He started for the stairs.

A shiver raced down my spine. I grabbed my tablet and yanked my backpack from my bottom drawer. I stuffed the tablet, some notepads, and a pen inside and raced to the elevator. If I'd known I'd be climbing in and out of a car chasing Myles, I'd have worn pants instead of a sleeveless summer dress with a flowing skirt. At least I'd bypassed heels for a pair of wraparound sandals.

Myles was waiting by the front desk, chatting with Braxton when I rounded the corner off the elevator.

Braxton was even grinning. When I approached, he was saying, "Of course, Mr. Foster. Thank you so much."

"Anytime, Braxton. Don't hesitate to come to me with anything."

Curiosity burned a hole in my head. Myles wasn't the type to make people smile. He'd been nothing but professional to all his employees, protective, even, as he'd explained their roles and the good jobs they did. I might've melted a little when I'd caught hints of fondness, but seeing him chat with Braxton was a new view into Myles Foster. His shoulders had relaxed, and I caught a flash of the teen I'd known.

Braxton winced for me and gave me a finger wave. "Bye-ee."

I sent an air smooch his way and breezed out, smiling. The front desk clerk was one of the highlights of my day. Everyone at Foster House treated me well, but I was nothing more than a temp employee to them. I was used to working with family, with all the employees being unabashedly up in my business, so it was hard to work where I didn't matter beyond my position. Braxton was friendlier and made each day a little brighter.

Myles hadn't loaded himself into the black SUV. He stood holding the door open. His driver was in the driver's seat. Weren't they usually the ones holding the door?

"I don't like to be late, Ms. Kerrigan," he said as I slid in.

Ho-ly shit. The interior was a sophisticated mix of black and wood accents that should have looked dated but only came off as expensive. The real shocker was the privacy shield between us and the driver.

"It's like a limousine." What he said finally sank in. "Wait—late for what?"

He adjusted his position and pulled the seat belt across himself. He gave me a pointed look until I did the same. Of course I always wore my seat belt. If he would remember who I was, he'd know.

"The lunch meeting with Cadillac Sam."

I only knew who Cadillac Sam was because the guy took out ads in every bathroom stall in every restaurant, club, and gas station in Colorado. But that was the extent of it. "I didn't arrange a meeting."

blocked out from eleven thirty to one.

"I saw that, but I didn't realize it was a business lunch."

"The blue is a standing lunch with Sam."

"You're on a first-name basis with Cadillac Sam?" The guy owned the most popular chain of liquor stores in Colorado and was spreading into every state that shared a border with Colorado. I hadn't dealt with him, but my oldest brother, Tate, had. Tate described Sam as charming, gregarious, and cunning, but a businessman first and foremost. He'd said Sam didn't tolerate people who couldn't look beyond his 1967 Cadillac DeVille convertible, ten-gallon hat, and bushy gray mustache.

"Sam and I go way back. He was the first major retailer to carry Foster House."

"And because he did, you were able to level up." The car kicked into gear. I studied Myles. This was my chance to learn what made him tick other than corn yields and the bottom line. "You feel like you owe him."

Myles tucked his phone away. "I owe a lot of people. Sam and I both like to talk business. He's...he reminds me of someone." He stared out the window. Conversation over.

Typical. The man filled me with more questions than answers.

The restaurant we pulled up to was not what I'd expected. Based on the car, I'd thought we would go to a downtown place with glass walls, a place that used wine-glasses for water and served their filets perfectly balanced on three stalks of asparagus. A pasta palace in Castle Rock wasn't where I expected to find the Myles

that still managed to be delicious. Myles didn't eat carbs.

I was seeing a new side of him. Interesting.

The driver stopped and opened the door. I waited while Myles murmured to him, and then we were heading inside. Sam was easy to spot. He had a corner booth. His hat took up half of it. A Western tie with a turquoise center was the same one Sam wore in all his pictures.

Sam scooted out, grin in place. "Myles, how's it going?" He shook Myles's hand and pulled him in for a hearty hug with a solid back thump.

I was riveted in place by Myles's almost smile. He had sexy-as-hell crinkles at the corners of his eyes and admiration shining in his gaze. "I'm well, Sam. You?"

"Eh, joints are noisy in the morning, and the back hurts more than it doesn't." He turned his wide grin to me. "Mrs. Crane finally ditch you for the gardening gloves?"

"She's out until the end of October. This is Wynn Kerrigan, her temporary replacement."

"Wynn, nice to meet you." He stuck his hand out.

My entire hand and wrist were encompassed in a warm handshake. "Nice to meet you, Mr.—"

"Sam," he said, saving me from having to remember his last name. Daddy and Tate would chide me—*Always know your colleagues*.

"Nice to meet you, Sam."

He ushered us into the booth. I was opposite Myles. Sam liked to engage us both. I took my tablet out to take notes on anything significant Sam had to say about

I was most shocked by the dish Myles ordered: spaghetti carbonara. A buttery, creamy pasta that had almost no protein. I had ordered the same since I hadn't been able to concentrate on the menu while listening.

When the food arrived, Sam tabled the business discussion and turned his attention to me. "How 'bout you, Wynn? Where'd you work before this?"

Thankfully, I'd rehearsed my vague background more since starting with Myles. "I interned in a couple distilleries in college, and then I went to more school and got my MBA."

Sam's expression turned incredulous. "And you're his temp assistant? I'll poach you myself." He snorted.

I chuckled, aware of Myles's focus on me as he steadily ate his food. "I'm trying to decide what I want to do with my life." I knew what I wanted to do. I knew where I wanted to work. But first I had to satisfy my obsession with the man who ate as if he didn't worry about one drop of sauce getting on his shirt. I was tempted to tie my napkin around my neck.

"You went to all that school, and you don't know what to do?" Sam asked. Humor laced his words, but there was more. Tate had described Sam as shrewd, too. He was the type of guy who'd keep pushing.

Myles didn't seem to care less about who I was outside of my assistant role, and Sam was too interested. I'd dabble in both satisfying Sam's question and giving Myles information I wished he would ask for.

"Honestly, I'd like to move closer to my family, but my dad's dying, and I can't stand to be around and watch him slowly waste away."

gently touched my shoulder. "I'm sorry about your daddy."

"Thank you. Losing parents is rough."

His bushy brows drew together. "You lost your mama?"

I only nodded, afraid the whole story would spill out. That I'd ruin my shot at getting time with Myles, time that I couldn't explain why I needed.

"Hell, kid. I'm sorry about that, too."

I gave Sam a thankful smile, then slid my gaze to Myles. His look was assessing, but he dropped it and returned to eating his food.

Right. I'd thought he would care about a scenario that echoed his own past, but no. For the rest of the meal, I questioned why I was still in Colorado.

◦○

Myles

The Rizz in Colorado Springs looked like its owner. Loud pops of color over a sleek and modern vibe. Wes Clayton used the youngest and trendiest designers when possible.

I was sitting at the bar, on fucking uncomfortable stools, with Wes acting as bartender. He was drinking a vodka gimlet, Ms. Kerrigan had ordered a club soda with lime, and I was having an old fashioned with whiskey from another Colorado-based company that put out a

The sun was high in the sky outside, but inside, the lights were low. Neon beams lined the wooden epoxy bar, and an indie band's melody flowed through the speakers.

A few minutes after meeting Wes Clayton, I'd realized I was way too fucking old for him. He talked like he was Gen Z despite being closer to my age group. He sounded like a social media influencer and constantly said *Fair* whenever I discussed a limitation in my distribution process.

Wes Clayton came off differently in person than he did online, and I didn't have high hopes for the outcome of our meeting. There'd be no contracts or agreements drawn up. He'd tell me he'd call me later and ghost me like he probably did all his much younger dates.

I didn't know for certain, of course. But I'd gotten adept at reading people, especially selfish dicks, during my time floating from home to home. Wes was as transparent as the frames perched on his nose.

"The thing is, Foster." He steepled his fingers. Wes had guffawed when I called him Mr. Clayton, but I had been taught not to assume anything about a potential client, or any client. Never assume, no matter how well I knew them. Business first, friendship second. Wes Clayton and I weren't friends. "Foster, Foster." He clicked his tongue. "I like to work with companies that are philanthropic first."

I'd never heard the word used like that before, but I knew an excuse when I heard it. "I understand."

"And, well, if I follow the Foster House trail, it only leads to money. I can't find community support, or spon-

Anger clawed at the back of my throat, hot and quick, reminiscent of my youth. This motherfucker. I was no longer that kid. I was a grown-ass successful businessman. "Can you spell it out?"

"You see, Clayton Enterprises pays out five hundred thousand a year in donations alone. We also have several internships and sponsorships and"—he laughed—"I also sponsor a little league team. As for scholarships, I've set up an endowment fund at three different colleges to provide scholarships for several students who major in entrepreneurship." He folded his arms across his chest, a smug look in place. "I prefer to collaborate with others who also pay it forward, including my suppliers."

At my side, Ms. Kerrigan had quit taking notes. She watched our exchange, wide-eyed. Tension rode through me. Having this exchange in front of her grated on me. What did she think?

Mrs. Crane would remain quiet. Later, in private, she'd cluck, comment on Wes's arrogance and ignorance, and we'd move on with our day. My regular assistant was apprised of the full scope of my business. She also knew I detested justifying myself.

"An admirable notion," I said and shot back the rest of my old fashioned, knocking my teeth on the round, neon-blue fake ice cube that assaulted my senses. Even his ice was pretentious. There was nothing wrong with a perfect cube of ice, slowly melting and softening the notes in the whiskey, drawing it out like a lazy melody.

"It's more than a notion, bruh."

I set the glass down with a thunk. Wynn flinched.

His arrogance glowed almost as brightly as my ice

My anger swelled larger, bumping against the restraints I'd locked it in. "Oh, yeah? How big's your house?" Goddammit. I could keep my cool better than this. But guys like Wes reminded me of the assholes I'd fought in high school. Entitled pricks who picked on me because they thought they could. They were wrong, and Wes would find out I didn't lie down and cover my head while taking a beating.

His conceited smile slipped. "Excuse me?"

In my periphery, Ms. Kerrigan rolled her lips in like she was trying not to laugh. The girl surprised me at every turn. She never acted how I expected. There was no wanting to scurry away, skittish. She was watching the show.

So I would give her one. "Your house. The profits. Don't you do fundraiser runs? Five Ks, correct?" He nodded once, still looking confused. "And you use that money, the money *other* people donated, to slap your name on little boys' T-shirts."

He opened his mouth, but I talked right over him.

"And that endowment fund has your name—at least the name of your clubs, and they're only set up in the towns the universities are in, correct? Because what's a donation good for if no one knows you gave it? The sponsorships serve you somehow. Whether it's a tax write-off, to get your name out there, to recruit from the over-twenty-one crowd on campus, or to seduce bright, young interns into working grueling hours for you so you can enjoy all the money you keep to yourself. In fact—if I were to buy this drink, would I be asked if I wanted to round up and donate to some charity your fingers are

helps people, that's a bonus. But you should know not all of us want the glory and the recognition. Some of us form corporations we run our businesses under so we can contribute without the fanfare. I don't need an invite to some bullshit charity auction so other rich fuckers can stroke my dick and call me good. I don't need to prove anything to myself, certainly not to you. You want to run your business that way, fine. I was taught by a mentor who made a real difference in people's lives not to assume facts about my colleagues. It's a good way to lose money."

Ms. Kerrigan stiffened next to me, but I couldn't look at her. I was holding Wes's scandalized gaze.

To his credit, he recovered quickly. After giving himself a little shake, he propped his hands on his hips. "You talk a good game, Foster. Are you telling me that you didn't use the play on your last name and your experience in the foster system to capitalize profits, yet do little to pay it back? You're not tugging on heartstrings about your poor, downtrodden childhood to make a mere living? What kind of house do you live in?"

"If you knew anything about how I grew up, you'd shut your fucking mouth, Clayton, and you'd know I don't owe anyone a goddamn thing." My voice cut between us like a serrated knife. I shouldn't have sworn. I strived to maintain professionalism with every breath, but this fucker made me slip. "You knew you weren't going to work with me, yet you wasted my time and brought me here to peacock about your *philanthropy*. How very generous of you." I pushed back. "Ms. Kerrigan."

get me to slow. I wanted away from Wes and the defensive asshole I reverted to around him.

"Good luck on your pitch with Mainline," Wes called. "I have a good friend on the board. I'll make sure to speak with him before next month."

I pounded out the door, rage fighting back the panic his words incited.

The driver scrambled out of the car, but I had already opened the door. I lifted my chin to let him know to load up and be fucking ready to leave. I tapped my foot while Ms. Kerrigan practically dove into the back seat.

I was pissed, my blood boiling, but I didn't miss the way her skirt rode up the backs of her thighs, giving me a tantalizing view of more bare flesh than I'd seen on her since she'd started.

She settled, pulling her skirt down, as I climbed in. Strands of her hair were hanging in front of her face. She puffed at them and snapped her seat belt in place. I did the same, glowering out the windshield. The privacy screen was down, and I was grateful for the view.

"Who was the mentor?" she asked quietly.

"What?" I snapped, then reeled my temper in. Again, she'd surprised me. I'd thought she'd comment on Wes's attitude, or ask me how I paid forward shit in the world.

She didn't shrink. She leaned forward, her expression earnest. "The mentor who taught you not to assume. Who was it?"

I worked my jaw, the story clamoring on my tongue to spill out. I never talked to anyone about the man I considered a mentor. "You wouldn't know him."

about what was said back there?"

The moment I dreaded. "Is it about what charities I support?"

"Not really. Just if what he said was true, that you don't support charities. You made it sound like he couldn't be more wrong, yet I'm sure he did his homework. Guys like Wes are calculating."

She was correct. "No. It's not true." That was all I'd give her. I kept my name out of all donations if possible. The less attention on me, the better.

"Did you know what his house looked like before you made the comment?"

"Ms. Kerrigan, that's two questions."

"Indulge me, Mr. Foster."

There was that damn purr again. If she used that tone again, I'd tell her everything about my company while getting on my knees and lifting that damn dress up her curvy legs. "I make it my business to know everything about the people I work with. I don't like to—" I chewed on my tongue. They were only words. She wouldn't know the meaning. "I don't like to go into a place unprepared. I want to know what to expect."

Her eyes softened as if she knew the exact reason I behaved the way I did. If she hadn't already known I'd been in the foster system, thanks to nosy interviewers, then Clayton had revealed the fact. "Oh. Right."

"And yes, he has a house in Washington Park that he bought for one point seven million, another home in Dallas where he built his first club, and a beach house that's more of a shack. He's financed to the hilt, and he compensates by paying his staff shit while creating a

Confusion dimmed her soft brown eyes. "Yet you wanted to work with him? You wanted Foster House on his top shelf?"

A question I'd asked myself once. "You have to make money before you can give it away."

Her gaze intensified. "Another tip from your mentor?"

"He had a lot of them." Of all the things that we'd done today, she'd gotten hung up on the tidbits of advice. "Are you going to write them down?"

"No." Her smile was faint, maybe a little sad. "I think I'll remember."

I turned my gaze out the window to watch the snow-tipped mountains in the distance. Usually I worked while commuting, but the entire drive back, my mind mulled over the confrontation with Wes Clayton...and the way Ms. Kerrigan's dress lifted when she got into the car.

CHAPTER FIVE

Wynter

The events of the meeting three days ago continued to run through my head. In six weeks, we'd meet with the wholesalers. Since the meeting with Wes Clayton, Myles had replaced the stick in his ass with a titanium rod. He'd been holed up in his office, demanding reports and data on sales and production possibilities. He had all the numbers, but he wanted it arranged in a million different spreadsheets with almost as many projections.

The master distiller was annoyed with me. The manager of the packaging plant was taking longer to respond to my messages, and I didn't dare piss off the grain suppliers. I knew how finicky they could be.

My stomach rumbled. It was almost time for an afternoon break. Since it was Friday, Myles had ordered in pizzas. I had made a comment to the HR manager about the delivery costs this far out of town, and she'd

Understated generosity must be his thing. He'd been upset enough at Wes's accusations that I knew there was more to the story. Did his response mean he was more than the meal fairy?

The edge in his voice when he'd sworn at Wes... Shivers danced across my skin. I'd liked it.

His voice had power over me.

I wandered down to the third floor. The break room wasn't a little forgotten room in a dim corner. Open windows in the brick bathed the room in light. Long wooden tables were rimmed with chairs comfortable enough to nap in. The savory smells of pizza filled the air. Braxton was sitting at the corner of one table. I grabbed a couple slices and a bottle of water and sat across from him.

His plate was empty. He pushed it aside and leaned in close. "What happened the other day? Mr. Foster has been a storm cloud." He spoke in hushed tones, like the room was wired and fed to Myles's office.

"I don't know what I can say." I was dying to tell someone. I couldn't tell my siblings who I was working for. They thought I was still looking for a job. If they knew I was with Foster House, they'd rush down here and demand to know why I was a traitor. Then *Myles* might think I was a traitor, gathering state secrets or something.

I did have access to his recipes, but I didn't care. Daddy always said being authentic was more important than being the winner. Other than the basics, Foster House's blends weren't like Copper Summit's whiskeys.

"I shouldn't have asked." Braxton looked around like

"Intense?" I asked.

He smiled, showing the dimple. "You picked up on that?"

"Immediately." I'd known that almost my whole life. Odd thought. But I was dying to get more information on Myles. Maybe I could give Braxton a little and get something new in return. "Someone accused him of not being charitable."

The dimple disappeared. "Like how?"

"Donations, scholarships, sponsorships, and stuff." How much should I say? How much did Braxton know? I had to give a little to get a little. "He even accused My —Mr. Foster of exploiting his foster kid history."

Braxton laughed. "Whoever said that knows nothing. I mean, just look around."

"How so?" My curiosity was spilling over. I wanted to shake every Myles detail out of the guy.

"Me, for one. I was a foster kid."

"Really?" I shouldn't be surprised. Myles hadn't been the only foster with me and my sisters. Children of all ages had come and gone, though none stayed as long as Myles. I hoped those kids had lost the stunned fear, the palpable loss by the time they were adults.

Braxton nodded solemnly. "He's even helping me get into college. The scholarship I have for the fall is somehow linked to Foster House. Full ride. And then there's Arya in IT. She was in the system, too. Hailey, Tanner, and Julio. Several more who have come and gone. He's hired us all and helped us move on if we want different careers." His sunny smile was back. "I'm going into fermentation science. I'd love to be a Myles Foster."

great."

"Thanks. My boyfriend doesn't drink alcohol, but I promised I'd make him a steady supply of kombucha."

"You'll save him so much money."

Braxton laughed. His gaze lifted to the door, and he blanched. "Mr. Foster."

"Braxton." That hard tone rumbled right through me, leaving need in its wake. "Ms. Kerrigan. I need you to take notes on my meeting in ten minutes."

"I'll be there." I shoved pizza in my mouth to keep from looking guilty.

"See to it." He sucked the cold air out of the room when he left, leaving only the hot sun radiating on us.

I chewed and smirked at Braxton.

He picked up his plate. "I wish whatever asshole upset him knew what he was putting us through."

I swallowed. "Don't worry. The guy got a severe dressing-down."

"Would've loved to have witnessed it." He tossed his plate and left the break room.

I'd seen Myles let loose just a hint of his temper. How spectacular would it be if he lost control in other ways? I had to fan myself while eating the rest of my food.

⁃◦

My eyelids drooped. I might be young, but I'd been told I had an old soul and that included being ready for bed by eleven. It was almost midnight, and I was still at the

Myles had the cuffs of his shirt rolled up, and I'd been drowning in muscle and veined forearm porn for hours. Dark hair dusted his skin, and my fingertips tingled at the thought of his strong chest under my hands.

Being tired made it harder to forget how attracted I was to my temporary boss. Add in the low level of anxiety rising thanks to the light pattering of rain on the window, and I wasn't thinking clearly. I would have to drive back to the city in rain. I hated driving in bad weather. I disliked bad weather, period.

I blinked at the blurry screen. We'd pored over tables, rearranged data, reinterpreted information to determine the various quantities Foster House could supply for a national distributor without sacrificing flavor and quality. We wouldn't be working this late if Myles thought the amount was satisfactory. He didn't say it, but he was worried he couldn't fulfill expectations with the facilities and staff he had. He thought Mainline Grocers would turn him down flat.

A few times, I'd caught him muttering, *We can't sacrifice the product for money. The money will come after the quality.*

Again, I was struck silent by the familiar phrases. Myles had been put to work on the ranch. As far as I knew, and from what I'd gleaned from my older siblings, Myles hadn't worked in the distillery very often. Was it possible he'd accompanied Daddy there more than we'd realized?

Frustrating that Myles wouldn't discuss it.

hand for several heartbeats, and tucked his phone back in his pocket. I'd noticed that before with certain calls and messages. Get lost in the screen, then ignore.

Who was calling him? A woman? Several women? Someone from his past? Who did he have in his present other than Cadillac Sam and the employees of Foster House?

More questions. No answers.

I rubbed my eyes as more tables and timelines flashed on the screen. No matter how Myles positioned the numbers, Foster House fell short. He'd need to make deals with more suppliers. More suppliers meant more corn and grain to use and store. More use meant more mashers, more stills, more space, more staff, more, more, more.

This place was big. There was room to grow, but not for a pitch weeks away.

"What if you came at them a different way?"

Piercing blue eyes that didn't show an ounce of fatigue shot my way. "How would that be?"

The yawn that was close to working its way out was crushed under the weight of his direct scrutiny. My idea had seemed revolutionary seconds ago, but verbalizing the thought was terrifying. I'd witnessed exactly how he felt over a week ago when he'd told Wes Clayton off.

"Um..." Adrenaline dripped into my veins and chased away my sleepiness. "You're trying to sell them on numbers, but it's the story that sells."

His gaze sharpened like the last time I'd spouted some of Daddy's advice. "I've already sold them the story. That's how I landed the meeting."

successful businessman." I scrubbed my face again. I was committed to saying what was on my mind, but I couldn't watch him turn to an icicle that could stab me when I did it. "Look, I know you told Clayton you don't want the recognition or the admiration, but other people need it. That's just the way life works."

"I don't need to cater to—"

"Yes, actually, you do."

"You're interrupting again, Ms. Kerrigan." This time, I might've heard humor, but I might just be that tired.

"Like I said, in order to be heard in my house, I had to talk over strong personalities. You're kind of in the same boat. In rural Colorado, you're becoming a big deal. But if you want to be the next Jim Beam—"

"I don't want to be the brand of the masses. I want to be the go-to top-shelf brand of serious whiskey drinkers."

I scowled at him. "Now who's interrupting?"

He pushed back and crossed his arms. Time for bicep porn. The thin fabric of his shirt clung to the bulges like I wanted to.

When he didn't speak, I continued. "So, if you want to be a nationally recognized top-shelf brand, albeit on a smaller scale than Jim Beam but a whole lot bigger than you are now, then you'll have to create a deeper story. You might want to consider sharing more of you."

His jaw turned to granite.

I held my hands up. "I know. I'm from a private family, too." Everyone in our small town knew our business, but outside of Bourbon Canyon, people only knew what Daddy wanted them to know. "And I get it, you

guy?"

He arched a dark brow.

"But what if you gave them those numbers? Since you started Foster House, how many kids who've been in the foster and juvenile system have you helped? If you've formed scholarships, how many college kids have the funds helped? How many adults got back on their feet because whatever umbrella company you formed made it possible? You don't have to divulge names or even specifics, but maybe tell them generals. Tell them why it's important to remain incognito." Another idea sparked. "Maybe you spin it as your contributions in the community are as customized and individualized as your product. Something like 'Foster House makes top-shelf whiskey, and we pay it forward, top-shelf-style.'"

I blew out a breath. There, I was done.

He dropped his gaze, something he didn't do very often. A small furrow formed in his brow. "That's a horrible tagline."

I laughed. "That's what you have marketing people for." I didn't mention I'd majored in marketing in college. I was sleepy, dammit.

He pinched the bridge of his nose, and for the first time, he seemed weary. A moment later, he was back to being sharp. "I might be able to work with that."

My triumphant joy was wiped out by a crack of thunder. I jerked, and Myles's attention was back on me full force.

"I don't like driving in storms." If I told him I hated thunder and asked him to read to me, would he figure out who Wynn Kerrigan really was? Didn't seem like a

He pushed away from his desk, stood, and went to the windows. Lightning flashed, outlining him against the night—broad shoulders, unshakable resolve, authoritative stance.

He pulled up his phone. "A large system is rolling through. Strong weather for at least an hour."

Anxiety clawed at my throat. "Shit, really? I *hate* driving in storms," I muttered again. Then it'd be really late, and I'd be driving at night while extremely tired.

"You're really worried?"

I could tell him. Reveal everything. I wanted to know how close he really was with Daddy. I wanted to know what he thought about the Baileys. I wanted to know why he'd formed his own distillery empire when he could've been invited into the Copper Summit world.

I wanted to know why he'd left me.

Yet the odds that he'd open up to me instead of driving me out of town were dismal. He was a vault. I'd now created a situation where keeping the truth from him only made the telling of it more complicated—and looked worse for me.

"It's a fear I haven't been able to kick as an adult," I explained. "And I'm not used to staying up so late." He kicked up another brow as if to ask why a young, single woman was in bed with a book by ten. "I don't have a good reason to be out late anymore."

His gaze hooded, and he looked away. I might be reading into his reaction, but from what I knew of him, he'd make sure I had a damn good reason to be up late, one that wasn't work related.

Fear skittered across the back of my neck. "I can't stay in the distillery alone." I sounded like a coward, but I'd be the only soul at the base of the mountains southwest of Denver. The security system would only tell Myles's team what bogeyman had attacked me and when, but cameras wouldn't help in the moment.

He gave me a funny look. "Ms. Kerrigan, where do you think I live?"

"In Denver?" Where else would he live?

"Here." More lightning flashed across the sky behind him.

"Like, *here* here?"

He pointed to a door on the far end of his office. I had assumed it was a closet. I'd ignored Daddy's advice about assumptions there. "When I got the loan for the place, I couldn't afford the payments on top of another mortgage or even rent. So I moved in." A muscle pulsed on each side of his jaw. Was this an admission he didn't want to make?

Wouldn't Wes Clayton be surprised? I was. Myles had a big fucking house, but his living space was only as big as a decent-sized loft. "You have a better view out here than any place in town."

The corner of his mouth quirked. "I doubt that. My windows face the mountain. It's a lot of rock."

Almost humor. I'd take it. "Good thing you spend so much time in your office. That view is stunning."

"Yes, it is. Wide open and full of possibilities."

"It's why you put your office on the top floor, facing this direction, isn't it?" He could see out. The mountains behind the building, but visible in the periphery, and

parking lot. "You don't like being limited."

"No. I don't." He drew himself straighter. "And you don't like to drive in storms. You shouldn't either. The road gets hard to see, and the highway isn't much better. I'll be right back."

He disappeared through the door, and I almost fell off the chair craning my head to see into his loft. All I caught was a dark, open space.

A few minutes later, he returned and dropped the blankets and pillows on the plush couch against the wall of his office.

"You actually use that thing?" I'd thought it was nothing more than decoration. A prop.

"It's quite comfortable. I've spent several nights on it when I was working late."

"With your loft next door?"

His gaze strayed to the window. "I like to work."

Or...he had nights where the past blocked him in with the mountains. His offer to sleep on the couch carried more significance if that was the case. It was like offering me his safe space.

I might have the best sleep of my life and then—shit. "What about the morning?"

"What about it?"

"I don't have an apartment next door. I'd like to clean up and change, but what will people think?"

A flash of heat lit his eyes, and he fisted his hands at his sides. "Right. You can get up when you feel it's safe to travel. Take tomorrow off."

The weekends were long enough. I had explored Denver, but I worked too much to make friends. Satur-

rifle-shot messages coming in at all hours of the night. "I don't need the whole day off. If you decide to pivot with your pitch, then you'll need help. I can run home and come back."

He ran his hand along his jaw. The scrape of his whiskers against his hand set a steady, inconvenient beat between my thighs. "Very well. I'll make tomorrow a lighter day. I need to think about what you said."

"Oh." The warm sensation in my belly was worse than the desire filtering into my veins. "Sure."

He glanced around, his gaze bouncing off the couch. I was afraid to move. The intimacy of making my temporary bed wasn't like when he'd sat with me and read. We were both adults now. The energy between us had changed from comforting and understanding to sizzling and tense.

"I'll let you rest." His tone was as clipped as his steps to his loft. He disappeared inside.

Was I so tired I was imagining a connection between us?

I shook my head. A peal of thunder rattled the windows, and I jumped for the couch. The glass was making the storm seem closer. Thunder bracketed the building. God, I hated the sound, but I could collapse from relief at not having to drive in this weather. I whipped the blankets out and climbed onto the couch. The booms were relentless, and my heart was wedged in my throat. His scent surrounded me and was the only reason I wasn't trembling.

I couldn't ask him to read to me. Even if he did know

Yes! I grabbed my phone, brought up one of the conversations with the master distiller. Ellie did most of the talking, but I fast-forwarded to a spot where they'd had a back-and-forth about different spices to add to a batch of mash.

The noise of the storm faded to the background, and after twenty-two years, I got to fall asleep to the sound of Myles's voice again.

CHAPTER SIX

Myles

I stared at the arched ceilings in my bedroom. The whole loft was my bedroom. I didn't plan to get married and have kids, so I'd made the entire space open. I didn't like being shut in. I hated being limited.

Sunlight poured through the windows. I was normally out of bed and in my gym by now, but I hadn't been able to rouse myself from the covers.

I had a girl under my roof.

Technically, she was sleeping in my office, but my dick didn't know the difference. My morning erection didn't care that she was an employee. The prick had no concerns about workplace fucking. I wasn't sure what Ms. Kerrigan would say about any of it, but I was better off not knowing.

Seeing her every damn day, wondering what different ways I could discreetly ogle her, was a steady torture that

If I was smart, I'd be figuring out a way to keep her on staff. She was intelligent, knowledgeable, and capable, and the rest of my staff liked her. She'd fit in at Foster House. I didn't know a thing about her, but I knew that. I trusted Mrs. Crane with a large portion of the inner office, and I'd trusted her with hiring a temp. I only cared they were proficient and interested in the industry, not me. Several times I was tempted to message Mrs. Crane and ask for details on Wynn Kerrigan, but the less I knew about the alluring woman with the big brown eyes and pale hair, the better.

Wynn.

A perfect name to breathe into her ear as I was thrusting—

Fuck. I needed to get to the gym. Run off this unwanted lust. When the pitch was over, I'd find someone to burn it off with.

My dick did not like that idea. A stream of longing went through me.

Fine. Fuck. I was lonely. I didn't have relationships. I fucked here and there, but pursuing women wasn't a priority. Enough of them chased me that I didn't have to go looking. I wanted it that way. I kept it that way on purpose.

I rolled out of bed and squinted out the window. The landscape already looked greener after the rain last night.

I ran through the shower instead of going to the gym. The pitch was on my mind and what Ms. Kerrigan had suggested. She was right, dammit. I didn't want to put myself out there, but I'd have to in order to go in as

I checked the time. No one would be here for two hours. Had she left yet? I'd slept fitfully enough I would've heard, but just in case, I put on a white T-shirt and tossed on a pair of gray sweats.

I should've gotten fully dressed, but last night had gone late, and I picked comfort over dressing for the position I wanted. Another thing my mentor had taught me, but I was wound tight and slacks would only be more constricting.

The lights had been left on, but my office was bright. I flipped the switches off as I made my way to a lump of blankets on the couch. Was she still here?

I approached. Pale hair stuck out the top.

My world tilted as I stood over her. Her small frame was tucked deep into the blankets I'd yanked off my couch from when I watched a rare movie after work or when Gianna was especially dramatic and wouldn't quit blowing up my phone. Wynn was sleeping in my things and the rightness of it settled into my soul, making a nest just as she had on the couch.

What do I do? Let her sleep?

She was afraid of what others would think. I knew what they would assume. An attractive woman with a sharp mind and round ass that wiggled when she walked, sleeping in my office? No one would think she'd taken the couch, and I'd been on the other side of the wall. Doubt would be planted, and it wouldn't be my reputation that suffered.

I couldn't have that.

If you borrow something, give it back in better condition.

Another mantra ramming through my head. I

"Ms. Kerrigan."

She didn't move.

"Ms. Kerrigan."

Still no response. How hard did she sleep? She was rounding on just over five hours if she'd been able to settle down right away. A short night, but still manageable.

"Ms. Kerrigan," I said louder.

A small moan left her, and she burrowed deeper. I liked that sound way too much. The corner of her phone stuck out from where it was buried between the back cushions.

"Wynn." Maybe her first name would work.

Nope.

I nudged what I hoped was a shoulder. Anything else would be highly inappropriate, and unfortunately enjoyable. "Wynn."

A whimper that was less appealing and more resistant to waking up came from the lump in the blankets.

I shook her shoulder. "*Wynn.*"

She popped up with a gasp. Her hair rained over her face in a tangled mass. "Oh my god. I'm late for chores."

"What?"

"What?" She aimed her wild gaze at me and froze. Her gaze fell to my chest, then south of the waistband of my sweats.

Christ, if she kept looking there, I'd be hard in seconds. I cleared my throat, and she jerked her attention up. Again her gaze dipped to my chest.

Ms. Kerrigan had an odd fascination with my collar line. I often caught her looking at the base of my throat,

caught her.

She's not for you, jackass. I'd given myself many things that I'd been deprived of, but this woman wouldn't be one of them. She made me think about things that were better left forgotten. Fun and free evenings. Someone waiting at home or that I could talk with, cook supper for.

I'd seen homes like that. I'd lived in one once. Twice. It was hell when it went away.

Then there was the way I'd started talking about my past, opening up. So damn easy around her—and I didn't even fucking know her. She was temporary. That had to be why.

I could handle temporary things.

"Oh." She buried her face in her hands. "Sorry. It took a minute to remember where I was." Her shoulders shook, but I caught the laughter. "I wasn't snoring, was I?"

"No." Her snoring would probably be sexy, too. She made taking notes alluring, with her eyes narrowed in concentration and her pert nose wrinkling. "No snoring. It's six thirty. Thought you'd want to get going before people started arriving."

She popped her head up. Her eyes turned amber in the morning light. "Right. My pristine reputation." She flung the covers back. Another gasp rang out. She flipped the blankets back, but not before I caught a swatch of bare stomach and a glimpse of sunny yellow underwear. Her skirt had ridden all the way up, and her shirt was half twisted around her torso and caught in her bra.

come face-to-face with morning wood number two. Or was it still morning wood number one, since I'd never taken care of the first round?

"I'll give you privacy." I strode toward my loft, desperate to put distance between me and something I wanted so much and couldn't have. I hated that feeling, but for some reason with Wynn, I craved it.

Ms. Kerrigan.

She could never be Wynn to me. She was temporary, just the way things I couldn't control were supposed to be.

CHAPTER SEVEN

Wynter

I had just hit the road back to work. My apartment was on the south side of Denver, the side closest to Castle Rock. At least I was used to commuting. From my house to Bourbon Canyon. From Bourbon Canyon to Bozeman. And from Bozeman, anywhere. To trek anywhere in the Montana countryside, the hours stacked up.

The drive from my place to the distillery wasn't more than a half hour if traffic was light. I'd get there by three, and I couldn't shake the feeling of being late. Myles had messaged me with a stern order to take my time, get a nap in, and eat some food. Then he'd followed up with a **Seriously, eat a good, late lunch, and be here by three**.

My radio went silent as a call came through. I recognized the number. Summer.

I answered. "I wasn't ignoring your messages."

I hadn't had time to respond. The nap I'd taken—

that was the sexiest thing ever, and sweatpants that didn't hide size.

"Really?" Summer's dubious tone held a lot of snark.

"Seriously. I'm going back to work, so I can't talk long."

"Wait—you got a job?"

I screwed my face up, grateful she couldn't see me. "Yes, but it's just a temp job. It pays well though."

"It should, for no benefits. You know who has good benefits?"

I chuckled. "Leave it alone, Summer."

"Have you at least called recently?"

Sadness bloomed hot in my chest. "No." I wasn't one to call home a lot. I'd stayed with Mama and Daddy for a few weeks before I'd moved to Denver. Being home had reignited the need to hunt down Myles.

I'd found him and called home, omitting details about where I was working and for who, felt deceitful. I didn't want my last conversations with Daddy to be of me lying.

"Well, he'd love to hear about you. He thinks you're lost and confused and wandering the Colorado countryside, finding sports bros to hang out with and make poor decisions with. Next thing you know, you're going to live in the city. Your husband will drive a pickup that's only hauled skis and not cow mineral or chicken feed. And your kids will say things like bruh."

"The kids in Bourbon Canyon say bruh."

"No, they'll say bruh next year, when something trendier has taken its place in more urban areas. Ask Autumn."

I missed them. "My contract is up at the end of October. Then I'll be home." For better or worse.

"I think you'll end up home before that," she said sadly.

The sense of impending loss collared me around my throat. "Shit, I'll call them, okay?"

"Tate's been worried about you."

Crap. Worried older brothers were never a good thing. "Tell him I met a real rugged outdoorsy guy, and he's keeping me busy." One thing about my three brothers—anything sex related, and they kept their distance while dry heaving.

"Have you?"

Myles wasn't really outdoorsy. Maybe he had a private ski slope on that mountain, but I wouldn't be in Denver long enough to find out. "Not really. My boss is hot, but he's a workaholic. Kind of like your man."

"Boyd knows how to have fun."

"Does he?"

"We're not talking about me," she said primly.

Why did Myles work so much? He'd done well for himself. He could afford to relax a little, but he seemed to block everything out on purpose. The way he chatted with Cadillac Sam didn't give me the impression he was a recluse. No one was watching him clock in and out. He didn't get cookies for working twelve-hour days. He was driven, but sometimes, it was like he was hiding.

"At least you have something good to look at while you're getting paid," Summer said.

"Amen. Hey, I'll call Daddy, okay?"

Guilt ate at my stomach lining. I should've thought of Mama Mae. She and Daddy were *#goals*. My sisters and I had been so damn lucky to fall into a home with another wonderful couple. The right kind of lightning hit twice.

I hung up with Summer and voice activated a call to Mama.

"Hey, buttercup," she answered. Her delight only magnified my guilt.

"Hi, Mama. I just wanted to check in. Summer said everyone's getting worried."

"Oh, you know how they are." Her chuckle was all the comforts of home wrapped in a sound. "I bet you're having a good time in the city."

"I am. I've met some cool people. I'm glad I did it. How's everyone?"

She gave me updates on Tate and Scarlett and their kids. My other brothers, Tenor and Teller, were helping Tate on the ranch and working for the family business. Autumn had thrown herself into helping on the ranch for summer break. June was trying to break into the country music scene. She traveled a lot, but last I'd heard, she was in Nashville.

"How's Daddy?" I asked once she was done with the updates.

"He's awake. Would you like to talk to him? Today's a...good day."

Good day. Meaning the pain wasn't fogging his mind. "Yes, please. Love you, Mama."

"All my love, Wynter."

Tears misted across my eyes. "Hey, Daddy."

"Having big Denver adventures?"

"Yes." The last few weeks built up. I wanted to talk about what I was doing. I didn't want to be vague and feel like I was lying. Most of all, I didn't want to wonder what Daddy would think. He was an honest man, and he wasn't prone to sharing business that wasn't his to spread. "Is, um, Mama close by?"

"You got some secrets, buttercup?"

I smiled at the interest. His days had to be hard, feeling like a burden, like he was waiting for the end. And here I was with piping hot tea. I only hoped he'd still be receptive after I told him. "Maybe?"

"She's in the kitchen getting a roast in the oven."

Good enough. "Okay, so—I got a temp position with Myles Foster. He doesn't seem to realize who I am though, and I'm not telling him."

"Well." More shuffling came through the phone. "Let me shut the door in case Tate stops in." His heavy breathing was audible. "Okay. Care to share why?"

"I've just been wondering about him. He built a product and reputation off the Baileys without acknowledging us, and he acts like his time with us never happened." He'd just left. He'd left like we meant nothing. He'd left when important people had already left me.

"And why haven't you told him who you are?"

"I don't want to ruin it, and I think it would. I think he'd banish me from Foster House." I had no proof, just intuition. Myles did not play games. "He's interesting, and

and a minimal personal touch, but he's not faking it and his tactics work. I don't want to get kicked out. He's got a weird chip on his shoulder that I can't identify."

"That chip is none of your business, Wynter. Like I tell Tate, that kid went through a lot we'll never understand, and he doesn't owe us a thing."

I sighed and turned off the highway. I'd be at the distillery in minutes. "I know. I guess another reason I don't tell him who I am is because he says things that he got from you."

"Mm-hmm." Daddy wasn't surprised at all.

"You trained him?"

"No. No." Daddy chuckled. "I talked with him. Like a young man, not like a troubled kid. He was a sponge, and I liked to talk. Some days, Myles listened better than my own kids, and that was a nice treat."

I smiled again. "He quotes you a lot."

"Oh, yeah?"

"I thought he just helped around the ranch."

"Oh, you know. Some days, he'd come with me to the summit." The distillery in Bourbon Canyon. "One weekend, Tate was sick, Tenor had a tennis match, and Teller was too young to care, like you girls, and he came with me to work each day. We talked, you know."

Daddy would never say about what. Myles had acquired that aspect of Daddy's personality, too. "I'm glad you did."

"He's doing well?"

"Yes. He works a lot. It's his life."

"It's safe," Daddy said simply. "You gonna tell him who you are now?"

state secrets."

"Sharing is caring. A rising tide lifts all boats. He should remember that."

"He doesn't need the stress right now." Myles ate a big bowl of stress for breakfast as it was. In those gray sweats.

"You're a good kid, you know that?"

"You made it easy to be a good kid, Daddy." I pulled into the parking lot. Cars filled over half of it. Right. Tastings were in the afternoon. More cars would fill in as it got closer to three—since I was twenty minutes early.

A knock came on the other end. "Ah, there's your mother. She worries about me. I love you bunches, Wynter."

I blinked back tears. "I love you more than all the snowflakes in the world."

When the line disconnected, I fought the tears. I sniffled and blinked. If I touched my eyes, I'd have red-rimmed lids and puffy bags underneath. I had to put the call with Daddy out of my mind, or I'd walk into Foster House a mess. I couldn't think about how that might be the last time I talked to him. I couldn't admonish myself to be grateful I'd actually gotten a chance to tell him everything I needed to instead of having him gone in an instant. My daddy was dying, and since I'd already lost one, I knew how hard it would be.

I swallowed hard. The clock was ticking. Fifteen minutes early. On time in Myles's world. I couldn't waste much more. I got out and rushed to the door. Instead of a loose top that could get twisted around my torso and flash my belly button at Myles, I had on a tighter-fitting

with the other Foster House staff.

Inside, Myles was chatting with Braxton, leaning against the front desk, one hand in his pocket. Long and lean, he wore another shade of gray slacks and white shirt. His cuffs were already rolled up.

"Morning," I said to him like it was a normal day, and I hadn't slept on his office couch. "Hey, Braxton."

"Ms. Kerrigan," Braxton greeted, more official around his boss.

Myles's sharp gaze stroked down my body and back up, centering on my eyes. Could he tell I'd been crying?

"Did I miss pajama day again?" I asked to distract him.

"We're doing a tasting." He pushed off the counter.

"We're doing the tasting?" I tugged my tote bag over my shoulder.

He didn't rush off this time, but waited for me to stop in front of him. "We're participating. Did you eat?"

I nodded. "Ham sandwich with grapes and a bag of chips." I eyed him. "You know ham? It's a fatty portion of pork people cure and enjoy as a deli cut or in roast form?" I didn't look at Braxton. The poor guy would die if I made him laugh at Myles's expense.

Myles frowned. "I eat ham."

"Do you?"

Humor lit his eyes, and I was tempted to pump my fist in the air. He'd gotten my joke and thought it was funny. He turned to Braxton. "In case I don't see you before you leave, have a good night."

"Night, boss. Enjoy the tasting, Ms. Kerrigan. It's a real treat."

His gaze stayed on me a beat too long before he tore it away and strode toward the tasting room on the second floor behind the merchandise selection.

Five people were lined up at the bar. Two couples and an older man. At least two different tours were going on. Friday and Saturday afternoons were the highest-traffic times at Foster House.

The older man behind the bar was Shelly. He grinned when he saw us approach.

"Now the whole crew's here." He didn't introduce Myles but launched into an introduction to whiskey, flavor profiles, and what smelling the product could do for you. "All right now. Hold your hands out."

We did as he asked, and he poured a couple drops of a clear fluid into our hands. I loved this part.

"Now clap your hands and breathe in. Don't smell your hands, or you'll be going home with burned nostrils." He clapped. "White dog is the whiskey right out of the still. It's got no color since it hasn't been in the barrel. We won't know what the finished product will taste like, but we can still tell a lot about what's going on. Now clap again and breathe."

Myles gave his hands a brisk rub and clapped.

"This is a strong one," I murmured, closing my eyes. "Mm, barley. Is that..." I took another breath. "Fruit?" I opened my eyes and met Myles's gaze. Copper Summit didn't work with fruit in the mash after one disastrous fermentation.

"Peach," he said, his voice thick. "I thought it'd go well with the caramelization from the barrel."

"Yes," I whispered to keep from disrupting the group

Satisfaction entered his gaze. "That was exactly how I sold it to Ellie."

"You had to convince her?" He was the boss, but he didn't throw his weight around.

"I defer to her expertise, or I wouldn't have hired her. If she thought it wouldn't work..." He lifted a shoulder, and his lips twitched. "I would've had her do a small batch anyway."

I laughed. "This is going to make a good honey barrel."

"A unique single batch, yes. Seasonal."

I inhaled again and let the memories of Daddy quizzing me about what I could tell from white dog roll over me. Tears burned behind my eyes again.

"You okay?" he asked softly.

So he'd noticed I'd been crying when I had arrived. "I talked to my daddy before I got here."

"I'm sorry." He touched my elbow. Shocked, I looked down. Skin-on-skin contact. The rough tips of his fingers were warm. I licked my bottom lip, my mouth dry. He was riveted on my tongue, like a bird of prey.

Shot glasses with amber fluid were slid in front of us, followed by clear glasses of water. He released me and faced forward, head down.

The spot he'd been touching was cold without him, like he'd taken all my body heat with him.

He was probably a furnace in bed.

I turned my attention forward and went through the motions of sampling the whiskey with different amounts of water.

"For tastings, I like neat. Otherwise how do you know what'll work well with it in a cocktail?"

He slid his bright gaze toward me. "You're into mixology?"

How else was a girl raised in a rural bourbon empire supposed to pass the time when she wasn't stalking a man from her past? "It's a hobby. My sister is a whiz with pairing flavors, and we liked to play around." An understatement. Our recipes were made and sold at the distillery's bar in Bourbon Canyon. "At the bar in town, she used to send the bartender recipes to try, and he'd keep some on the menu. We are determined to bring bourbon back." I hadn't had enough to drink to loosen my lips. For a man with a million walls, he was easy to talk to. He listened. I liked that.

"Bourbon?" Shelly made his way down to us. He rested his hands on the counter. "We appreciate a good bourbon around here, don't we, boss?" He lowered his voice to keep Myles from being outed.

"I respect a good bourbon," Myles agreed.

Shelly smiled at me. "Apologies for the stereotype, Ms. Kerrigan. I'm not used to the young ones choosing bourbon over whiskey."

"Bourbon's making a comeback. One Kerrigan at a time." Another of Daddy's sayings.

"That's what I like to hear. If only I could tell you where the really good stuff is hidden around here." Shelly's brown eyes twinkled.

I pretended to think. "Hmm... Could it be the lineup of bottles in a certain office on the fourth floor?"

guests.

"The really good stuff?" I asked Myles.

"I'm not a big drinker, so when I imbibe, I want to drink the best." He leaned to the side, our shoulders bumping. He was such a solid wall, I could wrap myself around his arm, tuck into his side, and stay warm in the strongest AC the building could pump out. "And keep track of the competition."

My insides were quivering, but I acted unaffected by his proximity. "I knew I spotted other labels in that line-up." There were five Copper Summit bottles, all over half empty.

"For work purposes only."

"Mm."

He threw back his shot and pushed the glass to the edge of the counter. I did the same with mine. The smooth flavor burned down my throat, a familiar sensation. His pupils dilated.

He slid his eyes closed and swallowed. When he opened them, his irises were a cooler blue. "Would it surprise you that there's straight moonshine with food coloring posing as whiskey on that shelf?"

At first I was startled, but I didn't need long for it to make sense. I put my elbow on the bar top and propped my head in my hand. "I bet you take a shot every now and then to keep in mind what cheap alcohol tastes like."

I knew where he'd gotten that habit from.

"I haven't had a skunk drink for a long time."

"Skunk? Isn't that beer?"

"Works for shit whiskey, though, doesn't it? Makes

His mouth spread into a grin, and he laughed.

I drew in a slow breath, afraid to burn my retinas as badly as sniffing straight white dog would burn my nose. A smiling Myles was devastating. His eyes crinkled, and his teeth were white, with sharp canines and a hint of unevenness that made him approachable. Attainable even. His laugh was deep and should be bottled up and sold for millions.

I giggled with him, giddy on rampant hormones. That smile of his made Braxton's enthusiasm seem dim, yet it could also melt my underwear right off.

If I didn't slip them off and throw them at him like he was a famous rock star first.

"You're staring, Ms. Kerrigan."

"You're smiling. Pajama day and comedy night?" I shook my head. "I wasn't prepared."

Another chuckle escaped him, like the plug had been pulled, and he couldn't help it. Shelly glanced over, looking almost as stunned as I felt.

"Would you like to do more sampling in my office, Ms. Kerrigan?" Myles asked.

"Give me your best and your worst, Mr. Foster."

Myles

Sampling the variety of whiskeys and bourbons in my office had been a bad fucking idea.

I was laughing and pouring Ms. Kerrigan shots. She

"My sister would say the best thing to go with that is the trash can." She shuddered and opened her mouth as if to blow off the fumes like a dragon. "Seriously, that stuff could make you go blind."

"Nah, they make it that bad on purpose. I met the owner. He makes his profits with the fast turnaround and cheap sales. Quantity over quality."

"I'm sure his doors stay open."

"It's cheaper than buying lighter fluid and just as effective."

She laughed a tinkling sound that made me smile. She wiggled her fingers toward a half-empty bottle of some of the best bourbon I'd ever had the pleasure to taste. I savored a drink every now and then. "I haven't had Wynter Summit in forever."

Wynter Summit was a Copper Summit bourbon. I didn't often buy a bottle, but I always had one on hand. I grabbed a small glass and poured her enough to cover the bottom. Since we were sampling, we'd been doing the same with whiskey in the shot glasses. I didn't want a drunk Ms. Kerrigan on my hands, but I also wanted to keep the tasting going. This was...enjoyable.

She took a small sip and rolled the bourbon around on her tongue. Her eyes drifted shut.

I relaxed, not realizing I'd tensed, waiting for her reaction. She always had one. A scrunch of her nose for the not-so-good ones. A suppressed gag for the paint-thinner varieties. But a good brand—watching her reaction would give me another shitty night of sleep.

"Mmm." She kept her eyes closed. "So good."

Christ. I was going to hear that in my dreams and

the chair next to it.

Her eyes fluttered open. "Had enough with the skunk drinks, too?"

"Yes." More of her moans would be nice.

She lifted her glass and inspected the amber liquid. "A bourbon is never shot. It's savored."

"And never saved," I finished. "Meant to be enjoyed with friends and family."

She rotated her glass. "And what am I, Mr. Foster?"

So much more. "I count a fellow bourbon enthusiast in that statement."

"Fellow? You specialize in whiskey."

"Bourbon's restrictive. So many qualifications to meet the definition of bourbon. I can play with whiskey. Besides, I've already had the best bourbon made. I don't feel like I have to improve on it."

She took another sip. "And what's the best bourbon?"

"You're drinking it." Copper Summit's products were quality. Were they the best in the world? Probably not. But they were the best in my mind, and I didn't care to compete with them.

She made a noncommittal sound and inspected her glass. "My first drink was when I was fifteen." She gauged my lack of reaction. "That doesn't surprise you?"

Most people would be shocked. Aghast even. But where I came from, young drinkers were a reality. "No."

"What if I told you my parents gave it to me?"

I lifted a shoulder. "The context makes all the difference."

The corner of her mouth kicked up. Her pink lips made the sauciest curve when she smiled. "You're right.

"Smart." She was my goddamn forbidden temptation. I'd shared a handful of drinks with Mrs. Crane in all the years she'd worked for me. She'd never accompanied me to lunches with Cadillac Sam, and I'd never wanted to learn everything about how she'd grown up.

"Daddy liked to test me on what I could tell from a small sip." She laughed, but I sensed the sadness underneath. "He'd never admit it, but I think he was disappointed I preferred bourbon cocktails over drinking it neat."

"You can't fix erroneous taste buds."

This time, her laughter was melancholy-free. "He'd probably agree with you." Her expression wavered, and the heaviness was back in her eyes. Then it was gone. "A good cocktail is hard to beat, but you know what's better?"

"I know what I think is better," I practically growled.

Pink dusted her cheeks, and her eyes flared. "Candy, Mr. Foster. Bourbon chocolate fudge, to be specific."

I poured myself a glass of Wynter Summit. "Sounds rich."

"It is. There's also gummy bears, truffles, cordials, and caramels. I once took a trip to Kentucky just for bourbon candy."

"Maybe I should stock some with the merch."

She finished her drink and set the glass down. "I bet they'd sell. I know candy isn't your moneymaker, but it holds a special place in my heart. I have a sweet tooth."

As much as I wanted to dwell on how sweet she'd taste, all those little samples added up. I didn't get the

"Mr. Foster. Second night in a row."

"Guilty. But you need a full dinner first. Let me order food in." The excuse sounded false in my ears. Was I only keeping her in my office as the evening wrapped up and people went home? Maybe, but I wasn't risking her getting behind the wheel. "What do you like to eat?"

She'd brought sandwiches and leftover pasta dishes, plus she always ate whatever I ordered in. No pickiness, and I'd tracked way too many of her habits.

"Unhealthy stuff that you don't touch."

I gave her a mock scowl. "I ordered in pizza not long ago. You even had some."

"I did. Did you?"

"I don't like pizza." I got out my phone and started a message to my delivery guy.

"Who doesn't like pizza?"

"A kid who had nothing else to eat but old, hard pizza when his mom spent all her money on drugs." Fuck. Why couldn't I keep my mouth shut?

Her ripe lips parted. "Shit. Sorry—no pizza, then."

"I'm ordering pizza. It's fine."

She scooted forward, keeping her legs under her until I worried she'd tip off the couch. She put her warm hand on my forearm. "No. I want something you'll like, too."

I liked seeing her enjoy the food I bought her. "I said it's fine."

"It's not. Get what you want, too."

"I'm surrounded by what I want." I couldn't have her reading into that. I wanted her. I couldn't have her, and that was a situation I tried to avoid—being around something I couldn't have. Like getting shuttled off to

reprieve, and honestly, I wouldn't have wanted to take me on vacation either. As a kid, it had fucking sucked. More proof I wasn't wanted and couldn't have the nice things.

My stomach growled. Lunch had been a while ago for me, too. "If I get wings, will that satisfy you?"

"I'll be so satisfied, Mr. Foster."

Her damn purr.

I shot off a message. When I was done, I found her gaze on me. "Something wrong? More bourbon?"

"Yes—to the bourbon. You know I saw that bottle of Old Rip Van Winkle."

I huffed. "You mean the six-thousand-dollar bottle of Old Rip Van Winkle."

She gave me a theatrical gasp. "Only six grand? You must've bought it years ago."

"The first year I turned a profit." I got up to retrieve the label.

"So the delivery guy, Cooper. He's, like, on call?"

I wasn't surprised she knew his name. She only needed to be told once to recall who each employee was and what department they worked in. Cooper Luis delivered to Foster House nearly every day. "He's my personal assistant."

Another dramatic gasp. "You're hiding assistants from me now?"

"No. He's been quite visible."

She rolled her eyes, and I grinned as I poured her a finger of the good stuff. She deserved more than a few dribbles.

I added the same to my glass. "I originally hired him

set the bottle on the coffee table.

She glanced from the bottle I didn't immediately put away like I had the others. I didn't react. If she wanted to swig the whole bottle, I wouldn't stop her.

"A lot of places work around students' schedules," she said.

Not for what I paid. "They do, but he also needs..." Cooper wasn't shy about his learning disabilities, but his personal story wasn't mine to discuss. "School takes him more time."

"Oh, right. He made a comment about summer tutoring." She held the glass loosely in her hand and leaned on the arm of the couch. "You're a softie."

"I'm understanding."

"Softie," she said around the rim of her glass.

I waited, my breath stalled.

There it was. The slow fall of the eyelids. The slight chin lift. The upward tilt of her lips. I couldn't see her roll the fluid on her tongue, but I knew she was doing it. The same flavor she was tasting played over my tongue.

She opened her eyes and sighed. "That's good stuff."

"Some of the best. I have a fifteen-year-old whiskey we're bottling next year."

"Fifteen? You would've only been—"

"Fifteen years younger."

She laughed, the sound so light and free. I was smiling again, dammit. "If you're sensitive about your age, you should know it's one of the first things that's printed in the interest pieces written about you."

"I know." Heat that had nothing to do with the alcohol wicked up my face. I hated the attention on

"You're a private person, Mr. Foster."

"And you're surprisingly understanding. You don't pry."

Indecision worked through her eyes. "Sometimes people have similar experiences, and they don't talk about it."

"You were in the system?" Pressure expanded in my chest, pushing at my ribs. Wynn was sharp and fun and light. Picturing her in some of the settings I'd been put in tore at my soul.

She chewed on her lower lip, then released it suddenly. She ran a finger around the rim of her glass and didn't meet my gaze. "My family took in kids. I always wondered if they felt like they got lost in the chaos."

"No wonder you interrupt all the time."

She laughed, but there was something hidden deep in her expression. A heavy emotion she wasn't sharing. And I wasn't going to be the one to pry. She'd respected my privacy. I'd do the same for her.

CHAPTER EIGHT

Wynter

I'd had my opening. It'd been right there. I could've done the "Well, actually..."

I'd chickened out. With all the admiration and gratefulness in his voice, I couldn't bring myself to admit that I didn't pry because I knew the main points of his life's story already. I remembered the way his head had hung down when he'd arrived, but how he'd studied everyone from under his long hair. The hunch of his shoulders was gone, but only circumstance had made him stand like that in the first place.

I took a bite of pizza. I didn't ask how he knew plain cheese was my favorite. He'd ordered a medium cheese and a Canadian bacon as if he'd also noticed I shunned anything pepperoni that wasn't on a charcuterie board.

Myles was finishing his chicken. He'd gotten his wings sauce-free. I couldn't have handled seeing him lick his fingers. A low burn was constant in my belly—and

Did his chest have a scattering of hair? Did it just cover his pecs or trail down to disappear underneath his waistband? Were his pecs as hard as they looked?

"So, one time," I said around my mouthful, not caring one bit about manners. The more deliberate he got with eating, the sloppier I became. Talk about work and spirits was tabled, and I was regaling him with my and my siblings' antics. Vaguely, of course. "My sister, the one who's two years older than me, said no to her boyfriend, that she wanted to wait, and he broke up with her and dumped her on the edge of our land."

"I hope your brothers castrated him," he growled, dabbing his fingertips on a napkin.

"Nope." I took another bite and grinned while chewing. I might look like a doofus, but Myles seemed to enjoy the stories about my brothers and never asked their names. He liked the stories, but he also kept his distance, even now. When I swallowed, I continued, "Every time he took a girl to the movies, we took his tires off and put them in the bed of his truck."

His low chuckle was my reward for the retellings. "How many times did you get away with that?"

"Twice. The third time, he came storming out, yelling and throwing a fit, his date in tow. So Ju—my sister asked him if she should drop him off miles from home because he wouldn't put out like he had done to her. His new girlfriend got a ride home with us."

More laughter. Success.

I polished off my last slice. Myles started cleaning up the food containers and dumping them into the bag they'd arrived in. Cooper had been prompt with the food

Hearing a little more of his story from Myles had rounded out Cooper more than Myles probably thought. Cooper needed more time in college, and that would affect his ability to work and earn money while going to school. So Myles made it happen, and I wouldn't be surprised if Cooper made sure he had an open session between classes during lunchtime. A win-win for them both.

For a guy who couldn't remember me and didn't speak of the family he'd lived with for over two years, he was considerate and generous.

I took my plate and napkins and helped him pick up. A comfortable silence settled between us. He set the bag of garbage by the door for the cleaning staff that came in the morning.

I should leave. I had no other reason to be here. I hadn't had any more to drink in the two hours while we'd eaten and talked. Cooper had brought water, milk, and juice to add to the collection in the break room.

But I was curious about what we'd talked about last night. "How's the pitch going?"

His jaw tightened. "Fine."

"Are you changing it up like I suggested?" I held a hand up. "It's fine if you're not. I'm just preparing for a change in prep duties."

"Yes, and you'll be there for the pitch."

A tiny thrill went through me. I was excited to see him at work. In this scenario, he wouldn't be in control. He hadn't been with Wes Clayton, not at first, but then he'd taken the reins.

I twisted my fingers together. "I will be there with you, but I'm starting to regret my suggestion. It clearly bothers you."

"I worked hard to forget a lot of my past."

I could tell. Echoes of hurt reverberated around my heart. Had he wanted to forget me? Had I been nothing but an annoying kid? He hadn't grown into an adult who acted like reading to a scared kid would be a burden, but perhaps he preferred distance. To use his money to help without actually touching or interacting with anyone.

What a lonely life.

"I'm sorry all of it was so terrible," I said, unable to contain my bitterness.

He went to the window and propped his hands on his hips. The sun had disappeared behind the mountains, leaving a swath of pinks, purples, and oranges in the sky. "It wasn't all awful."

I waited for him to continue. He didn't.

I crept up on him like I would with a horse prone to startling. Usually, with a skittish horse, my siblings and I could systematically desensitize the animal just by being us. "Not all of it?"

Why was I trying to get him to open up? Then I'd have to be truthful. Did I want to tell him who I was?

I did—but only if he had fond feelings toward that girl he'd made an impression on.

"It's hard not to look back and see everything I didn't have. It's hard not to remember why I was so resentful in those days." He glowered out the window. "Especially when there's one stark reminder I can't outrun."

He turned, towering over me. "You should go."

Standing this close, I didn't want to move away. Warmth radiated from him, but mostly I wanted to smooth the frayed emotion in his eyes. I shouldn't touch him, but I didn't care. I ran my finger down the side of his face, where the corner of his eyes pinched. "I know. I should."

The blue of his eyes darkened, his pupils crowding out the irises. "Christ, Wynn, you never act like I expect you to."

"Didn't anyone tell you never to assume?"

A low growl rumbled from him, and then a strong arm was banded around my waist, and I was pulled flush to his chest. He was a delicious, hard wall of muscle. His hot mouth crashed onto mine, and all I could do was hang on, my fingers curling into his shirt.

He didn't finesse the kiss. He dominated, licking between my lips. I automatically opened for him. His flavor was addicting. Soft hints of bourbon, seasoning from the wings. The demanding man was the perfect nightcap for my evening.

Was this what I had missed out on when I'd slept on the couch?

I twined my arms around his neck and stood on my tiptoes, my heels coming out of my sandals. He growled and plundered my mouth, taking control and stealing my breath until I subsisted on him and him alone.

A whimper left me. My body was on fire, and if he loosened his hold, I'd strip down and beg him to take me against the cool glass of the window. His steel-banded embrace didn't ease. He spun me, and my back hit the

around my waist and up to cup a breast.

I arched as much as I could into him, but I was stuck. He slid his other hand down my back and gripped a butt cheek. His punishing grip wasn't painful. Nothing but need vibrated through his body and into mine.

The crush of his mouth on me was my only lifeline. I slid my tongue along his, never tiring of his flavor and not caring how garlicky I tasted. Maybe I'd make bourbon and pizza his favorite.

A familiar ringtone sounded from his pocket, and he ripped away. The incredulity on his face was a bucket of ice water on my desire.

"You have to go," he rasped, his chest heaving.

"What?"

His phone rang again with that ominous tone he'd given it. He didn't dig it out of his pocket. "You're my assistant."

I was his temporary assistant for barely two more months, and we could do anything we wanted together afterward—if he was interested. He'd forgotten about the kid version of me who'd idolized him, but now he wanted to slam a wall between adult me and him, too? "Don't you let anyone close to you?"

Resolve hardened his features. "No. They only end up letting me down." He retrieved his phone, glared at the caller I couldn't see, and stalked toward his loft.

He was leaving me once again.

CHAPTER NINE

Wynter

"Did you get that down?"

I was sitting across from Myles's desk. It was Wednesday. We'd fly out Friday morning, do the whole private-jet thing, which, I couldn't lie, I was a little excited about. Then he'd give his proposal and hopefully be less of a dick after.

"Didn't you see me writing?" I replied, my pen poised over the tablet.

He scowled at his computer screen. Never at me. In the weeks since our kiss, he'd been avoiding me. Hard to do when I was his assistant, and he was preparing for a critical meeting to expand his company, but he managed with rigid efficiency. "We're done for the day."

I checked the time. It wasn't even five. "Already?"

"I have errands to run."

This was the first I'd heard. "Do you need me to—"

"No."

be getting on Friday?"

"What's wrong with me?"

"Kind of hard to spin a sympathetic story about your past when you're glaring and scowling and looking like you want to rip everyone apart."

"I don't want to share my story, but you convinced me it was necessary."

"I told you my opinion. You made the call. Own your decisions." Another quote straight from Daddy. Usually, he'd been yelling at me or my siblings when we'd fucked up as kids, but the sentiment worked on Myles nonetheless.

He stiffened. "I am owning it. I don't have to like it."

I sighed and coaxed myself into relaxing. I should respect that he didn't want to lose control and fall all over his assistant. He was in a tough spot, and of all people, I should understand. Recounting some of what had happened to him and using his history for sales wasn't comfortable for him. With the way he was behaving, the idea was hurting him, but he'd do anything for his company.

I didn't like sharing the story of my birth parents either. Luckily, most people I came across in Bourbon Canyon already knew the tragic story of the Kerrigan sisters. But I'd learned new details behind their death after I'd gotten older, and the information was personal. It was no one's business. I had to set aside my ego. "Do you want me to take a look at what you have?"

He blanched. "God no." He slid his gaze to look out the window. "It's bad enough you have to be there."

Ouch. *Remove my ego, remove my ego.* "Okayyy. Why

might not have troubleshot the way his pitch was falling short.

"You don't ask a national wholesaler to hold on when they're considering millions of dollars in contracts with you."

His snide tone was one I hadn't heard from him before. Embarrassment curled around my neck and cinched tighter until it was hard to breathe. I didn't like when he blew me off.

Since he was curt and short-tempered, and had ordered the most obnoxiously healthy foods for lunch all week, I should take him up on his declaration that the workday was done. I could grab a beer and a burger and grumble to myself about how kissing me wasn't life-changing for him.

Knowing what his lips felt like now was changing mine. I had a hard time falling asleep without having a little one-on-one with my toys. I woke up thinking about what it had felt like being locked between him and the window. And much of my day was spent pondering who was behind that ringtone and why they unsettled Myles so badly.

The tone played through the room. I blinked. Had I summoned the caller?

"Fuck," he said under his breath. He stared at the device that was facedown on his desk.

If he'd looked irritated before, his face was a mask of fury now. If a girlfriend no one knew about was calling, that was one toxic relationship. But Myles had said he didn't do relationships. So who was it?

He flicked his gaze toward me. "You're leaving?"

"I'd rather not be around for the"—I wiggled my finger at him again—"pleasing disposition you get after those calls. Have a good night."

I left him at his desk, phone still ringing.

In the parking lot, I ran through ideas of where I could have a burger and beer and still get home without having to drive. I didn't have gal pals to navigate the city with and watch each other's back.

I'd settle with picking up a six-pack, sticking a mug in a freezer, and pretending a bottle of beer in a frosty mug tasted as good as draft. Then I'd order in. In the morning, I'd be back to work. Dealing with uptight Myles was best when I was fully rested. Forgetting the sweltering kiss was easier when I wasn't in the same room as him.

Before I got in my car, I glanced up at the window. Heat licked my skin like he was watching me, but I'd never be able to tell with those damn windows. The building reflected him in that way. People could only see in where he wanted them to, and the interior was apportioned according to function. The really interesting stuff he walled off from everyone.

On the way to town, Summer called. I answered with "Hey. I didn't see any texts from you."

The second of silence was enough to tell me there'd been no missed messages. Tears poked the backs of my eyes. Was this it? The call I'd been dreading?

"He's in the hospital in Bozeman," she said. I nodded even though she couldn't see me. "He, um, will probably

Daddy wanted to be at home when he died. "Thanks for calling and telling me."

"Aren't you going to come home?"

"I told you I wasn't," I said, unable to keep from being defensive.

"I just thought..." Her sigh was loud. "I thought you'd want to be there when the time finally came."

I couldn't. I couldn't handle it. "He understands. I wish you would."

"No, I do..."

There was something in her tone that made the hair on the back of my neck stick up. "*You* do. Who doesn't?"

"The guys don't get it, but I told them why. They're trying. You and Junie aren't home. Autumn is, but I don't see her as much as I'd like. Boyd's been working a lot, so it's just been hard, you know."

Why couldn't her boyfriend be there when she needed him? I wasn't Boyd's biggest fan, and he wasn't the most enthused about small towns and big families, but Summer was into him. I didn't know why. She needed someone to lean on. She was always trying to save us from ourselves, and she shouldn't have to.

But she had Boyd, and I had memories that drove me away. I needed to take care of myself, and it hurt that my brothers didn't understand. "You told them I already watched two parents die and can't bear to witness another?"

"Don't be pissed at me. They don't know what it's like, and this is different."

I sighed. "I'm sorry. You're left dealing with a lot." She wasn't at fault, and being the oldest, they often got

coldhearted brat. "Is that why Tate hasn't checked in?"

"Tate's not the one with the issue. He's busy with a wife and kids and taking over for Daddy while making sure Daddy doesn't drag Mama through hell during his last days of being stubborn. You know how sensitive Tenor is." And Teller could get lost in his head and forget others had emotions.

"Thanks for sticking up for me."

"If I didn't, Mama would ream their asses."

My sad chuckle matched hers. "Take care of yourself. How are Autumn and Junie?"

"Junie's not home yet, but she should be any day. Oh —the doctor's going into Daddy's room. Gotta go—love you, bye." She disconnected.

"Call Junie," I said to my Bluetooth.

I wasn't surprised when she picked up. We were all dreading the call. "Where are you?"

"I have a layover in Denver." Her voice came through small and sad. "I missed my flight."

"Intentionally?" My sister was big into self-sabotage. She could handle her anxiety and get up on stage, but only if she could get past it to get on the plane in the first place.

"Maybe." She sniffled.

A flight from Denver to Bozeman was short, and flights were constantly leaving from Denver. "I'll pick you up. What airline?"

"Thanks, Wynter."

"Hey, we all have our thing." When she returned home, she could explain herself to our brothers. She just needed to be weak tonight. And I'd appreciate not being

and it wasn't like I could go to him for support.

Junie curled up on the couch with a glass of wine. She was the anti-bourbon girl. Like the rest of us, she could recite the taste profile of any bourbon without looking at the label, but everyone expected her to drink it. Therefore, she didn't touch it.

Her light brown hair had blond and pink highlights. The way she had the strands swirled and bound at the top of her head made her look like she had a snow-cone hat.

When I'd picked her up, she'd had on big sunglasses and a floppy hat. I'd teased her about going incognito, and she'd only rolled her eyes, claiming she wasn't famous enough for that yet.

She would be. June Bee was making a name for herself, slowly but surely, thanks to the work ethic our parents had instilled in us. Both sets.

"I don't want to go home," she said before she took a swig that drained half her glass.

"Nashville's going well, then?"

"Um...define well." She polished the rest of her wine off. "It's a pretty town, but you have to fit their cookie-cutter image and have their cookie-cutter sound. Lord knows they love their blond country singers, but they don't want my songs, and I don't want anyone else's."

A few more highlights, and she could be the blond bombshell country artist with a perky smile and a kill-

"So Nashville sucks?" I asked.

She wrinkled her nose and set her glass down. "It's fine. I'm just having an existential crisis, and I shouldn't be figuring a damn thing out when Daddy's dying."

My heart constricted. He was dying. I would get the call soon. "I'm glad you're going home."

She gave me a sympathetic smile. "Don't let Tenor and Teller get to you. They don't have to understand, they just have to respect your decision."

I nodded, almost wishing I was flying out with her. But the lingering terror from my bio parents' crash stayed with me, constricting my throat, and the closer I got to their place of death, the worse it'd be.

I'd almost suffocated the last time I was home, which was how I'd ended up in Denver.

"Enough about depressing shit. It'll catch up to us soon enough." She scooted around on the couch until she was facing me on the other end. "Summer said you have a hot boss?"

"He's so hot."

She grabbed her phone. "Tell me about him. Where do you work? I want to see a picture."

"Junie!" Panic sent my pulse soaring. She wanted to look him up. "Don't be nosy."

She gave me an appraising look. Her eyes were darker brown than mine, and sometimes I couldn't tell what she was thinking. "You like him."

"I..." I scowled at her and took a sip of my rosé. Better than the merlot from the night Myles had fired me but still not what I'd like to drink. One day, I'd quit

"Mm-hmm."

"And he's my boss. I want to keep the lines clear." And I wanted to keep his identity a secret from my siblings. Junie never talked about Myles much. She was too busy trying to forget Bourbon Canyon as thoroughly as Myles had.

"Do you, though?"

Damn her. "His real assistant will return in a little over a month, and I'll be looking for a job."

"Under him?" She snickered.

"Stop it." I tossed a throw pillow at her, and she batted it away.

"Seriously, though. Are you going to work at Copper Summit?"

"Yes. Once everything's settled."

She nodded. Cool relief that she knew exactly what I meant washed over me. Could also be the wine.

"Just don't move to Denver full-time," she said. "I like having all my siblings safe in one place while I travel the world."

She got the worst anxiety traveling, so I doubted that was true. "You mean you don't want to travel more to visit me on top of them?"

She stuck her tongue out.

"Uh, so immature." I suppressed a smile.

"We all have our things, okay?"

Didn't I know it. "I was working late one night, and it started storming. I slept on the office couch."

"How'd you hide that from the boss hottie?"

"He suggested it." I couldn't get into specifics. "He keeps a loft where he works because of his hours."

"Sure."

"June."

She rolled her eyes. "All the big shots are banging any young impressionable thing they can."

I mulled that over. Myles wasn't like that. I'd seen no indication of an active sex life. I wasn't being defensive just because. But there was more to what she'd said than she was telling me. "Is there something you want to talk about?"

"Nope." She got up to pour herself more wine. "Don't worry, I won't overindulge. There's nothing worse than flying hungover."

"Pour me another, then."

She topped off my glass. "You're keeping this guy to yourself, aren't you?"

"Yes," I admitted, grateful she'd read through me, and I didn't have to lie by omission again. "You'll understand once I tell you, but for now, I need to keep him to myself." I took a sip and let the woodsy grape flavors play over my tongue. A hint of smoky lilac and vanilla. A little reminiscent of the Foster Garden line. "I talked to Daddy about him, though."

Her smile was sad. "And he was as chill as ever."

"As ever," I agreed.

"I'm going to miss him." She drew in a shaky breath.

"Yeah. Me, too."

She lifted her glass and inspected the color. "Maybe I can fly a little hungover."

CHAPTER TEN

Myles

Where was she?

I tapped my pen on my desk. I didn't have anything to write down. I should be finishing preparations for tomorrow. Without Wynn, my world spun off-kilter. She'd become a stabilizing force for me since she'd started. Someone who didn't shrink away from me or leave me alone when I was especially grumpy. Except for last night.

I was in *one of my moods* as one of my foster moms used to say. *You get in one of your moods and expect everyone else to suffer with you, doncha, kid?*

I pushed a hand through my hair. I shouldn't have bothered with styling this morning.

Mrs. Crane gave me space when I was foul-tempered. Wynn faced me head-on. Until yesterday. She'd left.

Another damn phone call had chased her away.

All the calls before that I'd been able to break and

enough.

The problem was that my life hadn't stayed ruined. Now I was nothing but a resource for her. Another reservoir to tap that should've run dry years ago.

Stupid magazines splashing my face across the cover.

I was in a shitty headspace this morning, and then Wynn had messaged and said she'd be late. She needed to take a sister to the airport.

How long had her sister been in town?

Why hadn't she told me?

Why did I care?

I cared about a lot when it came to my assistant. After that kiss, I dreamed about a lot more. A few more minutes, and I would've had her stripped down and pressed against the glass. I would've been inside of her and in heaven.

My mood soured even more. Fucking phone calls. I could stay out of the past, but it kept tugging me back, like chains were hooked to my ankles, and when I was finally fully upright, Gianna gave me a big ol' yank.

Behind me, a drawer closed. Wynn. I was up and out of my chair, heading for the open door to my office.

Mrs. Crane would know something was up. I never kept my door open, but now I only shut the damn thing when Wynn was inside with me.

I had a problem.

I got a glimpse of her ass in loose linen pants. She had on a nice blouse that gave her a summer office vibe, as if Foster House was set in Hawaii. She straightened, brushed her hands down her pants, and turned. Her eyes had shadows under them, and she hadn't done

Had she and her sister cruised the bars last night? Had they found a party and some guys?

Didn't I sound like a crotchety fucker?

"What's wrong?" My question came out as a demand. "You look like hell."

I normally didn't lie. She looked radiant. Beautiful. She was my very own ray of sunshine cresting the mountains in the morning. But she wasn't mine. She'd move on for someone who was less of a jackass, and I would deserve it. Like always.

"Wow. Good morning to you, too."

Remorse and I were estranged friends. I ignored the feeling, and it was usually happy to leave me the hell alone. But not after insulting Wynn. "I'm sorry, Ms. Kerrigan. I only mean that you don't seem as chipper as usual."

She shot a skeptical look at me. My sudden change of tone could be taken as snark, but I was being sincere.

"I'm not. My daddy's in the hospital, and my sister was flying home, but she had a layover."

My remorse grew stronger, like lack of use gave it power. I'd been focused on her reaction to me. I'd forgotten she was losing a parent. For whatever reason, she hadn't asked to go be with him, and I could understand wanting to avoid grief. "I'm sorry. Nice visit with your sister?"

"Yeah, it was fine."

This wasn't the first time Wynn had held back information. I refused to plead for her to open up. There was no need for her to. We weren't a thing. She worked for me. But I'd grown to care about her in our time

way she didn't put up with my shit.

She'd left yesterday. It wouldn't be long before she left for good. That was just how it went.

Relationships worked better when I didn't try at all, or when I left first. Only bad things came from me hanging around.

She gave me a superficial smile, one that didn't come close to her normal cheer, and sat at her desk, back to me.

I'd been dismissed.

An old, raw wound opened back up in my chest, gnawing away the scraps of any decent mood I had left. I hated being dismissed.

Wasn't that what tomorrow was about? I'd bare a part of my damn soul, and they'd say *thank you, next* like I didn't matter.

Would it suck as much as Wynn shutting me out?

Wynter

I met Myles at the airport because I'd secretly wanted to sleep in after the late night talking with June and the hangover I'd dealt with yesterday.

The inside of the plane was as posh as I'd expected. A flight attendant rushed to take the luggage out of my hands even though I had to fend her off. I doubted the plane ride would mean less work, and I'd need my phone, tablet, notepad, and pens.

one side. When Myles nudged me from behind, I snapped my mouth shut and kept walking.

He was wearing a tie, as if I needed to see a tie to know today was serious.

Imani, the attendant, smiled at me. "Choose any seat you'd like. Once we reach cruising altitude, you can switch to the couch. If you need a quick rest, there's a small bedroom in the back and a bathroom across from it."

"A bedroom?" I sounded like the country girl I was at heart. A plane with a bedroom. I might be dressed in a black pencil skirt with a pink blouse and look like I flew private every day, but I'd rarely flown. And it'd been nothing like this.

Myles dropped into a chair and efficiently buckled himself in. All day yesterday, he'd been curt, giving me one-word answers. Mostly, he had messaged me. From his office, where he'd sat brooding with the door closed.

I knew I shouldn't have called off the morning to take Junie to the airport, but given her anxiousness about losing Daddy, I hadn't wanted to tell her to call a ride. I wasn't even going home, so I wasn't one to judge her for missing her flight.

I'd sat in the parking lot until she'd sent me a text that she was boarding.

Imani smiled at me, ignoring the grump in the chair. "Can I get you anything before we go over the safety briefing?"

"I'd love a water."

"Would you like a lemon or lime wedge? Cucumber water or sparkling water?"

be great, thank you."

"Absolutely." She shifted to Myles, and I took the seat across from him. "Can I get you anything, sir?"

"An uninterrupted flight." He flicked his gaze up. "After the safety briefing, I need complete privacy."

"Of course, sir." Imani was either a saint or used to asshole corporate fliers. "I'll run through the briefing now and then go to the front and close the partition. Press the call light if you need me for anything during the flight."

I could barely pay attention to how I was supposed to save myself and the grumpy jackass across from me in the event of an emergency. His attitude embarrassed me yet he wasn't ruffled at all. When she disappeared to the front and closed the little sliding door that reminded me of the RV Mama and Daddy had, I glared at Myles.

He continued working on his laptop. "Can I help you with something, Ms. Kerrigan?" He still didn't look away from the screen.

"Rude much?"

"I wasn't rude."

I pointed a finger at him. "Your tone was rude. Would a *please* or *thank you* hurt too much?"

"Depends on how I get punished for not saying it," he said through clenched teeth. "Do you think that's something I should put in my proposal?"

My hand dropped to my lap. Punished?

Suddenly, I was the one who felt like an inconsiderate idiot. He had to relive his past in front of strangers in mere hours, and I'd been salty because he was short with me.

going through. My sisters and I had gone to the Baileys first, and then they'd adopted us. An idyllic home for four scared little girls. Myles had been a handful of years older than me when he'd gone into the system. He wouldn't have made his way to fostering with Mama and Daddy as a teen if a previous placement had worked out. From what I'd heard, he'd been through several homes. Not all of the reasons he'd been pulled could be his fault.

"I'm sorry."

"Don't be," he snapped. "It's not your problem, and I don't want your sympathy. I want this fucking meeting over with, and then I want them to forget what I said." He slammed his laptop lid down, and I jumped. "God-damn it." He glared out the window as we started taxiing.

Static crackled overhead, and then the pilot spoke loud and clear. Did they have better radios in private planes or did the pilot enunciate more?

Tense, silent minutes ticked by as the speed ramped up, and we took off. I stared out the same window as Myles, the tall buildings of downtown Denver fading and the mountains growing smaller.

It wasn't long before the pilot gave us permission to roam the cabin. True to her word, Imani didn't come back out.

I studied Myles. His body was a two-by-four from head to toe, and it didn't matter that he was sitting.

The guy had to relax, or he was going to tank this pitch. He would glare at everyone and sound like the angry teen he'd been.

"Myles, is there something you can do to relax?"

could he shame me with one word?

"Yes," I said tightly. "You're worked up, and it's going to come across as you talk. You're not the professional you usually are, and that won't go unnoticed."

The muscles in the corner of his jaw bulged so badly I worried teeth would crack. Then he'd be a storm cloud in pain, and the deal definitely wouldn't happen. He jerked the seat belt loose and rose. His laptop fell on the floor, and he stormed into the room with the bed and yanked the pocket door closed behind him.

Well.

He was already in pain. Those mystery phone calls hadn't helped. They'd poured nothing but fuel on his already raging fire. I didn't know him well enough to talk him down. I couldn't ply him with shitty spirits to loosen up. The energy coursing through him was eating him alive.

I doubted he was going to nap in that bedroom. If only there was something else to calm him down. The only time he'd been as intense was the earth-shattering kiss.

I eyed the door. Flutters danced through my belly. He wasn't calming down, but could his emotion be redirected?

No. Bad idea.

But. This meeting was important to him, and I wanted to help. Just so happened, I'd been wanting to do other things, too.

CHAPTER ELEVEN

Myles

I tossed my suit coat on the bed to keep from wrinkling the damn thing by tugging on the sleeves. I couldn't run my hands through my hair, or I'd mess it up. I couldn't risk getting sloppy. Mainline needed professional, like Wynn had said. I didn't need to be the kid who fucked up yet another opportunity because of his shitty personality and even worse history.

I propped my hands on my hips. Anger undulated under my skin. Anxiety. Fuck, despair. I didn't want to do this. Not on the tail of what Gianna had said when I'd told her I couldn't help.

The pocket door opened. Wynn stepped through and closed it again.

I was risking everything by being in a poor mindset. I couldn't add the tension of being closed in a tiny room that had a bed with Wynn. "I'm fine, Ms. Kerrigan. Leave."

"You need to fucking go."

"And you need to fucking relax."

Fury—at my situation, at my pitch, at my worry, at Gianna—pushed against my temples until my vision narrowed. I wasn't a violent guy, and I'd never lay a hand on Wynn that wasn't caressing her soft skin, but if she stayed, my blood pressure would skyrocket, and I'd stroke out. I was sure of that right now.

Then she reached for my belt buckle.

My lungs stalled. I couldn't believe what I was seeing as her small hands worked the clasp open and slid my zipper down. If I didn't take a breath soon, I'd black out. "Wynn?"

"I'm helping you relax."

That purr kept me immobile. I had to be mistaken. I'd already had a brain hemorrhage and had passed out. This was my afterlife gift. Here, have an erotic trek to the white light.

She tugged my underwear down and freed my rapidly swelling cock.

Nope. This was real.

"Wynn," I groaned. Now my sight was blurry for a completely different reason. Her touch was warm and firm and more than I'd had for months.

"Just try to be quiet so I can look the crew in the eye when we leave." She dropped to her knees. "Oh my god, you're so much bigger than I thought."

A tremor racked my body. "You don't have to—"

"Oh, Myles—I've been dreaming about doing so many naughty things to you. Shut up, and let me suck you off."

ciative sound, I was done. I was in her hands in so many ways.

Then she put those full lips around the tip, and I tipped my head back. "Fuuuck."

She answered with a moan.

I had to watch. Pure awe crowded into me, barely able to fit around the lust. She looked like an office siren, on her knees, pleasuring her boss. Which was exactly what she was.

I couldn't hold back the buck of my hips. She gazed up at me, her cheeks hollowed, her breasts rising and falling as she took in air through her nose.

The thought of how forbidden this should be went out the window. "You're so fucking beautiful like that, taking me deep."

She responded by sucking in more of me.

My groan was ragged. "Can you take it all, baby?" Her hum reverberated right down to my balls. "So fucking good. Do you know how often I pictured you just like this? Then I'd bend you over the desk—"

She did something with her tongue that should be a sin. I tipped my head back again. My balls were tightening and energy raced down my spine to coil at the base of my cock.

My timing today would be the worst ever. I'd never come so fast. "I'm not going to last much—"

She swirled her tongue along my length as she pulled back, then swallowed me deeper.

"Fuck, Wynn." I had to clench my teeth before a shout echoed through the plane. "Fuck, fuck, *fuck*."

The energy turned into a lightning bolt, circling

hard and long, and she sucked, prolonging the climax until I had to prop a hand on the nearest wall.

She took everything, every last drop. When I sagged, she released me. My cock bobbed in front of her face, and she gazed up with a smug expression. "Are you relaxed now, Mr. Foster?"

That "Mr. Foster" splashed a few drops of cold water on my face, but it wasn't enough reality to make me regret anything. "When my cum is still on your tongue, you can call me Myles."

Her swollen lips curved up, and she rose. I put a hand on her elbow and helped her stand. Then I gripped her chin and kissed her. I couldn't afford to get lost in the kiss like the other night. She didn't need body fluids on her clothing, and I couldn't afford the new erection that would sprout up within seconds of having my mouth on her, but I wanted to show her how much her blow job meant. She could've let me be an incorrigible asshole and ruin my goals, but she'd taken care of me.

I hadn't had anyone take care of me in a long time. I pulled back. "Thank you."

"Just nail that presentation so I can have my regular uptight boss back."

Wynter

Myles's pitch was a work of art. He'd done as I suggested and kept the details vague, generalizing the concepts and the feelings that were all his own.

The way he'd shared those emotions, of being a lost and confused kid surrounded by strangers, it was an experience I knew intimately. The constant doubts about being enough, about proving oneself. He'd ended with how he'd turned those insecurities toward being productive, toward creating an environment where his employees had a place at Foster House. He paid it forward with his actions and didn't care who knew. That wasn't who he was.

I'd dabbed at tears throughout his speech, struggling to keep from bawling. The others in the room, the marketing execs and the vice president and the distribution team, had been as affected as me, discreetly wiping their eyes.

And through all that, Myles had managed to sprinkle in the data we'd toiled over, collecting and rearranging the information until it satisfied Mainline's requirements for suppliers.

If this was what he could do when he got a blow job, he'd be unstoppable with a girlfriend. I bit back a smile, but he must've noticed and caught my eye. I lifted a brow and let my pride shine through.

No matter what Mainline's answer was, he'd accomplished what he'd set out to do. Their decision would not be about him or what he did or didn't do to pay it forward.

Even the friend who'd specifically outed himself as Wes's buddy when we arrived had sniffled a time or two.

"So that's it." Myles spread his hands. "Foster House is my legacy. It's also my life, and just like I didn't care to

lighted for their trauma or their struggles. The quality of the product speaks to the strengths, the compassion, and the dedication of those involved, including me." He folded his hands. "I'd be happy to answer any questions you have."

The undercurrent of his tone said he'd only be okay answering questions about whiskey.

I took notes as he was peppered with questions about production and his plans for expansion. Everyone seemed content to stay away from his past, and it wasn't long before we were marching out of the headquarters building and into the warm Omaha air.

A car was on the way for us, lapping around the parking lot. We waited. No one had walked us out. One of the things I loved about the spirits world of the Midwest was the expected informality.

"You did it," I squealed under my breath. "That was amazing." I hugged my tote to my chest. "You feel good about that, right? I mean you should."

When his ice-blue stare connected with mine, the world narrowed to just the two of us.

"If you think I've forgotten what you did for me in that plane, Ms. Kerrigan, you're sorely mistaken."

My heart sank. He was back to being glacial Myles. "I was out of line. I didn't know what else to do and..." I licked my dry lips.

His gaze followed my tongue like a predator planning his attack. "You said you've been wanting to. Was that true?"

The edge of his voice sent shivers coursing down my spine. "Yes. I thought you could tell by that kiss."

closer to my ear. "I've had my own fantasies. Tell me, Ms. Kerrigan, would you like to know what they are?"

So badly. A tremble went through my body from head to toe. "That depends, Mr. Foster. If your head's between my legs, are you going to call me Wynn?"

CHAPTER TWELVE

Wynter

His direct stare bored into me as he spoke to Imani. "Thank you, but no. I need complete privacy once we take off."

"Of course, Mr. Foster." Imani deposited an old fashioned made with his Foster Garden whiskey line that was infused with hibiscus and rosemary. No bourbon old fashioned for him.

I was having the same, only with a twenty-year-old, single-barrel special from Copper Summit. I could down the drink in one whole gulp, but the liquor wouldn't be enough to dull the lust and excitement and anticipation swirling inside me.

Energy crackled between us. My body was a live wire. He hadn't touched me—yet—but the promise was in his eyes, written over the tension in his body. Need vibrated through me, and the way his body had felt plastered

This was going to be an achingly long flight.

He turned his attention to the window for takeoff. I did the same. So flat. Sprawling. I was used to flying out from mountainous places, the complete opposite of Nebraska.

"Beautiful," I murmured.

He didn't reply.

Several minutes later, the pilot announced that we could roam without our seat belts.

Myles's eyes met mine. My breath caught.

With efficient movements, he unbuckled his seat belt. I went to do the same.

"Don't move, Ms. Kerrigan." He didn't stand, but slid out of his seat and to his knees. He shrugged out of his suit coat and draped it across the empty chair next to his. He loosened his tie but didn't take it off.

I pressed my thighs together. His kiss had wiped out the memory of ever being kissed before. How badly could he ruin me?

He flicked open my seat belt and carefully laid the straps aside. "You're going to have to be quiet, Ms. Kerrigan. The crew is on the other side of that flimsy door."

I nodded, my legs quivering. "Are you saying you're going to make me want to be loud?"

He only arched an arrogant brow as he ran his hands up my legs, pushing the skirt up as he did. Then he gripped my hips and yanked me to the edge of the seat.

I gasped. The move had me immediately widening my legs to catch myself, but he had me in his hold. He released me only to shove my skirt higher. "I'm going to

you're not going to need these."

Clutching the armrests, I did nothing as he slid my underwear off. My pussy was bare to him and his greedy eyes.

"You're wet, Ms. Kerrigan."

"You have that effect on me, Mr. Foster."

His eyes darkened, and he pushed my legs open farther. "I'm going to call you Wynn now." He descended.

The first stroke of his tongue unraveled me. Pleasure radiated and expanded to fill every crevice of my body. The tip of his tongue hit my clit, and I caught my cry before it left my lips.

I gritted my teeth, riding on the waves of ecstasy he created. He licked, he nibbled, he sampled, he took his damn time.

My body shook, and my knuckles were white. Trying to stay quiet while he did amazing things to me with nothing but the tip of his tongue was harder than I'd imagined. The erotic show we created made it even more difficult—my legs bracketing his wide shoulders. The way he was still in his dress shirt with his tie on, and my blouse was tucked into a skirt that was circled around my hips. I'd never forget how we looked.

I wasn't normally a voyeur, but the thrill of getting caught only heightened the sensations.

He added pressure, his strokes speeding up. I didn't have a lot of room to move, but I undulated my hips. I needed more.

"Myles," I hissed. "Oh my god." The delicious pressure inside me built. I was a bomb ready to detonate,

He looked up at me and gave me a long, deliberate lick.

I groaned, and my right leg started shaking uncontrollably.

He paused, and I was tempted to yank him by the hair and push his face back where it was. "Do you want to come, Wynn?"

I nodded, my body rigid. What was he doing?

"You're fucking dripping, and you taste so sweet." He slid two fingers through my seam. "Your pussy is like warm velvet. I could come undone when I think of what it'll feel like around my cock."

"Myles," I whimpered.

He pushed those fingers inside me, and I groaned. Too damn loud. The way he filled me just now only meant he'd obliterate me when we had sex.

When we had sex. Was this really happening?

When his thumb hit my clit, I moaned.

"I knew you'd be responsive when I first saw you," he growled. "It's why I fired you."

I was flying as high as the plane, but his words rooted me. "What?" He'd run me out of his office because he wanted me? So unfair, but also flattering.

He pumped his fingers in and out. "I saw you in the parking lot with those long legs and that obnoxiously pink top. All I could think about was how sweet you'd taste, what kind of sounds you'd make."

He dropped his gaze to where his fingers were leisurely thrusting in and out of me.

I was so damn close to exploding, but he was edging me as deftly as he handled projection reports. I should

grasp.

"Then you gave me attitude, and I wanted to shove my dick between those smart lips and learn if you were as good at sucking me off as you were at cocking off." He lifted his gaze. "I know now I was right. Put that pillow over your face and get ready to scream, Wynn."

Oh my god. I grabbed the pillow and braced myself as he buried his face back in my pussy. He was relentless. His fingers filled me, stroking just the right way. His tongue was dialed in to exactly what I needed, and when he paired them both, I was done.

A tsunami crashed into me, hitting me hard at first and then keeping me underwater. The torrent was so powerful, my vocal cords didn't work. I should be screaming, but only squeaks were coming out as I muffled the sound with the pillow.

Wave after wave of pure unadulterated pleasure pulsed through me, never ending, just like Myles. He kept working me, coaxing either a really long climax or bringing a second one on the heels of the first. I was too consumed to tell.

I arched, rubbing myself over him until it became too much. I was out of energy and oversensitized. When I sagged against the back of the seat, he backed off.

Gently, he removed the pillow. His chin glistened with my release. "Look at how well you come, Wynn. This is only your first one of the night."

"First," I echoed. I should be ashamed of how I was slumped with my knees crushing the side of his head, but his expression was so supremely satisfied, I couldn't be bothered to move an inch. He dropped a kiss on my

"I don't want to be done yet. I want you to come back to my place tonight and spend the weekend in my bed." He ran his hands up my thighs. "But I have to warn you, this doesn't change anything. I still don't do relationships, and you're still working as my assistant."

"So you're not going to bend me over your desk?"

He made an appreciative sound. The bulge at his crotch was undeniably large, and I knew his size intimately. "I might not be able to stop myself if you tempt me."

Another anticipatory shiver went through me. The whole weekend? I'd trade my soul for that experience. "What are we going to do until we land?" I asked innocently, but heat curled through my belly. We were in prime position to continue what we were doing, but he was proving he was a businessman first. His base needs came after.

"You're going to clean up." He backed up and helped me sit up. Disappointment flickered through my center, dimming the rising desire. "I'll straighten up out here and think about crop yields until my erection gives my brain some blood supply back. And then you'll meet me at home." His thumb was stroking circles on my thigh. "Is this what you want?"

Thinking was hard when his hands were on me, but my answer to his question was crystal clear. "Yes."

Myles didn't touch me for the rest of the trip. When we landed and Imani appeared, he acted his same perfunc-

I could barely look at her and mumble a thanks to her and the pilot. My feet hit the tarmac. My car was in the lot. All I had to do was drive to Foster House, and I'd get more of...*that*.

The effects of my orgasm were lingering, waiting for another. The distillery would be empty, and we'd be in his loft anyway. I could be as loud as I wanted. Would he get noisy or keep that low rumble of dirty talk in my ear?

I didn't care. I wanted him inside of me.

"I'll walk you to your car," he said. His hand hovered at the base of my back as if he couldn't help the slip of impropriety.

This man could do the smallest things and make me feel special. "Thank you."

His driver was parked next to me. Myles opened my door, his gaze shadowed from the parking lot lights. "Drive safe."

"You, too." I smiled and glanced at the ride waiting for him. "I'll wait for ten minutes so he doesn't see me going to the distillery with you this late in the evening." I had the code to get into the distillery, so he wouldn't have to wait for me to arrive. I could let myself in.

His lips thinned. He didn't want to wait either. "See you soon, Wynn." He closed me in, and I could take my first full breath in a week.

The man was potent. This would be the longest ten minutes of my life. I took my phone out of my bag.

Shit. The screen lit with a ton of messages. From Summer. From June. Tate. Mom.

No. Icy cold washed through my veins, bleaching out the heady, lust-filled anticipation from a heartbeat ago.

"He's gone, Wynter." The words were all she could get out before she started crying.

Daddy was gone. Hot tears streamed down my face. I'd known this call was coming, but that didn't make it any easier. Neither did knowing what I had to do. "I'll be home soon, Summer. Tell Mama I'll be there soon."

I hung up and stared at the phone screen. A tear splattered against the glass. The urge to run for home was strong, to be among my family, and comforted by them. But that meant I couldn't go through with tonight. If I stayed with Myles, I'd break down. I'd tell him about me and ruin the connection we'd formed. I'd rather keep what we had, hold it close, and continue on with my life knowing that the kid who'd read me books had grown up to be a decent, if icy at times, man.

All I'd have of him were the memories, but at least this way, he wouldn't learn I'd been lying to him about who I really was. He'd had enough betrayal in his life.

I called him.

"Ms. Kerrigan." There was a hint of worry in his voice. Was he scared I'd changed my mind?

"I have to go, Myles." My voice cracked.

"Your dad?" He wasn't shocked or confused. He gave me the benefit of the doubt and guessed correctly.

"Yeah. I, uh, don't know how long I'll be with my family. After the funeral..." I blew out a heavy breath. "I just want time with them. I'm not—I'm not coming back."

"I see."

"I'm sorry." The words came out a whisper. I didn't think it'd be this hard to say goodbye. Would it be easier

was Ms. Kerrigan, or Wynn when he was getting me off, and nothing more.

He'd never know he was my hero. "Goodbye, Myles."

CHAPTER THIRTEEN

Myles

I'd worked all goddamn weekend. It was Monday, I was in a shitty mood and hadn't left the distillery for days. Some fresh air would help. So would getting laid after suffering blue balls for days. Weeks. But my gut told me that a random lay wouldn't satiate me. Nor would another girl match the sounds Wynn had struggled to hide when I was between her legs.

Fucking heaven.

I liked sex as much as the next guy. Sometimes, I craved it. Being with Wynn had elevated the act to a transcendental level. I wasn't the same man once she'd come on my tongue. I could never be the same.

And she'd left.

My sympathy welled for what she was going through, but my cynical brain also wondered if she really had a dad. Had he indeed passed away?

stories she shared had made me wonder what it would've been like to have been incorporated into a real family. To have siblings who cared. To have fun stories to tell some uptight boss who lived vicariously through them. To share them with a pathetic man who was grateful a girl like Wynn had happy memories and none like mine.

I caught myself glowering at my black computer screen. For fuck's sake.

I should be busier than ever. I had no assistant, and I wasn't going to comb the temp agency looking for someone to fill in for a month. Mrs. Crane had backed off my schedule to keep her replacement from getting overwhelmed. She'd probably been astute enough to know I'd need a breather after the pitch.

I'd planned to take a good three days off and bury myself inside that pretty temporary assistant with a taste for quality.

Pressure grew behind my zipper. Sitting at my desk was worse, but I couldn't bring myself to stand and have it be obvious. I needed to bury myself in work instead. More than anything, I wanted Ms. Kerrigan to walk in on a cloud of sweet lemongrass and give me some sass about being moody.

My screen lit up at the same time that dreaded ring-tone came through. Gianna.

I let three more rings chime before I answered. "Foster."

"Hey, Myles." Her roughened voice came through the line and I let my eyelids fall closed. "I didn't think you were going to answer."

You know that."

"I know, honey. You just work so hard. You and I both know what it's like to toil away all day."

"Sure." While I found no fault in the work Gianna did, grilling hamburgers and running the fry vats wasn't quite like being responsible for over fifty employees' livelihoods and health and retirement benefits, even more people depending on your business to keep a roof over their head, and never being able to walk away from the work because too many people counted on you.

"Listen, about what we've been discussing..."

My shoulders cramped with the tension. She could spin the story a million ways. "We haven't been discussing anything. I told you no."

"Come on, Myles-high."

"Don't call me that." She couldn't see how inappropriate the nickname was. It burrowed under my skin to rot. The "high" part of it was the worst, and she was oblivious, which just fucking stung.

"Right, Myles. Sorry. Old habits, you know."

I fisted my free hand. Otherwise I'd bust the phone. "The answer is still no. I've paid your rent for the year, and you have groceries delivered every Saturday when you're not working."

"But it's my car."

The car I had bought her. "I told you, take it to the repair place, and I'll settle the charge." I shouldn't be doing any of it. Not the groceries, not the rent, not the repairs. Nothing. But I wasn't the one who abandoned people.

disgusted sound. "Did you hear? Darin Bailey died. His funeral's Thursday."

I flinched. A well of emotion I couldn't identify swelled in my throat, choking off a reply. Darin had passed away?

The past I tried not to remember pushed at the doors of my brain. I'd had to crack the door way too many times in the last month, but Darin had never been fully blocked behind that door. Not even I was that coldhearted. "What happened?" I asked gruffly.

"I dunno. Cancer or something I heard. Bet he thought he was too good for cancer."

"Jesus, Gianna."

"You act just like him sometimes."

I couldn't respond, or she'd get more belligerent, more insulting, and I wouldn't be spared. "Listen, I've gotta go."

"Gotta make all that money."

"Someone has to do it," I said. This was how we usually parted. A tradition that should fill me with warmth but left me empty.

"Wait—I need a deposit for the car's repairs."

Was that a thing? "Have them call me. No, you know what, let me know, and I'll call them." I'd look up the repair shop online and make sure they were legit and not someone Gianna had conned into talking to me to get cold, hard cash. "Goodbye, Gianna." I hung up.

I let out a long, heavy exhale. Another call with her was done. The relief was short-lived.

Darin Bailey had passed away.

And then there was Mae. She'd been lumped in with people I tried not to remember, but when I did allow myself memories, she was a fond one. Mae and Darin had been one of the good homes I'd been in. They'd been resilient enough to let me stay.

Mae must be devastated.

She had a ton of kids. She didn't need me bugging her.

I want you to call—anytime, Myles. Do you understand? You'll tell yourself you're going to bother me, but listen to this and listen hard. You are never a bother. Pick up the damn phone and call.

I had once. And she'd given me much-needed advice during my time at the Baileys'. I owed her, too.

Pick up the damn phone and call.

Since when had I listened to anyone?

Wynter

When my bio parents had died, my sisters and I had been in the hospital for much of the funeral preparations. All I could remember were hushed tones and dour expressions. I'd been too young to be of use, and there'd been no one to help us until Mae Bailey had arrived at the hospital.

Darin Bailey's funeral was the opposite. My brothers were home and staying with Tate and his wife. His house was on Bailey land and large enough to fit the guys.

was inside with Mama. We were on constant rotation, but if Mama wanted a moment to herself, she wasn't getting it.

When my sisters and I first came to live with her, she hadn't let up on us until she'd known we would be okay, and I was doing the same for her.

"Have you decided where to live yet?" Summer asked. Her blond hair was kissed by a reddish tint and secured in a high ponytail. Somehow she still looked office ready when she was in worn jeans and a camisole. Her cowboy boots were almost as colorful as the ones Junie wore on the road.

"Not yet." I kicked the toe of my own plain brown boot in the grass at the base of a metal fence post. "Scarlett offered me a room, of course, but I don't want to be in the way. I mean, I could be Super Auntie and help Chance with his homework and be on baby duty so Scarlett and Tate can nap, but I can do that from here, too."

"She's pregnant again." Autumn snorted and scratched at the star on the forehead of Tenpin, a roan gelding who loved attention and treats and knew when we were home he'd get both. "I don't think it's napping they're doing."

"Gross." I snickered anyway. When I was at home, when we were all home, I devolved into the youngest, allegedly most spoiled, child. "Tenor said he wears earplugs at night, just in case he might overhear anything."

"Teller is probably ready to record it and use it for blackmail." Summer combed her fingers through Tenpin's wiry mane.

Scarlett might blush like she was embarrassed, but you know she's proud as hell." Sadness crashed over me, a surprise wave of grief that wouldn't go away. "I'm glad they're having a baby. Gives Mama something to look forward to."

"Yeah," Autumn said sadly. "Daddy Bailey loved welcoming babies into the family."

"Daddy Bailey had two passions—bourbon and family." Summer started a small braid in Tenpin's mane. "Ranching was a close third."

"Probably why he kept taking on fosters. He loved working with children." And with one foster in particular who Daddy must've taken an interest in more than any of us knew. "Are any going to be at the funeral?"

Myles wouldn't show. He wouldn't leave the empire he'd built with his own hands. How long would pass before he even knew?

How'd he handled my departure? I'd thought of him constantly in the days I'd been home. His strong, talented hands. That wickedly skilled tongue of his.

I almost groaned.

"Looking a little flushed there." Autumn squinted at me. Her gaze narrowed on me the same way she must study students who claimed to have a tummy bug. "Jet lag?"

I rolled my eyes. "I was in the same time zone, Autumn."

"And what were you doing in that time zone?" she asked primly.

"Work." More than the sun heated my cheeks. I was a terrible liar, and my sisters knew it.

buckle rivaled the size of a top bull rider's, but her jeans were a pristine blue, so sharp they should crackle while she walked, and her button-up purple shirt wasn't buttoned but tied at the waist.

"Geez, Junie." Summer put her hands on her hips. "Are you putting on a performance tonight?"

Junie glanced down at herself with a confused frown. "What?"

Autumn groaned. "Don't tell me that's so normal for you that you don't even know you look like the Bourbon Canyon rodeo queen."

Junie pouted her expertly tinted and glossed lips. "I've never done rodeo."

Junie could seem like a clueless, high-maintenance diva, but she was smart and used to being underestimated. She used it to her advantage.

I smirked. "Going to town and afraid you're going to run into your ex?"

Her frown deepened. I'd hit on a real nerve. "No. He'll probably be with his kids anyway."

"Who have June Bee posters on their walls?"

She smiled, and her dimples flashed. "I can't help it that girls between the ages of two and forty-two love June Bee. It's the men of America I'm working on. I have a better chance of making it if I hit sex-symbol status. Anyway, I stopped to ask if anyone wants to go to town with me. Mama got a call and told me to go get more groceries."

"Mama's fielding so many calls, and she refuses to give the damn thing up. We need to go to Bozeman to

pets from Junie. "I'll go. I can swing by home and pick up a few things and check in on Boyd."

I exchanged a covert glance with Autumn. Shouldn't Summer's boyfriend be checking on her?

"Mama's going to get you to move back home eventually." Junie's smug look said she thought she was exempt from the lure of Bourbon County.

None of us were. I was back. Finally and for good after ten years of being away. Autumn had only left for college, being the biggest homebody of us all. Summer hadn't gone far, but Bozeman was too far for Mama. Same with Tenor, but he split his time between all the locations. Teller was such a recluse and lived in the cabin he'd built on the far edge of Bailey land in the shadows of the mountains. The distance was almost a commute, almost impossible depending on the weather, which was why he was staying with Tate until after the funeral.

He claimed to prefer game trails over bike paths.

Summer waved her off. "I'm a city girl, even if that city is getting kind of bougie." She pointed a finger in my direction. "Don't think you aren't getting away that easy. Who is he?"

"No one anymore." The empty chasm close to my heart yawned open. "We didn't have a chance to be a thing, and now I'm here."

I was yanked into Summer's warm embrace. Her strawberry-and-sugar scent surrounded me, as much of a reminder of home and family as the scents of musty barns and wildflowers on the wind. "I'm sorry, honey."

My face was crushed against her bony shoulder, and I

She squeezed me tighter. "You'd better not be, or Daddy is going to return from the afterlife and haunt you."

Laughter burst out of me, but tears pricked the backs of my eyes. "He would, wouldn't he?"

"He'd do it for posterity," Autumn said, both humor and sadness in her voice. "But I caught him drinking beer a few times."

"Me, too," Junie said. "I think that's why he helped me move to Nashville."

We all laughed. Our family enjoyed alcohol as a hobby. Daddy would visit breweries to taste products, study their marketing, and siphon details about their processes, but he always ended the day saying, "Spirits are better for the spirit."

He'd claim the distillation process was a metaphor for life. Leave the worst behind and take only what you need to make you the strongest.

I blinked away tears but lost the fight. "God, I miss him."

Junie and Autumn added themselves to the hug.

"Aw hell, am I going through puberty again?" Teller's voice drifted to us. To others, he'd sound disgruntled, but I could hear the thick emotion he was fighting to hold back. Teller would never join in on a group hug, but he was hurting like the rest of us.

Summer pulled away, and the rest of us broke apart. She put her hands on her hips and squared off with Teller. As the oldest of the Kerrigan girls, she and Tate might have felt like competitors, but it was Teller she often faced off with, like both of them were vying for the

stand what she'd been through as the oldest sister and the one who remembered our parents and the crash the best out of all of us.

Teller wasn't oblivious, he just wasn't going to let her trauma bamboozle him into doing her chores like Tate used to do.

"You might have to go through puberty again and learn some manners." Summer pulled herself up to her diminutive height. "Did you really tell Finley Porter that she didn't need to stop by and see Mom?"

He strode toward us, and Tenor rounded out of the barn. I'd never admit this out loud, but I often wondered if Tenor was a foster kid, too, and our parents just forgot. Where Tate and Teller were wide-shouldered, bearded mountain men, Tenor was not quite as tall. He was lanky and clean-shaven, and he dressed in baggy T-shirts and loose khakis—jeans, if he was working the ranch like he was today.

Tenor had been the smaller kid with two adored older brothers. When those two were around, he was forgotten. When they weren't, he was teased and bullied. Tenor had a streak of pride buried as deep as the coal veins of Montana, and he hadn't told anyone. Four nosy younger sisters had found out and put a stop to it.

Tenor might've grown up to resemble a lighter-haired version of his brothers, taking after Mom's side, but he still dressed and acted like that kid who'd been afraid to be noticed.

"Tenor," Summer called, knowing he'd never disagree with her. We were all baby sisters to him, but Summer had headlocked the worst of his bullies and

her boobs instead of revealing what Tenor had been going through when he wanted it to remain a secret. Tenor had let Summer get away with murder ever since. "Your brother was rude as hell to Finley, wasn't he?"

"He's rude as hell to everyone," Tenor replied, pushing his glasses up and keeping to his typical middle ground.

She rounded on Teller. "To *Finley*? She's as sweet as molasses. You know Mama would enjoy her visit."

Teller was unrepentant. "Mama has a full house and has a million calls to make to finalize all the funeral arrangements. Everyone's coming out here after the funeral. Until then, I want Mama to have a chance to rest and catch her breath. You know how the last few months have been."

Mama had taken care of Dad to the end, minimizing his hospital stays and keeping him from dying in a stale room surrounded by unfamiliar scenery.

I'm a part of this land, he used to say. *And you are, too*.

Teller crossed his arms over his impressive chest. "You and Junie come back with groceries only. No people."

Summer wasn't cowed. "Mama thrives on company as much as Daddy did."

"She has a house full of seven kids, a daughter-in-law, and two grandkids. Thursday is for everyone else." The muscles in Teller's jaw flexed, and then I understood. *He* needed a mellower environment. We were all grieving.

"You know, I'm with Teller on this one," I said, or Summer would invite all the residents of Bourbon

Grief ran through Junie's eyes. Tenor crossed his arms, but he was hunched over like he was forming a wall like Teller.

Autumn nodded. "Low-key sounds nice. I know we were expecting this, but it's an adjustment, and we're going to have visitors stopping by no matter what. Might as well encourage the masses to wait until the reception."

Teller shot me a grateful look, and I dipped my head to him.

"Then we'll have Daddy's party, just like he wanted." Junie lifted her hat, ran her hand through her silky hair, and put the hat back in place. "Ready, Summer?"

Summer studied all of us. Would her stubborn side overrule common sense? Some days, she could argue until sundown with a fence post, demanding it move out of her way.

"Anyone need anything from town?" she asked sweetly.

Teller's shoulders unknotted, and the rest of us relaxed.

"Toilet paper," Tenor said. "With all of you back under one roof, I can't imagine the amount we're going to go through."

"I'm going to sneak a roll every time I use the bathroom just to piss you off," I teased.

Teller gave me a shocked stare. "You mean you don't?"

Laughing, I punched him in the shoulder. Dammit, now my fingers stung. He put an arm around my neck and noogied my hair. My laugh grew stronger.

ing. Just like I was getting used to not driving to an office by the mountains every morning and seeing a scowling, stern, handsome man in a suit sitting across the desk. But at least I was back with my family.

CHAPTER FOURTEEN

Wynter

For the most part, visitors were minimal. The funeral was still two days away. Mama was getting a ton of calls, but between me, my sisters, and my brothers roaming through town, talking to people at the gas stations, the grocery store, and the distillery, we'd managed to convince people that the reception at the Bailey ranch after the funeral was the best time to talk to Mama.

I was at the kitchen table. Dad's spot was empty and would likely stay that way for months or years. I had my boots on with a yellow summer dress. Cool, easy. I'd felt like dressing up after a morning of getting dirty and helping with chores and cuddling with barn cats.

Lunch was over. Autumn and Summer had dumped bread, lunch meat, and produce on the table, and Junie had taken a tray of bars out of the freezer one of the neighbors had brought over right after Dad had died.

As if food were a silent signal to the boys, Teller and

Tate and Scarlett and baby Brinley were welcome, too. When Mama hinted at something, she got it. We'd been programmed from an early age and had copied Daddy. Whatever Mama wanted.

Now the food was put away. Chance was in the living room with Scarlett and his baby sister, listening to Junie pluck her guitar strings. The quiet melody of her voice filtered through the house.

Mama hovered by the door like she was waiting on something. Every time Tate tried to shoo her into the living room, telling her we'd take care of the after-lunch cleanup and would let her know when the brownies were thawed, she brushed him off.

Every few minutes, she'd look out the window.

I paged through a *Rodeo Magazine*. Back in the day, I used to look through the pages and dream about the cowboy husband I'd marry. Now the way they tucked their faces down, their expressions lined with concentration, and the rigid hold of their bodies while a bull or bronc tried to dislodge them, didn't compare to the clean lines of a well-tailored suit and flashing blue eyes.

Autumn was cutting the bars. Summer was in the pantry on a work call. Teller and Tate were talking about the cattle and Tenor was peppering the conversation with numbers about calves, how many and when they'd be ready for sale, and the conception rate for the year.

Mama hitched a breath. We all stopped and looked at her. She stiffened and turned from the window. Determination was steeped in her brown eyes, and her mouth was set in a stern line. "I want you all to be on your best behavior."

driving on country roads."

Mama put her hands on Tate's shoulders. For a short woman, she loomed over him like he was a six-year-old who'd sassed off to her. "The main thing you need to know is that he's been invited here, personally, by me. You all need to remember that."

Teller frowned, glaring out the window. "What *the fuck* is he doing here?"

My belly swirled, slowly tying itself in a knot. I didn't like when my family argued, but worse, alarm bells were going off in my head.

There was a knock on the back door, the one between the house and the garage. Only people familiar with the sprawling family home knew that we never used the front door. Even delivery companies knew to use the kitchen door. That was where Mama would be.

"I don't want to hear it." Mama's tone was sharp. "He is my guest."

I exchanged a stunned glance with Autumn. Tenor's eyes were narrowed, and he was frowning in the direction of the door.

Was it someone he had a history with? A former bully and Mama didn't know?

Mama swung the door open, and my lungs seized mid breath.

Oh no.

I recognized those broad shoulders. That dark hair combed into submission. That impeccably tailored suit.

"Come in. Come in. I'm so glad you could make it." Mama squeezed his hand and dragged him inside as if she knew a hug would send him running.

"Nice to see you again, Mae."

His deep voice rumbled over all the nerve endings he'd lit up less than a week ago. Desire flooded my body, heedless that this moment was highly inappropriate.

My brain was spinning for a solution, for some way to save face and not look like I had ferreted myself into his organization to get close to him. Which was exactly what I'd done.

His attention swung over my brothers. His body was stiff, and Mama had let go of his hand. He narrowed his eyes on Autumn, like he was trying to place which sister she was even though she'd had distinctive red hair her whole life. The struggle for recognition stayed in his gaze when Summer appeared out of the pantry.

I felt Tate's wall of disgruntled attitude before he growled, "Mom, what's this all about?"

Myles dismissed him and continued scanning the room. Panic rose in my throat, choking me. Then that hooded blue gaze landed on me. Recognition flared as bright as a wildfire at midnight, followed by confusion, then startling hurt.

"Wynn?"

Myles

She was here. Wynn.

Blond hair hanging loose, long legs sticking out of a

Wynn.

I barely recognized Autumn. Summer or June was the one in the pantry and the other with pink in her hair was behind Tate.

But I knew who Wynn was.

Her wide eyes, open mouth, and stunned expression burrowed into my consciousness. Paired with her impeccable knowledge of bourbon and whiskey and all things distilling, I came to one disturbing conclusion.

She'd tricked me. "Or should I say Wynter Bailey?"

The guys crackled with restrained energy. They'd been about to kick me out, putting their mom in the middle of our beef, but the situation had changed.

Because one important fact had come to light.

My temp assistant, the girl I wanted in my bed more than anyone I'd met in my life, was a Bailey. The girl from a bourbon family who hated my guts would know damn well who I was.

So many tidbits clicked into place. Her sick dad. Her big family. The way she hadn't shared specific details. I had been glad she hadn't showered me with casual factoids. I'd wanted that distance.

Christ, I was an idiot.

"Myles, I can explain—"

Burning up with rage, I pushed backward out the door. Deep in my consciousness, I reprimanded myself for walking out on Mae like this, but I couldn't stay for another second. Betrayal had been building, but the confirmation she'd known who I was detonated a bomb in my chest.

Did Mae know, too?

for and take it for themselves like so many other foster families I'd had?

I stormed to my car. The squeak of the door resonated in the summer air.

"Myles, wait!"

Wynn's boots clicked on the sidewalk from the driveway to my car.

I opened my door, not even looking at her. I couldn't speak to her.

"Myles."

The house door creaked open again. "Wynter, what's going—"

"Not now, Tate," Wynn snapped, her tone frantic. "Myles, come on, talk to me."

I started my car and kicked it into reverse. I took my foot off the brake, then slammed it back down. A blond head was in my rearview mirror. "Fucking A, Wynn!" I yelled loud enough for her to hear. "Move!"

She pounded the trunk of my car. "Talk to me first."

Growling, I contemplated how to leave without running her over. Baileys were piling outside. I could see them out of the corner of my eye, but I refused to look in their direction.

Ghost fingers walked up my spine. Memories started assaulting me. The stares. The leaving. The garbage bag full of shit thrift stores wouldn't bother shelving. Coming or going, the feelings were too similar to now.

She skirted around the car, and I almost floored it backward. But her hands were on the car, and no matter what, I couldn't risk hurting her. I had too many onlook-

She ripped open the door and dove in. Before the door was closed, I hit the gas.

"Whoa." She rushed to close herself in and gave her family a reassuring wave. As if that'd put their mind at ease.

Fuck, what'd it look like? Angry Myles storming out of the house and abducting their youngest sister?

Goddammit.

"Myles."

"Wynn?" I bit out as I fishtailed down the driveway. "Oh, I'm sorry, it's Wynter, isn't it? Wynter Bailey?"

"We kept our last name. It's Kerrigan. Remember?"

That got me to look at her. Same beautiful face. Same wild eyes. Her hair was mussed with a hunk sticking up on top of her head. My fingers twitched to touch her, to stroke across that soft skin and smooth the lines of worry on her forehead. "No. I don't remember."

When hurt darkened her brown eyes, I looked away and skidded onto the main gravel road. I would have chips in the paint galore after this drive.

"I knew it." She slumped in her seat and stared out the window. I couldn't look directly at her, or I might soften. "I knew you'd forgotten all about me."

"Why would I remember you, *Wynter* Kerrigan? I was a teen, and you were like five."

"I was six when you left. Without saying goodbye."

Guilt lit deep in a pit in my gut. I refused to have regrets, but if I did, it would be the way I'd left the Baileys. Thanks to Gianna, I'd learned to be proactive. "I had to look out for myself."

"And you've been doing that ever since."

"Do you know where this goes?" she asked.

"Yup." The Bailey land had a ton of roads that led to open areas, and I'd had time to explore them all. *Vehicle-accessible roads for hunting*, Darin had laughed. *But I don't let no one hunt out here but us.* He'd hunted to fill the freezer and feed all the kids under his roof. I'd gone from discount beef that looked and smelled funny to wild game—elk steaks, moose roasts, and venison. Sausage and jerky and homegrown vegetables—that I'd had to help weed and water. I'd been a brat about it, too, until I'd tasted what Mae did with food that came out of the ground.

"Myles, talk to me."

"We're going to talk." This road led to an open vista. Ponderosas lined the mountainous terrain on one side and looked out above one of the many side channels of the Madison River.

It had been one of my favorite places to get away from the noise of everyone packed under one roof. The house was bigger than I remembered, but I recalled the feeling of not being able to get away.

When I reached a loop in the road, a turnaround point, I pointed the car out to face the water. To go any farther, I'd need a four-wheeler or a Ranger, and the land dipped down toward the basin.

I took a moment to inhale and straighten the jumble of thoughts in my mind. Fresh pine and crisp mountain air made it through my car vents. Green valley spread out in front of me. Darin had mentioned once this would be a good place for a house or cabin. The water would never get this high, but the setting wasn't so

Wynn's sweet lemongrass scent surrounded me. I'd never get the smell out of my car, just like I'd never be able to scrub the smell or taste of her from my mind.

"Why'd you do it?" I asked.

"Do what? Work for you?"

I ground my teeth together. "Trick me."

"I didn't trick you. *You* didn't remember *me*. I gave you my full name."

"Wynn?" I met her militant gaze.

Her resolve slipped. "Fine. I thought you'd run me off if I told you who I was."

"Good guess." A Bailey working for me? No, I wouldn't have trusted it. "Your brothers think I stole all your family's distilling secrets and got rich off it."

"Why don't they know you and Daddy kept in contact?"

"It's not their business."

"And Myles Foster doesn't want anyone in his business."

The slight mocking in her tone burrowed under my collar and itched. "No, Wynn. I don't. People are always after something for themselves."

"You were so nice to me," she blurted. She twisted in her seat to face me. "I remembered this cranky kid who was a little punk to everyone but so damn sweet to me. And then my brothers would talk about you and how you were copying Daddy and that you were nothing but a thief, and I had to know if I was wrong and they were right."

I leaned in, our faces inches apart. With the sun streaming in the car, I could see amber specks dancing

breathe.

"No," she said quietly. "I think Daddy helped you. I think you respected him—and Mama—or you wouldn't be here. What I don't get is why they don't know he was your mentor."

"He was more than that. He was my first investor."

Her eyes flared wider, and I liked that shock on her face. I'd put it there. She was so damn expressive, and this close to her, I could hardly think of more than those needy moans and her cries, my name on her lips. "Daddy helped you start Foster House?"

"He did. He argued his boys needed a proper competitor. That if things kept coming easy to them, they'd never keep Copper Summit at the level it needed to be."

A scandalized gasp left her lips, and it was all I could do not to capture that lush mouth for myself. "But you just make whiskey."

"Yes. Because Foster House is mine. If I made bourbon, your brothers would get involved, and they'd think it was theirs."

"Oh, Myles, they wouldn't try to take your business."

"No? Then why were you really there?" My anger ramped up again. This temptress was exactly that. A pretty doll to tempt me away from my goals.

She poked me in the shoulder. "I was a little obsessed, okay? You were this older boy who was sweet to me and then disappeared in the middle of the night. When I next learned about you, you'd become this devastating enigma who gives very limited interviews, has no social media, and only lets one headshot out into

"That'd make me a pervert, Wynn." I hadn't thought about her. I hadn't thought about any of the sisters.

She poked my shoulder again. "You know what I mean."

"No, I don't. You said you were six. I read you a few books. I didn't think about you or your sisters after I left because you were getting adopted. Which meant you would be just like the Bailey brothers, and I'd be nothing but a foster."

Goddammit, I couldn't shut my mouth around her.

Her lips parted and understanding filled her eyes. Normally, I hated to see that sympathy. Hated the way social workers tried to hide it. But Wynn was different. She *knew* what I meant. She wasn't feeling sorry for me like adults had done then. She didn't look at me like she pitied the horrible future that awaited a kid like me. She knew what it was like to not know if you'd have a home in a year, two years, hell, in a month. She might've been taken in by the Baileys right after her parents had died, but there'd been a time she'd experienced some of what I had. And that shit didn't leave a kid.

"Myles, you were more than a foster to me. You were a lifeline." She cupped my cheek.

I gripped her wrist and took her hand off me.

Her eyes sparked. "You are so damn stubborn! I went to work for you because I was nosy. I liked you. And you're writing me off because of who I grew up with?"

"I have no idea who you are!"

She sucked in a breath and leaned in close. "You knew whose lips were wrapped around your cock on that flight." She stuck that damn finger into my shoulder

liked it."

"That doesn't change that you're a lying little—"

"A lying little what?" She was practically over the console. "Go ahead. Finish what you started."

"I finished you—I didn't hear you complaining about that."

"You didn't finish a thing, Myles Foster." She shoved me back and crawled over the seat, kicking her cowboy boots off as she went.

I didn't do a damn thing to stop her. "Get back in your seat, Wynn."

"No." She reached down and laid the seat back. Again, I did nothing to stop her. Instead, I clamped my hands at her waist and ground her down into my erection. I'd been half hard since she'd jumped into my car.

She flattened her hands on my chest, her hair hanging over her shoulders. "We have unfinished business between us."

I wrapped her hair around my fist and brought her closer. "This changes nothing."

She wiggled her hips over me. "I know. Just fuck me already."

I didn't trust her. I didn't want to get to know this new grown-up version of some little girl who was supposed to have stayed in the past. But I wanted to be inside Wynn, and that wiped out any other thought.

I lifted her dress, baring a swath of creamy skin. She was wearing simple white underwear and a plain lace bra. I'd never seen anything so sexy. I tugged the dress over her head and palmed her breasts.

Wynn struggled with my belt until I abandoned the

hitting the roof and she was tipped over me, her breasts begging to be freed.

I acquiesced, dragging the cups down and baring her pink nipples just as she wrapped her fingers around my erection.

"Fuck, Wynn." I lifted her to get those pearled nipples close to my mouth. Finally, I wrapped my lips around a peaked tip and sucked.

"God, Myles." Only last week, she'd have called me Mr. Foster, and for some reason, that got me harder when the reminder should've chased blood from my dick.

She wrestled with her underwear, but between the door and the console and the roof of the car, she couldn't get it off with her nipple still in my mouth. Grudgingly, I released her.

Now for the underwear.

I gripped the hem and ripped. The sound of fabric tearing mingled with our heavy breathing. I tore the other side and pulled the underwear free.

"That's so hot," she breathed. She sat back until her ass hit the steering wheel and honked the horn.

We both froze like we'd fired a flare into the sky and let everyone know where we were. Then heat filled her gaze, and I was captivated by a naked Wynn. My goddamn assistant.

She stroked a hand up and down my shaft. I gripped her hips again but she tensed. "Myles."

I cut off my groan. I was standing on the edge of paradise and getting denied entrance. I'd survive, but I'd never recover. "Yeah?"

The words *fuck protection* almost left my mouth. What the hell was wrong with me? With jerky movements, I dug a condom out of my wallet and tossed the wallet in the same direction as her dress and underwear.

I tore the damn thing open, hating I was grateful she was the one to have some sense. I'd never planned to have kids. Yet I'd been ready to forget that when I'd thought of her belly growing round with my kid.

I slammed the condom on like it had personally insulted me. I'd think clearer after an orgasm.

She leaned over me again and placed me at her entrance. Sweltering heat covered the tip of my cock, and it was all I could do to keep from slamming her down.

Her pink tongue licked out, dampening her lips.

"Nervous, Frosty?" I jerked. Where the fuck had that come from? Nothing in the moment should've brought back a nickname I hadn't used for twenty-two years.

Surprise dilated her pupils, and she melted, sinking that sweet, wet pussy down, taking me in inch by inch until a frayed groan left us both.

"Fuck." How could she feel that good? How could she fit around me like she was made for me? How could I live without being so deep inside her I forgot about everything?

I fisted my hand in the strands of her hair again and brought her mouth to mine. She rode me, but I was in complete sync, thrusting up into her wet heat. Our foreplay had been an argument, and she was soaked. All for me.

She'd known who I was the whole time.

probably heard the gritty details from her family. She knew I was Myles Foster, the kid no one wanted.

Yet she was here, in the car with me.

Her hands were all over my hair, tugging at the strands. I kept her pressed to me, my tongue dominating her mouth. I swallowed her moans and whimpers.

She picked up the pace, freeing my mouth to toss her hair to the side. Her breaths were coming hard and heavy. "Myles."

"What do you need, Wynn?" I rolled my hips into her, and her eyes went glossy.

"You."

"Do you need Mr. Foster to suck that pretty little clit of yours again?"

Pink dusted across her cheeks. "I need Myles Foster to keep fucking me."

She said it like she knew I had to hear my name on her lips. That I had to know she knew exactly who I was.

Lightning coiled at the base of my spine, my climax imminent.

I took my hand from her hair and stroked down her neck, brushed over her tits, and skated my fingers down her abdomen to where we were connected.

I circled the tip of my finger over her swollen nub.

"Yes," she hissed.

My balls were tightening. I was coming soon, but my pride would not let me go first. "Come for me, Wynn. You're so goddamn tight, I'm not going to last much longer."

How had I held on this long?

I circled her clit. She let out a cry. Her hair curtained her face, and her body undulated. The way her legs were bent and straddling me, I had a full view of her. Her knees might have bruises after this, and I hated how I liked her carrying proof we were together.

"Myles!" Her pussy fisted my cock, demanding I careen over the edge with her. Her cries grew louder, and I took over, my hands bracketing her hips. I lifted and lowered her, my release needing no extra coaxing.

Heat flooded my hand and her walls rippled around me, catapulting me straight over the edge. "Fuck, Wynn."

My release hit fast and hard. The ends of her hair tickled my cheeks, and her breath wafted over my face.

"I knew it'd be intense with you," she murmured moments later.

"Just like I should've known this was a mistake."

She blew out an exasperated breath and shoved against my chest. "Is it something you can't help? Pushing people away?"

She tried to crawl off but I held her in place. "What do you mean?"

"You know exactly what I mean. That's why you're so upset about me and why you're trying to convince yourself I had some nefarious reason to get close." She dropped back down and feathered a finger down the side of my face. "When you know damn well there are no trade secrets under your roof that aren't already Bailey secrets."

I turned and sucked her finger into my mouth and

But Darin had taught me what he knew and encouraged me to use it all.

He'd also taught his children. He'd told me he planned to do the same as soon as each kid turned sixteen. They'd start by mopping the distillery floors and then move up. All of them had one major advantage I didn't—more time with Darin Bailey. Wynn was so knowledgeable about the product, she could probably take one of my proprietary recipes and deduce what had gone into it from taste alone.

She drew her finger out of my mouth and squeezed my chin. "You know I'm right."

I wasn't admitting anything.

She rolled her eyes and reached for her bra, which was half falling off the front seat. With me still hard inside her, she slipped it on. "I wanted to get to know the real Myles Foster. And now I know why I was so forgettable."

Dismay swept over me, settling heavy on my chest. She knew the real me better than anyone on the planet. "So you're done with me?" While I was still inside her?

Was I ready to be done with her?

"No, Myles. You're going to stay for the funeral. You should've seen the way Mama waited for you. If you leave, none of us will forgive you. And you're going to talk to my brothers." She leaned down to get her dress, which was draped over her boots.

If she kept wiggling on me, I'd have to test the capacity of the damn condom. "Christ, Wynn. You need to get off me, or we're going to break the condom."

Hurt flashed in her eyes, and she scrambled to get

glove compartment to wrap it in.

"I don't owe your brothers anything," I said as I stuffed myself back into my pants. Straightening my clothes was more difficult.

She shrugged into her dress and puffed hair out of her face. "You can do things without owing people." She gave me a pointed look. "Or without them owing you."

"I don't have to explain myself, how about that?"

"You don't have to, but you can."

"Fuck no."

She picked up the remnants of her underwear and frowned. I snatched them from her and stuffed them into my pocket. The little scrap barely made a bulge. She lifted her gaze to mine. "The tension between you and my brothers will be hard on Mama. My brothers are Mainline right now. Think of them like that."

Grinding my teeth, I glowered out the windshield, ignoring her steady gaze on me. I owed Mae. Directly and by proxy for everything Darin had done for me. Mae would never collect, and that was why I couldn't just drive away.

I was here, and leaving would make Mae feel like she'd done something wrong. "I'll go back with you, but I'm not explaining a damn thing."

"That's fine," she said sweetly. "You can stay with me while I explain."

"No." Her underwear was in my pocket. I wasn't facing her brothers while she still glowed from an orgasm I'd given her.

"Please, Myles. I've felt like shit lying to them, but I

She'd shielded me? Technically, she would've been the one bringing trouble to my doorstep, but I was stuck on the way she'd protected me. "You want me to stand in front of your family with your underwear in my pocket?"

"Yeah." She adjusted in her seat until she was sitting on her dress. "Let's go."

CHAPTER FIFTEEN

Myles

This was a bad fucking idea.

"I need you all to be quiet and let me talk," Wynn announced as she pushed into the house. "If you don't, I'm going right back out this door and taking Myles with me."

Okay, then.

I stepped into the kitchen behind her and hostility closed around me like my suit coat—which I had put on to cover any lingering stains from Wynn's release.

Mae's arms were crossed, and she was giving her kids individual hard stares. A woman I didn't recognize was tucked under Tate's arm. In his other arm was a baby. Fuck if I knew the age. An older kid slipped out of the kitchen and disappeared into the living room.

The house looked the same, but new appliances gleamed in all their stainless-steel glory, the cabinets had been updated, and the hardwood floor must've been

It'd peak in the open-concept living room. An upper level over one-half of the main floor had a couple bedrooms, and the lowest level had four more. Unless they had remodeled, or Wynter had moved to a different room, her bedroom was downstairs.

"Well. Explain," Tate said.

The three brothers glared at me. Tate and Teller were dressed much like they had looked when I lived here. Jeans, boots, and T-shirts. A utility knife was clipped to their belts, and they wore the same scowls. Tenor looked the most different, and if he hadn't been one of the three guys in the Bailey house, I wouldn't have recognized him. He looked like a lighter-haired version of his brothers, but with an aversion to snug clothes.

As for the girls, their names were easy to remember. The seasons, except June was named that instead of spring. *June—because most of June is technically spring*, she'd told me once.

Memories flooded back the longer I stood in place and soaked in my surroundings. I'd already figured out Summer was the highlighted blond with the suspicious look in her eyes, a lot like her brothers. Autumn was the redhead, and June had the pink streaks and wasn't fighting the mirth dancing through her expression.

I remembered avoiding Summer. She'd been a bossy little thing, and the one time I'd told her I wasn't listening to someone whose feet didn't touch the ground at the kitchen table, she'd burst into tears and told me she'd been in the car when her parents had crashed and died.

of them, details poured back. Wynter had been in the car. All the girls had.

I couldn't soften toward her. She'd lied to me.

You *were the one who didn't remember* me.

I had changed the subject whenever Darin had tried to talk about his family. The last thing I had wanted to hear about was family. And here I was with Wynn, with all her siblings and Mae, too. A group of people I'd never been a part of even when I'd lived among them.

Wynn scooted closer to me. "I wanted to get to know Myles because I remembered him as a thoughtful boy who read to me when I was scared."

I did not want to be here right now.

"He did not," Teller said.

"He did," Mae said and lifted her chin. "I wasn't sure how I was going to survive those first years. The tears and the crying and the storms. I didn't know how to console Wynter. Then Myles started reading." She looked at me fondly. "I never had to ask. He just did."

"He just did a lot," Tate snapped.

Wynn held her hand up. "We'll get to that later."

"No, we won't," I said.

She gave me an *are you serious?* look. "Nothing, Myles?"

"It's not their business."

"The hell it isn't," Teller shot back.

"Whatever Myles did, he did with your father's blessing," Mae announced.

Silence descended. I squirmed under their stares. Darin wasn't around to speak for himself. I felt like I was feeding him to the wolves. "Mae, you don't have to—"

father's decision."

I wouldn't let her take the heat for me. I tossed out the only thing that would take the focus off her. "Darin was my one and only investor."

"What the hell?" Teller held his arms out like I'd lifted his wallet.

"That's where the money went," Tenor said, and everyone's heads swiveled his way. He shrugged. "Dad withdrew a large amount of money, gosh, must've been almost twenty years ago."

"Nineteen," I clarified. "I was twenty-one and was... stuck. He put up money and told me to use what I knew to make a living."

"So how much do you owe the company?" Tate asked, his biceps flexing while his arms were crossed.

"He doesn't," Tenor said before I could respond. "The same amount went back into holdings. Five years ago."

Darin hadn't let me pay interest. I had tried. It'd taken him long enough to accept the money, and only when I'd told him I'd sell and find another career if he didn't.

The pleasant tickle of Wynter's attention was on me. How much had I missed that sensation in the days since she'd left?

Summer tapped a sandaled foot on the floor, her arms crossed and her expression incensed. "This is the guy who was a dick to you and made you drink a bottle of wine?"

Wynn's eyes widened, and she shot Summer a *why'd*

My people skills were rusty when I only thought of fucking my assistant and not reviewing reports. She'd told Summer I'd fired her? Did I have a bottle of wine to thank for her storming into Foster House to tell me off? Then I'd hired her without checking her background. Mrs. Crane wouldn't have known what to look for when it came to Wynn's résumé.

"I was right not to trust why she wanted the job," I said.

Summer's lips thinned. "You hired her for her qualifications. Or was there another reason?" she asked, deceptively innocent.

"I was in immediate need of an assistant," I replied smoothly. If I thought about this as a pitch to a distributor I wanted to work with, perhaps I wouldn't get irritable and tell the whole family to fuck off. "She had experience, and I had no choice."

"It's true." Wynn nudged my elbow. "But you were extremely picky, which didn't leave Mrs. Crane with many choices."

"I don't get it," Teller interjected. "How could you not remember her? It's not like Wynter Kerrigans grow on trees."

I tugged hard at a cuff link. The AC was going, but the heat of the Baileys' stares was death by a thousand laser beams. "I might've recognized the name Wynter Bailey, but that's not how she applied."

"He didn't know we stayed Kerrigans." She pulled at the hem of her dress. The one she wore no underwear under.

I was tempted to drag her out in the car and return

furnace ramped to unbearable levels.

"And I went by Wynn."

"To make sure I didn't connect any dots," I growled.

She rolled her eyes at me. "Can you blame me? I was a perfectly qualified assistant, and you barely let me in the door. You're not the easiest man to work for, you know." She tipped her head. "Actually, that's not true. You were completely professional, and except for long work days, you respected my time off."

Justifying myself in front of an audience was the equivalent of one of the circles of hell. Getting complimented in front of that same audience was being trampled by an angry herd of cattle and left to rot in the sun.

"Is that what you two were talking about when you both ran out of here?" Autumn asked. The twinkle in her green eyes was my only warning that this family meeting would get more intolerable. "Your *long* work hours?"

Junie's lips quivered, and her shoulders shook. "Maybe about how *hard* the job was?"

Autumn snickered, and Junie lost control of her suppressed laughter. Summer sucked in an audible breath. I couldn't bring myself to look at Mae.

I briefly closed my eyes. Could I sink through the floor? Not once had I had to explain myself when it came to a girl. I was either chased off because no one wanted their daughter to date a moody foster kid, or I was an adult and the woman wanted the prestige of being with a guy who wore a suit and drove an Audi.

I didn't have to look at Wynn to know her face was beet red, and she was as stiff as a board.

"Boys," Mae chided. "Stay out of Myles and Wynn's personal business." When I opened my eyes, Mae was directing her strongest mom glare at the girls. "That goes for you, too. Don't think I don't know what you did." Her face broke into a smile when she looked at me, and I was propelled back in time to when she'd seen me reading to Wynn. First, she'd sagged with relief that Wynn had quieted down, but then, and each time after, she'd grinned, thinking I couldn't see her, and tiptoed away. "Now, Myles. I wanted to let you know we have room here for you."

"No, that's not—"

"No, we don't," Tate said, cutting me off.

"I can't sleep with a strange man in the house!" Summer exclaimed.

"You don't even sleep with your own man in the house," Tate retorted.

"Because he never stays here," Teller added.

Summer narrowed her eyes, her jaw tight. "Boyd is working and will be here for the funeral."

"Stop." Mae held her hands up.

"I got a room in Bozeman." I wasn't crazy about being so close to Gianna, but I counted on the anonymity of a larger population.

"I'd love for you to stay and update me on everything Myles and Foster House," Mae said firmly. "I've only been able to keep up through Darin and snooping online, and we both know there isn't much out there about you. As for the rest of you—Myles is my guest. And I know all of you are keeping visitors away until Thursday because you don't want me overwhelmed.

guff about him being a stranger. I've known this man for over half his life, and I couldn't be prouder of him." Her eyes misted over.

Tate let out a heavy but silent sigh. Teller exchanged a defeated glance with him. Summer glared at Wynn, still being a brat when she didn't get her way. Autumn and Junie looked like they couldn't wait to witness the fallout while staying at the Bailey house.

Should I?

Mae had said her piece, but, to be juvenile, she wasn't the boss of me.

I glanced around the room. I'd expected more arguing, yelling at the very least, but they succumbed to Mae's wishes rather quickly. Did that mean I had to look for rattlesnakes in my blankets and mice in my shoes?

A large part of me wanted the refuge the Bailey home provided. Gianna wouldn't come close to the funeral or Bourbon Canyon at all. However, if she caught a glimpse of me in Bozeman, then she wouldn't let up. I'd be dealing with more than phone calls.

Being in the house was bringing back memories, but something inside me wasn't chasing them away again. Maybe if I let them come, that'd be the end of their power over me. The Bailey house held the best memories of my childhood. The Bailey boys hadn't been cruel. They'd been dicks, but no less than what I'd witnessed between other sets of brothers. At the time, it had felt personal, and in a way it had been, but not because I hadn't been good enough. It was because they'd known I could do better and didn't want to pick up my slack. They'd forced me to prove I *was* better.

roof, and her presence was a far larger factor in my decision than I cared to admit.

"If that's what you'd like, Mae, I'll stay."

Wynn stared at me, and this time I was the one avoiding her gaze.

Tate grunted. "Rules are still the same, Foster. You stay under this roof, you're getting your hands dirty."

CHAPTER SIXTEEN

Wynter

I was supposed to meet Myles in five minutes. When Tate had declared that Myles had to help with ranch work, Mama had been ready to ground Tate like he was ten.

But Myles had taken the challenge. *In that case, I'll stop at the tractor supply. Is it still open?*

The thought of him roaming Bourbon Canyon without me by his side to glare at any female who looked his way was strong. I couldn't let him go to town alone, and he'd agreed to let me tag along.

When he'd gone out to the car to get his suitcase, my brothers had started in on me as soon as the back door had closed. I'd fled the kitchen to my bedroom. If I'd thought I could get a few minutes to process what had happened this afternoon, I was mistaken. Autumn, Junie, and Summer burst into my room.

I could take her. This once. Maybe. She usually over-powered me, having the most experience and sheer stubbornness, but I was riding high on Myles-fueled adrenaline.

"You each get one question, or Myles is going to leave without me." We'd probably have to go to Bozeman, and Myles likely hadn't thought of that. The tractor supply store closed early on weeknights. I couldn't miss spending hours with him. Now that he knew who I was, would he be more open with me?

What if he wasn't?

"Did you bang him?" Junie asked, clutching her hands like she was praying the answer was yes.

They were going to get it out of me. Resisting was pointless. "Yes."

She pinched off a squeal and fist-bumped Autumn.

"Was it just now in the car?" Autumn asked, her eyes bright. The girl lived vicariously through others. She'd never stayed out past curfew, was always ten minutes early, and religiously put her shopping cart away—along with all the others sitting in the lot. Autumn loved kids, loved being a teacher, and wanted a family of her own but believed herself cursed with singledom. "Where'd you go? Was that your first time together, or have you been sleeping with him the whole time?"

"Yes," I said and held up a hand when she opened her mouth. "*One* question. Summer?"

Summer lifted her chin. "Is he a good guy?"

"Yes," I said quietly. "I think he really is."

"But you don't know?"

"He hates explaining himself and all that it comes

their future goals. He works hard because I think he's afraid to close his doors and leave his employees with nowhere to go."

"You think, or you know?"

"*One ques-tion*," I sang, and Junie winced. None of us had gotten her musical gifts. I threw the strap of my purse over my head to hang across my body, then remembered why I'd really come into my bedroom.

I went to my dresser and pulled out a pair of underwear. Keeping my back to my sisters, I balanced on one foot at a time while I stepped into them. Then I turned around and smoothed my skirt down.

Autumn grinned. "Nice."

"Oh no, Wynn. What happened to the pair you were wearing?" Junie smirked.

I walked up to Summer and stood until she moved. I opened the door. The hallway was clear, so I turned around and stuck my head in the doorway. "They're in his pocket." I darted out on Summer's annoyed "Oh my god!"

Myles was by his car, talking to Chance. Tate was likely inside, trying to talk sense into Mama, but Chance was fascinated by the sporty car.

"My mom used to have one like this." He kicked his beat-up athletic shoe against the tire. Tate couldn't get the kid to wear cowboy boots twenty-four seven like him.

"Oh, yeah? What's her name?"

"My mom is Tamera. Scarlett's my stepmom, but she likes driving Dad's pickup."

"Pickups are fun, too." Myles had changed into a pair

dollar bill into the casual Friday fund.

"Where do you live?"

"Outside of Denver."

"Cool. I used to live in Bozeman." Chance craned his head up to look at Myles.

Myles lifted his gaze to look at me. I gave him a cheerful smile, but damn, they made a cute picture.

"I used to live in Bozeman, too," Myles said, and I slowed my steps.

He didn't admit to a lot of his childhood. That he'd been a foster kid yes, but he'd never given me details about where and how many homes he'd gone through. Not once had he touched on the reason he'd been put into foster care. I'd heard drugs. I'd heard orgies. I'd heard abandonment. I hadn't heard the town. Had he been born in Bozeman?

Chance bobbed his head. "Bozeman's a nice place."

"It can be."

"I like it better here."

Myles's gaze stayed with mine. "I do, too."

"Heya, kiddo." I ruffled Chance's hair. "Did you know that Myles helped train Nugget?"

Nugget was the twenty-five-year-old sorrel gelding in the pasture with Tenpin.

Chance lit up. "Really? I ride him when I help Dad with the grid moves."

Myles lifted a brow. "Grid moves?"

"A fancy way to say they're moving pastures," I explained. "Tate and Teller blocked the pastures off into grids to keep better track of land management."

I nodded. "It was easier when he was the only one in charge. But Tate and Teller gravitate more toward running the ranch than being at the distillery. They don't want to be in an office all day. Tenor is the CFO of Copper Summit, but he puts in a lot of hours with the cattle, too."

"And the chickens," Chance added.

"Tenor spoils the chickens."

"Do you know we have two donkeys?" Chance asked, unwilling to let his rapt audience in Myles go. "Buckshot and Pudding."

"Do I want to know how they got their names?" Myles asked.

"Probably not," I said. "Chance, I have to steal Myles so we can get to town before the store closes."

"Everything closes early here." Chance had made the move to Bourbon Canyon well after Daddy got sick, and Tate had to take over the ranch, but he was still adjusting, according to Tate.

I smoothed out the mess I'd made of his hair. "Tell your dad I said you could have an ice cream sandwich."

"Thanks, Aunt Wynter!" He ran into the house.

Myles chuckled. "That was dirty."

"Yes, it was."

"Nugget's still alive?"

"He's the most mellow horse. Tate could put Chance on him when he was five and let him ride on his own." I went around the car and got into the passenger seat. My phone buzzed.

Grinning, I tucked my phone away. Aunt privileges.

Myles and I got in the car. He backed out.

"You guys all seem close."

"We are. Sometimes, it was us against the foster—" I clamped my mouth shut. I might not be a menace, but I'd sound like a shitty person.

"Go ahead and say it." The muscle in his jaw was tight as he drove with one hand on the wheel.

"I'm sorry, Myles. Not all kids were as well adjusted as you."

"A lot of us learn to hide how maladjusted we are. Sometimes, the pretending becomes permanent."

I put a hand on his leg. He flexed under my touch, like he would've pushed my fingers off if he weren't driving. "Some of them were very troubled. Mama and Daddy tried to get them the help they needed and offer them the support they should've had from the beginning, but it was still hard. From our point of view, as kids, it was...scary at times. Some experiences were worse than others."

The tension leaked out of him. "I know."

He knew the effects of his families being unable to have him under the same roof. "I think that's why Tate and Teller took such issue, thinking you stole from Copper Summit."

"All the recipes are mine. Darin helped me buy the building and set up the processes and hire people. He taught me leadership and management and the industry, Wynn. The product comes from me."

"Why do you think I stick to whiskey? I have no lines of bourbon."

"Why?" I needed to hear him say it. With Myles, I doubted the answer was one-dimensional.

"The Baileys do bourbon, and they do it well. I like to play with the whiskey."

"Which Daddy never did."

"He was a purest. Your brothers are, too."

Talking with Myles like this was different than before, when I hadn't revealed who I was. Instead of shutting me out because of the deception, he was opening up. He probably didn't realize it, or he'd shut down. "They are. They'd rather have me play with the flavors as a mixologist since the younger generations are more likely to drink bourbon and whiskey cocktails."

"So you *are* a mixologist." His hand tightened on the wheel. And there was his reminder that I'd been deceitful.

"It's more like a side gig. I was hooked as soon as Daddy taught me how to sniff the white dog." I'd been well under the legal drinking age, but Daddy had wanted me to study the sample he took straight off the still before the alcohol was poured into the barrel. "I did an online bartending course and then continued from there. Daddy wanted to draw a bigger crowd into the distillery in Bozeman by opening to the public, so I worked there after college. I'd help with the marketing by day and bartend at night. In between, I'd create Copper Summit signature cocktails and teach them to the other bartenders. I'll start up again after the funeral."

to keep creating recipes, but I think I got burned out for a while there. Then Daddy got sick, and I couldn't stay."

"Why not?"

Was he making conversation or was he really interested? My family knew why I couldn't stay, but I rarely talked about my past to non-family members. Myles was easy to talk to. Perhaps because I knew he wouldn't talk about what we said to anyone. Or perhaps because he understood. "The accident."

"Your parents' accident?" We were on the outskirts of town, and he was looking around, probably cataloging the changes from when he'd been here last. He must've driven from Denver straight to Bourbon Canyon without going through town.

"I witnessed two parents die already. I couldn't take watching a third."

"Jesus." He slowed to enter city limits. "I'm sorry, Wynter."

"Thank you." I was putting too much significance into the way he used my real name. Why did I even want us to grow closer? I wasn't delusional enough to think having sex earlier had meant anything other than that we'd finally succumbed to the raging chemistry between us. "Anyway, I'd love to live closer to my family. We're all around Bourbon Canyon, except for Summer. She's in Bozeman."

"I'd never live there again."

"There's no reason for you to, so you're in the clear." I caught a small flinch out of the corner of my eye. "Right?"

"That's good." The tractor supply store was coming up. "Then you won't mind having to run there for your clothes."

He whipped his head toward me. "What?"

"The store closes at four most days." When his incredulous gaze turned toward me, I shrugged. "They can't keep help, and they claim it's workforce shortages."

"It's awful management."

"Probably. The owners are in their eighties and think kids should want to work full-time after school."

"And there's nowhere else to shop."

"No. There's really not."

The level of dismay rolling off him only hinted at what was bothering him. There was someone in Bozeman he wanted to avoid. He was back to being rigid Mr. Foster.

I could ask why, but he wouldn't tell me. I couldn't imagine a day Myles would ever open up to me, but I couldn't stop from wishing someday he would.

CHAPTER SEVENTEEN

Myles

The trip to Bozeman last night had been uneventful, which was more than I could've hoped for. I had cheap jeans, a plaid shirt, T-shirts, and boots to wear working outside.

I hadn't tried anything on. I knew my size and only had to suffer in them for a few days if they were ill fitting. Afterward, Wynn and I grabbed some food. I'd taken Wynn to an upscale place that Gianna couldn't afford even the cheap alcohol in.

Morning chores were finished, and I lingered outside. The guys had sent me to let the chickens out and collect eggs. The job was usually saved for the youngest on the ranch and meant to be a low blow to my pride, but I'd rather hang around the chickens.

Instead of a big chicken run, someone had built paths for the chickens to walk through. On the other side of the chicken wire were plants. The chickens could

"Morning." Wynn wandered toward me, her hands in her back pockets.

Fuck. Office Wynn had been too sexy to let me think straight. Ranch Wynn made me want to haul her over my shoulder and find a clean spot in the barn.

Could I throw her in the car and go back to that spot?

I'd bought more condoms, knowing damn well what an epically bad decision it would be to keep sleeping with her. Being under the same roof as her all night was torture. Having a houseful of people was a special mind fuck. After seeing her today, it'd be impossible to get my erection to go away.

She'd put her hair in a long braid and clipped the shorter front strands behind her head. She wore no makeup and a pink T-shirt like she was the first version of Cowgirl Barbie ever made. Her jeans were worn at the thighs and torn at the knees in ways that hadn't been done in a factory. She had on the same boots as yesterday.

"Morning," I said and carried my bucket of eggs into the shop.

"Where are you going?"

"To clean the eggs." Nothing had changed at the Bailey ranch, but at the same time, there were differences. A new shop. Another outbuilding by the chicken shed. The donkeys had thrown me, and the pen with the goats hadn't been around when I'd been here last. Those were Chance's 4-H projects. Along with some chickens, but he kept those separate from the egg layers.

"We use the sink and egg washer in the garden shed

I switched directions, and she followed. When I got to the counter, I stared at the contraption in the bottom of the sink. "What the hell is that?"

"An egg washer."

"I thought that was me."

She hopped onto the counter and let her legs swing. "When we got older and started moving away, and my parents took in fewer foster kids, Mama invested in some time-saving devices."

"Do you still sell the eggs?" They used to be a mini business the Baileys had used to teach the kids entrepreneurship. I hadn't relished being a teen and delivering eggs with a much younger Wynn and her sisters, but I'd damn well pocketed the money and saved it.

"Mama gives the leftovers to the food pantry." She leaned over and her sweet lemongrass smell wafted over me. The fly of my jeans grew uncomfortably tight, and it had nothing to do with the fit and everything to do with where my blood was going.

I couldn't get addicted to her. Her life was in Montana. I'd never leave everything I'd built for a woman. My place was my job.

"You just put them there and run the water. The stream will jumble the pads enough to rotate the eggs and get them clean all over."

I grunted and did as she asked. She was quiet and stared out the door of the shed. A horse whinnied in the distance. Summer had gone out with Tate and Teller. Junie was staying in town with Autumn.

I had questions about them. And about Wynn. I could surmise what it'd been like growing up in the

questions flooded in. The sisters had been annoying, but in a little-sister way. I'd been protective of all of them—they'd been so haunted—but I'd only known how to help Wynn.

Being around the guys today had been easier than yesterday. They still looked at me with guarded contemplation, but if I didn't give them attitude, they didn't return any. We'd slipped into the same role we had as kids.

"Can I ask you a question?" She continued swinging her legs.

I laid out the eggs on clean rags to dry. "No." She wouldn't ask anything I wanted to answer.

"I'm going to anyway."

"Then why seek permission?"

"Because I didn't think you'd be that stubborn." She flicked the brim of my ball cap. I hadn't gone full Western. All I needed was to block out the sun while trying to avoid a hat-head sunburn.

"It's not stubbornness. It's called privacy, Frosty."

The self-satisfied look she got warmed my insides until they were molten. Frosty was a goddamn nickname and not even a sexy one, yet she beamed like it was some French endearment.

I'd call her Frosty and search for that expression from now on.

For however long I was here. "I left so I could start a life that was my own." I propped my hands on the counter and stared at the wall of tools—trowels, claws, markers, and little sticks to write on.

"Why couldn't you wait?" Her smile was sad. "I was

Junie made a song for you, and Summer complained about having to do your chores." She tapped her fingers on the edge of the counter. "I think the guys' feelings were hurt, too."

I comprehended none of what she said. "No one missed me."

"I did," she said softly. "Honestly, we all did."

I huffed out a laugh but stared at the floor, my arms braced on the edge of the counter. I'd only thought of myself. I'd had to. I'd been in places where people either didn't care I was there or wished I was gone. "I don't see Tate missing anyone."

"He did. I think he thought you guys were friends."

I worked my jaw back and forth. If I had to pick one person I'd considered a friend from those days, it'd have been Tate. The guy who'd tried to run me off yesterday wasn't friendly, but then he didn't understand my actions hadn't been about him. "You were a decent family. All of you guys." I pushed off the counter and paced. "You have to understand that I lived under constant fear I'd lose everything. At any moment. One phone call, and I'd have to pick up and go to another home."

"That's why you were so angry?"

"Part of it. Before your dad set up an account for me, I had no money. Scratch that—I'd had no money I had been allowed to keep. Or it was outright stolen."

"That's awful."

It was who'd taken it that made it all worse. "Not everyone is like your parents. Some are using the system. Some genuinely want to help but have no understanding of the mental and emotional needs of the kids. Some are already full. But in the end, sometimes it's me, and they don't deserve to deal with my shit."

"I'm so sorry." The sympathy glimmering in the depths of her brown eyes cut through me. Usually, I hated sympathy, would rather gouge my eyes out, but she made me feel seen.

I went to stand in front of her, and she uncrossed her legs. I wedged myself right in the middle. "I left because of me. All my early decisions were made for me. Then your dad helped me out, and I grew determined to give back."

"The investment money?"

I nodded. "I was in jail. For fighting." She knew so much already, I'd give her this.

Her pretty lips parted, and her eyes grew wide. "You were in jail?"

"I was stupid and quick to anger. I had no one to call. So I called Darin." To my surprise, he'd actually come. Then he'd bought me lunch. He'd driven through the night to save my ass. "He was frank about my options. I told him my crazy plan and thought he'd chew into me for copying him."

"Of course he didn't."

"He's a goddamn saint."

She twined her arms around my shoulders. Before this week, she'd been forbidden. Yesterday, she'd been unexpected. This? As natural as breathing. Why couldn't I wake up every day, suck in fresh morning air, wash eggs, and make out with Wynn in a garden shed?

"I think you're more like him than you think," she said softly.

tongue inside to taste her minty flavor. Lust soared in my blood until I was yanking her to the edge of the counter. She let out one of those needy moans I loved.

"What the hell is this?" Tate said from behind us. "I was checking on you, and I find you tonsil-deep in my sister?"

I jerked away, but Wynn wouldn't let me go far. "Tate, dang it!" She craned her head to look over my shoulder.

I wouldn't turn around and show off the monster erection in my pants. I looked over my shoulder instead. "Got anything else for me to do?"

Tate ignored me. "Isn't he a little old for you?"

She tightened her legs around me. "I like the grandpas."

I made a choking sound. "Christ, Wynn."

"Grandpas that read to you when you were a kid?"

"Don't let him get to you," she said to me as she played with the back of my hair. "We helped his wife buy him at a bachelor auction, so he's not one to talk."

The information did make me feel better. Wynn was twelve years younger than me. I hadn't felt like an old pervert until Tate had pointed it out.

I respected him. His disapproval...bothered me. "I hadn't seen Wynn for twenty-two years before she marched into my office—late."

"I was right on time!"

I smirked at her, and she mock glared at me. I'd kiss her again if her brother weren't right behind me.

Another shadow appeared in the doorway. "Oh my god. What did you catch them doing?"

more protective with age? "Washing eggs," I answered.

"Is that what the kids are calling it these days," he grumbled. "Mama's gotta go to town to meet with the pastor and finalize some details for tomorrow. Who wants to go with her and Summer? Tenor's going, too."

"I got it." Tate spun on a heel and jogged out.

A shudder ran through Wynter. What she'd said about watching her parents die had been real, from the heart. No wonder she'd stayed away from Montana until she'd gotten the call.

Teller eyed both of us. "I've gotta cover for Tate on the ranch. Autumn and Junie are getting the food arranged for the reception. You mind figuring out supper for tonight?"

"Myles and I will figure something out."

I would what?

"Does Foster House know how to cook?" Teller asked.

No.

Wynn must've seen the answer in my eyes. "He's very talented with his hands."

I let my eyes close again. She was going to get me beat up.

"Wynter Kerrigan, if you make any more innuendos, I'm going to ground you." He sounded as perturbed as I felt.

She laughed. By now, my erection had faded enough I could turn sideways and watch their interactions. One thing had been the same in all the families I'd lived with —the sibling camaraderie. Some were closer than others,

What would that have been like? But not having siblings had been a blessing.

"I'd like to take him through Copper Summit," she said.

I remained still while Teller measured me with his appraising gaze. If I was banned from the distillery, I'd own it. They didn't trust me, and they had no reason to. I'd built a nice life for myself off their family's hard work.

Teller ran his thumb across his fingertips. "I guess there's nothing there he don't already know." Teller shifted his dark gaze to mine. "We don't have fancy fruit mash, so there's no recipes to steal."

"Good thing I like fancy shit."

His expression didn't crack. He spun on his heel like his brother had and strode out.

Wynn wrapped her ankles around me and forced me around to face her. "Now, where were we?"

"Aren't you afraid someone else will walk in?" My dick had no fear, but this wasn't my property. This wasn't my home, and this girl was clearly loved by everyone who stepped foot on this land.

"Not particularly. We can shut the door."

The lust was back, flooding my veins and going straight for my dick. "God help me, Frosty. I'm on shaky ground as it is. Let me clean up, then show me the distillery."

Instead of getting pouty or looking hurt, she smoothed her hands on my shoulders. "You respect the hell out of this family, don't you?" She leaned closer and whispered, "I'll keep your secret."

After the hot and heavy make-out session in the shed, I should've taken a cold shower, but I was too excited to see Myles in my domain.

He parked in the parking lot that surrounded Copper Summit. He'd insisted on using his car even though each trip assaulted his paint job with rocks.

He stared out the windshield at the building in front of us. Admittedly not as impressive as Foster House's headquarters, Copper Summit was still gorgeous. Daddy's grandpa had built a giant wooden building with simple windows at first. Then he'd added the timber accents on the outside as he started to profit. From one end, long wooden tunnels winged out. The barrel rooms, done to look like an old mining shaft as an ode to the copper mines in the area. Grandpa had thought open-pit copper mining made blemishes on the countryside. Daddy had added on a wing to sell locally made products like huckleberry taffy, caramels, and lemonade mix, and then finally a bar for the public to enjoy our cocktails.

Copper Summit had been like a playground for me when I was finally old enough to legally play with the spirits and flavors.

"Even this looks different," he muttered.

"The bar was added once we were all out of the house. Daddy liked to joke that he suddenly had a lot of money as soon as he wasn't feeding hungry teens." Tears

Another tear escaped, and Myles tenderly wiped it away. "I'm almost jealous." Lines of concern crinkled his eyes. "You got to experience two sets of good parents." He wiped at another tear. "But I'd never want you to know the life I had."

I grabbed his hand and smoothed my thumb over the moist tip of his finger. My tear. "My Kerrigan parents were loving, but I think many would argue about how good they were."

He lifted a brow. I kept hold of his hand. "I don't remember specifics. Neither does Junie. Summer and Autumn have filled in what they know, and Mama finally told us what she heard from the social workers." I took a fortifying breath. I'd never told anyone about them. People heard my parents died in a crash when we were camping, and they got caught up in the sadness of four girls going through the trauma of an accident that stole their parents. They didn't think further about the details. "We were homeless."

He frowned. "I thought you guys were camping."

"Because we had nowhere to go. Mama said there was nothing. No money, no accounts, no assets. The house was foreclosed on. They left everything, and we camped. Summer said she remembered Mama Starr or Daddy Bjorn being gone for a day, like they got work for a day, and then we'd go to another campground."

"You didn't know you were homeless?"

I shook my head. "I thought it was fun. Mama Starr would tell us stories while we looked at the stars." I smiled, remembering some of the conversations I'd had with my sisters over the years. "That must be why I was

"Adults don't let the presence of kids stop them from having sex," he said darkly.

No wonder he'd formed a hard shell. I feathered my fingers over the grim set of his mouth. "I'm sorry for what you've been through."

He kissed a fingertip. "We're not talking about me. You were homeless, but were you living well?"

The crease in his forehead needed to be smoothed out, too. He was worried about my childhood. "Yes. The blissful ignorance of youth."

"Then they were good parents. If they kept you ignorant of their hardships and hid the dark side of life from you, then they were good parents."

My poor Myles. "You know why storms bother me?"

"The crash?"

He'd probably heard about it from Mama. "Yes. With the heavy rains and where we were camping, we had to get to higher ground. I remember Dad saying we'd get a hotel for the night. I don't remember how it happened, if a deer ran out in front of us or if the van had bald tires, but we slid off the road and rolled. For all their faults, they were strict about car seats. Summer and Autumn had the worst injuries. Me and Junie were in the third-row seat and took the least amount of damage. But Mama and Daddy..." The sadness and loss were present, but they paled compared to the fresh grief of losing Daddy Darin. I was recounting a story I'd heard told to me. I didn't remember more than the raging wind, rain, and thunder. And the crying. "Thankfully, someone saw us go off the road, but we had to wait until help arrived."

"And you still have a hard time in storms."

you were. It was in front of my face. I was too busy trying to ignore how attracted I was to you."

"You liiiike me," I sang.

He slid his gaze toward me. "You know that it can't go anywhere."

Wasn't that a cold bucket of water over the head? I swallowed my hurt. This was a hard enough week as it was. "Are you afraid I'm after your mega fortune and the penthouse in the mountains?"

The corner of his mouth kicked up. "My fortune is tied up in the company."

"Plus, you co-op a jet. I'm looking for straight-up owner-level rich."

"And the penthouse?"

I smiled smugly. "I'll build my own. You know where we had sex?"

His pupils dilated. "Yes."

His energy crackled over my skin. I could crawl into his lap again. But this spot wasn't as secluded as the last. "It's mine." I pointed off toward the mountains in the distance. "We all have a portion that's ours. Tate built over there. Daddy didn't work on those roads for hunting, but to give us access." My grief pooled inside me again, adding a heaviness I wasn't sure I could shake. "His dream was to have us all living on Bailey land. I can't help but feel like I disappointed him."

"Do you really think so? Truly?"

I sniffled. "Just a little."

He shifted in his seat. "Look, Wynn. We didn't talk about you guys the few times I connected with him after I left. I didn't want to. He told me not to worry about

ating with pride, and he wasn't the type to hype himself. It came from all of you."

"I told him what I was doing. With you." I tensed. What would he think?

He drew his brows together. "He approved?"

"No, but I told him I'd wait to tell you after the big meeting." I twined my hands together. "He said you were a sponge whenever he'd talked to you, and that you don't owe us a thing."

"And what do you think?"

I had a lot of thoughts when it came to this man. "The real question is, does it matter?"

If I expected a resounding *Yes, Wynn, it absolutely matters what you think of me as we've slowly been getting to know each other these last two months*, I didn't hear it.

"It shouldn't," he finally said.

Okay, then.

Did that mean it shouldn't, but it did, and he didn't mind? He did so mind? It shouldn't matter so why bother asking?

"Let me make you a drink." Because I sure as hell needed one.

CHAPTER EIGHTEEN

Myles

I never thought I'd be sitting in Copper Summit again. Or that the Bailey brothers wouldn't be trying to kick me out. I wish I could enjoy the experience.

The bouts of sadness that had struck Wynn through our time together the last two days bothered me. She had a valid reason for her feelings, and I was grateful she had all the support too many others didn't. But seeing her mourn brought back memories I'd locked even deeper than my foster years. I had no wish to revisit that part of my life, and I wanted to cheer Wynn up.

I found myself rooting through my brain, looking for a joke that clung to some unused neuron. Nothing. Mixing drinks made her happy, and I let her. I'd drink fucking pond water if coming up with her concoction smoothed the crease between her delicate brows.

"Okay. Try this." She slid a glass in front of me. She'd used crushed ice in a squat old-fashioned glass.

"I countered with a really sweet orange juice one of Mama's friends makes from her trees in Arizona." She tapped the bar top. "You can only get this cocktail here because the products are limited."

I would down the entire glass, but I liked the way she lit up when she talked about her creation. "I thought Darin was big on locally sourced. What's your motto?"

"Montana made. Montana proud. But!" She grinned, and her brown eyes danced. "Mama's friend was born and raised in Montana, and she only goes down for the winter. So it's a little work-around." She leaned across the counter. My gaze naturally slipped down to the cleavage visible in the tugged-down collar of her top. "We're honest in the description. We call it Fool's Gold."

Her smile was so broad, I had to chuckle. "You came up with the name?"

She nodded.

I lifted the glass to my lips and kept eye contact as I drank. Her gaze dipped down to my mouth, then up to my eyes, and down to my throat as I swallowed.

She crimped her lower lip between her teeth.

Flavors danced over my tongue. The bitterness and sourness were offset by the orange juice and honey syrup. Impeccable bourbon carried the whole set and the natural charred flavors were softened and transformed by the bitter. "Christ, that's good."

She straightened, her triumphant expression tying all sorts of knots around my heart, caging it in, and making her the only one with the key. "It's one of the recipes I'm the proudest of."

"What's another one?"

fruit."

"I'm man enough."

Grinning, she spun away and got to work. As she dug out bourbon, huckleberry liqueur, huckleberry syrup, and a container of fruit, she talked about how she'd created the concoction. "And then Junie found a patch of huckleberries on our land. So we hired a few high schoolers to pick and process them all. You should've seen the kids when we candied some of the batch. It was like..." She laughed. "Kids in a candy shop."

The muscles around my mouth began to ache. Was I smiling that much? I wasn't used to it.

"Daddy—" Her voice caught. She faltered but squared her shoulders and kept going. "He made it an annual thing. Bailey's Huckleberry Festival, he called it. We didn't do it the year we found out he was sick. And we didn't do it last year either." Her smile faded, but she slid a tall glass with a flirty umbrella and speared candied huckleberries in front of me. The liquid inside was a soft purple. "Tell me what you think."

This drink was so far from my type, I'd walk away if it was anyone else who'd served it to me. I picked it up, considering the bourbon she was using. "Wynter Summit? Your favorite?"

"We all have our lines."

I shook my head. I should've put two and two together, but I'd been too successful at putting the Kerrigan girls out of my head. I took a sip.

Sweet, but not so much that the bourbon was crowded out. A poor-quality bourbon wouldn't hold up under the other ingredients. "It's good."

the flavors and the spirits."

She lifted a shoulder. "It was my side hustle. I'd come home from college and create recipes." A wistful sigh escaped her. The melancholy returned. "I missed being home. Do you think—"

"No."

"You don't even know what I'm going to ask."

"You're questioning your decision to stay away." I'd done the same thing since I had called Mae after hearing about Darin's death. Wynn's question would be on a greater scale than mine. "No, you weren't wrong. Darin would've wanted you to take care of yourself, and he's one of the few people in the world—your sisters being the others—who would've understood."

She had her hands folded close to mine. "I'm really glad I can talk to you about this."

I stroked my finger over the back of her hand. Soft damn skin. Every inch of her was satin. Yesterday's quick fuck in the car roared into my head. Bad timing. All of it. Us.

There was no us.

I took another hearty drink, polishing the whole damn drink off. Then I grabbed the Fool's Gold. "You're going to have to drive, Frosty."

***

The family meal was big and chaotic and full of laughter. Chance had planted himself next to me. He'd asked if I played football in school, if I'd gone to elementary school in Bourbon Canyon and knew the

like he was trusting me with top secret information, about their new boats, and that his baby sister woke him up with her crying, but he liked to sing her lullabies.

I'd listened and nodded, working overtime to ignore the furtive glances from all the family members around the gigantic table. Tate had sat on the other side of Chance, a bodyguard of sorts. His wife, Scarlett, was next to him, and Teller had boxed me in. Chance's other bodyguard.

Tenor had taken a spot across the table beside Wynter. Her protector? I wouldn't write him off. He gave off a nerdy vibe, but that was all it was. I'd seen him manhandle pushy cows when he was filling the water tanks earlier today, and the hunch in his shoulders didn't hide the strength in his arms from someone who cared to look.

Not many people looked deeper. Tenor was probably the type of guy who counted on that.

"I heard you used to read Aunt Wynter stories. Did you sing?"

I had just shoveled in a forkful of mashed potatoes—my contribution to the meal along with digging up the carrots. Wynter had seasoned and prepared the crockpot roasts and gravy and even made homemade buns. I'd washed the veggies and peeled and cooked them.

How long had it been since I'd prepared more than a single serving of any one dish? How long had it been since I'd used the kitchen in my loft?

I slowly finished chewing, all eyes on me. "I didn't sing."

Now I did. Her giggles the first time I'd sung could've scared me away from reading again, but instead, I'd smiled and made sure to include that damn cat book in the regular reading rotation. "Yes, I remember."

"Does he still sing for you?" Junie asked sweetly. "Or are they grown up now? Like a real bourbon lullaby? A little alcohol, a few sweet words, and—"

"June," Mae chided. "There are children present."

Chance's head was swiveling around, trying to catch every nuance but too young to understand. I hoped.

"I don't read to kids anymore," I answered to make it clear I wasn't talking about me and Wynn.

What would I say? I was leaving after the funeral. There wasn't a me and Wynn.

The ache was back behind my sternum.

"You can read to Brinley," Chance offered.

Tate grunted. He might've said something akin to "Fuck no," but his mouth was full.

"You'll do a better job than me," I said. "My reading days are over."

"You don't have kids?"

I fisted my hand around my fork. My visceral rebellion against having kids warred with the sudden thought of what my kids would look like. Would they have dark hair like mine or lighter hair like—hell, what was I doing? "No."

Chance's wide eyes weren't releasing me from his curiosity. "Do you want them?"

"Chance," Scarlett said. "Those are personal questions we keep to ourselves."

"It can be a sensitive subject, but ultimately it's none of our business," she answered while Tate bobbed his head to punctuate each word as he was wiping his mouth with a white napkin.

Chance wasn't persuaded. "Then he can tell me it's none of my business."

I chuckled at Chance's logic. I didn't miss the startled gazes turning my way. I took a drink of water, the humor in his frank response growing.

Wynn's eyes were sparkling, and I liked that even more.

"Don't worry, kid. I'll let you know." I wouldn't have. I'd have figured out an answer to keep from shaming him in front of everyone. I'd spare anyone that if I could.

"It's Chance," said Tate. Would Tate ever not be a dick?

"Carter?"

Chance snorted, his little head swiveling between us.

Tate shot me a glare. "You heard me."

"Cranston?" More chortling from Chance, and I smirked at him. "Nice to meet you, Cory."

His giggles filled the air. Tate's siblings were holding back grins, including Tenor. I couldn't tell with Teller. He was a stony wall on my right. But even Tate's lips were twitching, his son's laughter his kryptonite.

"Just be careful, Chance," Teller started, and I tensed. "If Myles reads to you, the books will be watered-down versions of what you like the best. His stories won't be the really good, quality books you're used to."

When I glanced at Teller, I caught the shit-starting

the nation? A book with a little flavor?"

Teller lifted a shoulder, the shine in his gaze growing. "You don't need to flavor perfection."

"I've never been a boring guy," I countered, distinctly aware of how much I was enjoying the casual interplay.

"Maybe we should ask Wynter," Summer said, as much of a troublemaker as Teller.

I reclined in my chair, mashed potatoes forgotten. "Well?" I asked Wynn.

Her eyes widened. Was that a bad sign?

"Oh, uh, I mean..." She winced. "You do work all the time. And you live in the distillery."

"Is that allowed?" Tate asked, incredulous. "A residence under the same roof as a distillery? The regulations are pretty fu—darn tight."

"It was tricky, and it took a few years to get approval." I would've lived in the loft anyway. Fuck regulations. But if I wanted a place for people to come to work every day, I couldn't flaunt regulations. "The way the old mine was built, it was like a series of additions. I kept that in mind during the remodel."

"Always figuring out how to work around the rules and get what you want, Foster." Just when I'd thought Tate had meant it as a dig, he shot a playful glare at Wynn. "Just like someone else I know."

She fake gasped. "I resemble that remark."

Laughter filled the table until Tate bugged Junie about the record deal she was working on. After we were done eating, and everyone was vacating their chairs, I started gathering plates.

Mae put her hand on my arm. I hadn't realized she

I'd meant to help clean up, but I wouldn't argue with Mae. The porch was the quiet area. If Mae was on the porch with a kid, no one else would be allowed out until she was done.

At the edge of the dining room, Mae went to a wooden bar about four feet tall, the top lined with bottles. I'd gotten the idea for my office from this. She withdrew two glasses from a bottom cupboard and poured two fingers of a Copper Summit bottle I didn't recognize.

She handed me a glass with a sad glint in her eyes. "Darin's special barrel, just for us."

I dropped my chin. This family had a way of making me feel like so much a part of them, a lifeline for the next moment when I was back to being a kid with no real home.

On the porch, we were surrounded by uncharacteristically humid air and the sound of frogs and crickets. I'd had a hard time adjusting to the sound of the city after I first left Montana. Part of the reason why it'd been so important for me to live at Foster House.

Mae sat in a wooden rocking chair I doubted was from a big box store. Darin and Mae went out of their way to support local crafters. She gestured to the one on the other side of a small round table. "Have a seat." She took a sip and slowly rocked.

I did the same. Smooth notes of vanilla, oak, and caramel caressed my tongue. No one would think Montana could make better bourbon than Kentucky, the birthplace of bourbon, where the weather was perfect for production because the drink was literally a product made product in the heart of Montana. Either way, the shit was good.

"How's it really going?" She pinned me with her direct gaze. "Do you still talk to—"

"Apologies, Mae. But remember what Chance learned?"

She smiled, pride in her eyes. "I always admired the limits you set for yourself. You needed them."

Grateful for her understanding and surprised at the intensity of my desire to tell her anyway, I answered her first question. "I'm fine. I really am."

She rocked, the soft brush of wood against wood mingling with nature sounds. "What are your hobbies?"

"I love what I do."

She gave me that sharp look. The undercurrent of sadness was new, and likely permanent. I'd never embraced my empathy, but I let it out tonight. I felt for Mae. "Do you really?" she asked. "It's not just a way out, and you don't work all the time because you have to show everyone what a good kid you are?"

"I never cared about proving I was a decent person."

"Not really." She took another sip. "Unless it was to someone you cared about. We saw that. You wanted the boys to see you were a good worker and that you'd never hurt the girls. You wouldn't tell them, but you wanted them to be smart enough to see it. And they did."

I latched on to the sound of her steady rocking. For a guy who'd been invisible much of his life, it was unnerving to be seen.

She tapped a finger against her glass. "Darin saw it. It was easy. You were a bundle of chaotic, defensive energy,

waited. The boys still see it, or you wouldn't be under the roof."

"I really am sorry about Darin, Mae." I didn't say it to distract from what she was saying. When I'd first called her, she'd been so surprised, so delighted, my condolences weren't more than perfunctory.

"I am, too," she said quietly. "But you know, if he had to die, I'm glad it happened like this. He even said it. The long months of feeling like shit, being sick from chemo, he said he'd gladly suffer if it gave the kids time to process his loss. If it'd make the funeral a time to celebrate and reflect on all the good memories and bond over having been his kids, he'd gladly bear the burden. It's, uh…" She inhaled a shuddering breath. "It's why he did chemo when his chances were so low. He was okay with dying, he wasn't okay with dying quickly."

Goddamn. The burn was back, but instead of my chest, the pain went from my head down to my toes. He hadn't been my parent, not really, but Darin had been one of the very few adults in my life who'd truly cared. To use Mae's words, I wouldn't be here if he hadn't been.

Was this what Wynn had been hiding from? I would've moved her out of her city apartment and into my loft to keep her from being by herself with this loss.

"He was a good man," I said roughly.

"He was." Rock, rock, rock. She stared into the distance where the sun had sunk below the horizon and thick, building clouds blocked its fading rays. "Looks like rain tonight," she murmured and gave me a sidelong glance. "Judging from the humidity, might even storm."

CHAPTER NINETEEN

Wynter

I was nestled in my queen bed with the covers to my ears. I was in a snug sleep top and shorts, my preferred sleepwear, and the AC was on but not pumping frigid air, yet I was burrowed into bed like I was in the middle of a blizzard with no heat.

I'm too old to behave like this. Was it the combination of being home, losing Daddy, the funeral tomorrow, and the storm?

Thunder cracked, and I jumped. Having my room downstairs was supposed to help muffle the noise, but my bedroom wasn't a bunker.

God, Wynter! I rolled over and curled into a ball, my old stuffed ox, Bunyan, in my arms. I wasn't normally this bad. Usually it was low-grade anxiety. I'd put on a movie, listen to music, or clean. I avoided driving in a storm, like when I was in Myles's office, but here I was, shivering in bed.

I'd tried those already. Mama had been against TV in the bedrooms. I could go to the family room, but also I didn't want to wake anyone up.

A low, steady rumble had been haunting me for twenty minutes, with strobes of lightning playing through the blinds, but the storm was close, growing louder.

Another peal of thunder rent the night.

I squeezed my eyes shut and put the blankets over my head. I was being childish, but if that'd get me through the storm, fuck it.

A weight pressed down on the bed. I whipped the blanket away from my face, a cry in my throat. A strong hand pressed over my mouth.

"Don't be scared, Frosty."

Myles. He'd snuck into my room, opening the door and shutting it, without me noticing. It was storming out, and he'd come to me.

I nodded, and he pulled his hand away.

"It's stupid," I whispered and put my stuffed animal next to my pillow. "But I can't seem to not be a scaredy-cat."

"It's not stupid. It's this week."

And just like that, he understood. No explanations. He got it. Like he had before.

He pulled the blankets back and crawled in next to me. Already my anxiety was dipping to nonexistent levels. His warmth surrounded me, and yes, he wasn't wearing a shirt.

"Are you naked?" I didn't wait for an answer, but slid my hand down hard pecs to rippled abs to— Oh.

holding back his erection. My fingertips played over the tip budging past the waistband.

"Fuck, Wynn." He clamped a hand over my wrist. "I came here to distract you."

"Are you going to read me a book?"

He paused, and I could imagine his half-amused expression. "My tongue will be busy." He dipped his head closer to my ear. "Can you be quiet?"

"Yes." The next thunder blast barely made me flinch as fire swept through my body, more electric than the lightning outside.

He kissed a path to my mouth and licked inside. I was centered on him. My eyes were closed and flashes of light made it through my lids, but I didn't care about anything other than the man moving over me.

He released my mouth and moved his way down. I widened my legs to nestle his big body between my thighs. He skated my shirt up.

I tugged it over my head.

"I want you naked, too." My room was dark, but the light from the storm highlighted his face as he hovered over my bare breasts with my peaked nipples straining upward.

He held my gaze as he took his shorts off, the bed dipping with his movement. He dropped a foil packet by my head on the pillow.

I loved a prepared man.

Then he dropped his head to suck a nipple into his mouth. I groaned, forgetting I had to be quiet, but fuck his mouth felt good. Starbursts of pleasure lit inside me in time with the shots of light through the room.

of the way he'd bound me up and unraveled me on the plane flooded my veins with desire.

"Myles," I said on a low moan.

He nudged my legs farther apart, hinging my knees up. "Hold on, and stay quiet, Wynn."

"One day, we're going to fuck where I can be really loud, and we can both be naked and sprawled across the bed—or counter—or against the wall."

He gave me a neutral look, but heat burned in his eyes with startling intensity I could make out even in the shadows.

I was in trouble.

His hot breath wafted across my pussy.

The blanket fell to cover his head. I fisted my hands in the sheets. I could make out the peaks of my knees and the large bulge he made between my legs. A muted, yet erotic, sight.

He licked through my folds, his tongue soft but firm and oh so wickedly talented. This wasn't the needy retaliation from the plane. He took his time, circling my clit with his tongue, dipping through my pussy and inside me.

"Oh god." I should put a pillow over my face, but I'd miss the erotic shadow show.

Soft licks alternated with firm until I was on the brink. The blanket quivered with the shaking of my knees. Myles kept me on the edge longer than I'd ever experienced. My breathing had turned to pants, and I squirmed so much trying to get more, to jump over the edge, but he clamped his hands on my ass and held me in place.

house.

Too much pleasure filled me, chasing away any fear.

The strikes of lightning were strong, casting more light through the room. I lifted the blanket. He brought his gaze up to meet mine and continued lapping my clit.

"Oh god, Myles." I dropped my head back and let go of the blanket.

A boom of thunder pushed me over the edge. I arched my back, digging my heels into the mattress. He continued, relentless, and I shattered.

I had to bite my lip. My hands were tangled in the blankets, and ecstasy rocked through me. He drank me up, using only his tongue to have me at his complete mercy.

Then he was crawling up my body. The stroke of his hot skin against mine kept my desire stoked to an over-flowing level.

"I need you inside me," I gasped.

He found the condom and ripped it open. Within seconds, he was at my entrance and thrusting inside. I forgot to be quiet. I cried out, and he captured the noise with his mouth, leaving me to whimper against him while he filled me so damn perfectly I could cry.

I needed this. I needed him. Storms scared me, and hollowed me out, like everything was getting taken away, but not with Myles.

He was in me, moving, angling to hit all the right spots, but not needing to try at all. Just being inside me was enough. He kissed down my neck, and his hot hands massaged my breasts. He took the other nipple in his mouth this time.

thing, but I could only say his name. Feeling.

He released my flesh, his warm breath sending shivers down my spine. "I crave the way you come, Wynn." The force of his thrusts grew. "I fucking love the way you taste. I could have you every night."

He said there'd be nothing between us after he left, but I couldn't believe it. Did he?

"What do you fucking do to me?" he growled and planted his hands beside me, swinging his hips.

Flashes of light turned us into a disjointed slideshow. Him on top of me. My knees bracketing his hips. The fall of his hair over his forehead.

I arched again, needing to be closer, like we could become one if we tried hard enough. Another peak built inside me as he pumped, my sensitized clit stroking against his body when he thrust inside.

He rested his thumb on my swollen nub. "Christ, Wynn. You're so fucking responsive. Getting you off is my favorite damn thing."

That was all I needed. All the building emotions and sensations slammed together inside me, creating their own explosion.

I cut off the cry as my mouth opened wide. I shook against him just as he went rigid, his strokes shortening. Then he threw his head back, his teeth gritted as he came.

I'd never forget this. I'd never forget that he'd thought about me when it stormed, that he'd come to check on me. And when the thunder prompted fear, I'd remember when he was buried deep inside me, and we were as close as we could possibly be.

I woke up alone, my body humming, satisfied and ready for the day. But also ready to find a sexy, naked man next to me.

He was not there.

But Bunyan had taken his place.

I rolled to my back and stared at the ceiling. That man. He had a hold on me. He had since we were kids, but now? After getting to know the guy he'd turned into? Would he ever accept that there could be an us? That we could figure out how to be together?

Except I wanted to live in Montana. I had plans to live by Mama. I literally had the blueprints for the house I wanted to build. I had a job—one I loved, with family I loved even more.

But my feelings for Myles Foster grew stronger the more I was around him.

So maybe it was a good thing he was leaving.

He'd never said when. Tomorrow? After the weekend?

A small spear of panic wedged right next to my heart. What if he was gone? Just like when I was six, and he helped me get to sleep, and then he left?

No. He'd stay. For Daddy.

Would he ever stay for me?

As much as I didn't want to move to Colorado and leave everything and everyone behind, he didn't want to move to Montana for even stronger reasons. All of his bad memories were here.

I rolled out of bed and dressed in work clothes. It was early, the sun barely up, and we'd have to get the house ready for guests.

everything up. No one was coming out here until late afternoon. Myles, Teller, Tenor, and Summer were roaming the yard, picking up branches and small debris.

Myles gave me a dark, hooded look that turned all those branches he was raking into kindling. His green shirt was untucked, and he wore the same jeans from yesterday. The boots, though. I'd never tire of seeing him in cowboy boots.

Summer clapped her gloves together. "Wynter, wanna help me get the chairs from the shop? The guys will get the tables from the garage."

Myles dropped his gaze, and I could breathe again. The air around me cooled.

In the musty shop, she turned to me. "You doing okay?"

"Yeah." Did I look that bad?

"You sure? I slept through the storm, but it must've been bad." She gestured out the shop door. "Teller said there was a ton of lightning. If I'd woken up, I'd have checked on you."

I bit the inside of my cheek, and my face grew hot. "No, I made it through fine." My voice was unnaturally high.

She narrowed her eyes on me, then her mouth fell open. Her shocked stare shot toward the door. I glanced over. Myles and my brothers were walking toward the garage. Three tall, rugged men.

She swung her attention back to me. "He *read* to you?"

I groaned. "He read so hard, Summer." A small tremble ran through me, head to toe. She noticed, and I

She frowned, her brow furrowed as she thought. Grateful she wasn't going into overprotective-older-sister mode, I waited.

"Do you have to stay?" she asked. "I mean, if he can't leave his business, can't you go there?"

And there was the rub. There was the issue that really bothered me. "He's not asking me to." Her questioning expression crumbled into sympathy, echoing what I felt. "He's even said there's no us after he leaves."

"Oh, Wynter. You really like him." She pulled me in for a hug.

I gave her a brief squeeze and pulled back. "I can't get sad over him, Summer. Not today of all days. It's going to be hard enough."

She rapidly blinked away tears. Summer didn't often lose her composure. "Today isn't going to suck. But the funeral sure is. Then we'll have the party Daddy would've wanted us to have." She gave me another hug, a hard, quick embrace that squeezed my lungs. I was released to take another breath. "I hate funerals," she said darkly and spun away to the stacks of chairs we had to set up for the reception.

Good thing the sleep I *had* gotten last night was solid, otherwise today would be hell. I had Myles to thank, and I wished I could cling just as tightly to him all day as I had last night.

CHAPTER TWENTY

Myles

My hand continued to tingle from the punishing grip Wynn had had on it during the funeral. The church had been packed, and I'd expected to stand up at the back, but Mae wouldn't hear of it. She'd insisted I go with her and the others when the family met at the church. Then she'd shoved me into a pew after Wynn's sisters. I had been on the end, next to Wynn in her simple black dress. On her other side had been Autumn.

Hearing Wynn cry tore my heart to shreds. The sadness lingering over her sisters and brothers hung heavy in the air. Thankfully, that was over, but I'd never regret going.

What a way to live. Darin had made a positive impression on so many people. He'd been the first person to confirm that I was worth more. Part of me had known it, and maybe that was why I'd been so rebellious. So damn angry.

levels with the doors open and people spilling outside had attested to the same.

I'd driven Wynn and Autumn to the cemetery, where my hand had finally lost feeling for the day.

The reception was pleasant. A table full of bourbon products was available, but no one was drinking even as the sun sank in the sky.

Summer, Tenor, and Autumn beelined in and out of the house, refilling food and drinks. I'd been quickly introduced to Summer's boyfriend. A good-looking guy who'd jittered in his suit like he had a thousand other better places to be. He'd roamed the reception for a half hour and then made some excuse about an international phone call.

Tate held his baby girl and talked with an old teacher who looked familiar. No one had asked about me or recognized me, and that was just fine. This day wasn't about me.

Teller and Wynn were talking to people who Wynn had introduced as employees of Copper Summit. There were workers from all the distilleries here. They were all closed for the rest of the week into the weekend.

An older woman who looked vaguely familiar stepped between me and the punch. "How bad do you want to spike this?" she asked under her breath. She shook her head. "Feels disrespectful, but Darin would've approved."

"He would've."

She peered at me, her nose scrunched. She pushed her glasses up. "May I ask...are you Myles?"

I ducked my head, wishing I could tell her it was

woman's fault I didn't care to be recognized. "Yes."

She put her hand on her heart. "Oh my. I've heard about everything you've done." She nudged my arm and grinned. "Mostly from Darin and Mae. But seeing it for myself is just a dream come true." She must've noticed my lack of recognition. "I used to work..." A big sigh. "I drove you to the Baileys. That night."

The night I'd pissed off the self-proclaimed man of the house at the home before the Baileys, and he'd shown me how a fifteen-year-old should behave—with his fists. I'd gotten good at defending myself. "Katherine." Her name came to me, along with all the other regrettable details of that time. I wouldn't return to the past. I strove to lighten the mood. "Did you call me a dream come true?"

Her serene smile was indeed dreamy. "In that profession, Myles, we never know if we're making a difference. You go in so ignorant, so ready to save the world, and then you realize you're an ant in the entire wilderness. You feel so lost. So hopeless. Then the kids you try to help grow up, and a lot do so well for themselves." Her smile fell. "A lot don't. But then I get to meet someone like you, who did so well once he got exposed to the right environment, and call it selfish, but it makes me feel like my entire career wasn't worthless."

"It's not worthless," I said, needing to clear emotion out of my throat. She was fucking proud of me, and I wasn't ready for that reaction from people who knew me. "It's not your fault you don't get much to work with in a broken system."

I lifted my gaze to connect with Wynn's. She sent me an *are you okay?* look. I nodded and by then Katherine was pulling away.

She dabbed at her eyes under her glasses. "It means a lot to hear you say that." She patted my shoulder. "Don't you kids worry. I'll stick to Mae's side tonight. You all go do what you need to do." Then she strode off.

I was puzzling over her meaning when Wynn crossed to me. Her black skirt swished around her legs. Tendrils of hair were falling out of the bun she'd put it in to frame her face.

"Did that go okay?" she asked.

"Fine." I didn't care to talk about it, but also, I didn't know what to say. Katherine had helped me make peace with another portion of my youth. She and others like her who'd tried to help me were just as constrained as I had been.

"Teller said we should go to the distillery and have our own...memorial."

"A toast to your dad?"

She nodded. "You're invited."

I doubted that. "By who?"

She squeezed my elbow, her expression concerned. "Haven't you noticed they're not running you out? You're helping with chores and other work around the place. You're one of us." Her grin turned knowing. "But not so much one of us it makes last night wrong."

Last night had been right in all the best ways. After holding her while she fell asleep, oblivious to the storm, I wasn't sure how I'd return to Colorado, to the big, open loft, and go to sleep on my own.

did indeed seem more accepting of me. They'd also had the funeral of their father to contend with, so there was that. More importantly, I wanted to go.

"When do we leave?" I asked.

She smiled. "Now."

After a ride in the back of Tate's pickup bed with the wind whipping our hair, we piled into the distillery, leaving all the lights off except one lone light in the bar. Laughter filled the little space. Had it been just yesterday I'd been here with Wynn, getting privately served?

She was behind the bar again, mixing cocktails and taking requests for drinks the others made up.

"I'm not adding an egg," she declared, shaking her metal container, the ice inside clanging. "Gross, and the house doesn't have enough bathrooms if I give everyone diarrhea."

"The alcohol will kill it," Tate said. He was on a stool, Scarlett perched on his lap. Mae had plenty of hands to help her at the house with the kids. Chance was sleeping over and so was Brinley. Mae had practically demanded it.

"Don't care. No raw eggs." Wynn poured out the golden-yellow drink she'd mixed. Something with lemon and honey, two of her favorite ingredients. She added a candied wedge of lemon to the glass.

Tate grabbed one of the glasses and gave the candied lemon to Scarlett. She nibbled the sweet treat, and Tate

Summer made a disgusted noise. "Get a room, you two." She tipped her head toward Wynn. "You don't see these two crawling all over each other. You wouldn't even know one of them wasn't in their own bed last night."

Wynn's eyes flared, and my stomach hit rock bottom. It was one thing to have veiled permission from Mae to visit Wynn in her room during a storm, but the brothers didn't need to know. Summer knowing was bad enough. Autumn and Junie would just chortle and give us a hard time.

They were quickly becoming my favorites. They stayed out of shit that wasn't their business.

Teller put his glass down with a thunk. "I didn't need to know that."

Tate studied me, his expression unreadable. His wife put her hand on his forearm, and I sat still and waited. Whatever he sent my way, I'd take. I'd been in his sister's bed the night before her dad's funeral. That was how he'd see it.

Tate's gaze shifted to Teller. "Remember when Dad busted you sneaking Becca Smith into your room your sophomore year?"

A beat of surprise went through Teller's face before he laughed. "Goddamn, I try not to. He made me carry around a baby doll for a week and even woke me up every two hours each night to feed her. 'You gonna fuck around, you gonna find out, son.'"

Tenor snickered. "Dad was literal about that saying."

Teller's grin was wide. "I held on to my V card for

We all laughed, but more than relief flowed through me. Tate's change of subject really was acceptance. He'd allowed me into his childhood home, under the same roof as his mama and sisters, and he knew I was doing more than reading to Wynn these days, but he wasn't making an issue of it. Teller had gone along with it, and well, they'd been more than tolerating me all week.

Wynn slid another glass of her latest creation toward me, then came around the bar. She put a hand on my shoulder, and next thing I knew, I had that sweet ass perched on my lap.

I automatically put an arm around her.

"Jesus, Wynter," Tate grumbled. "You tryin' to butter up the next Jim Beam?"

"Jack Daniel's," Tenor added.

I rubbed her back. "Nothing's been offered yet."

"He had a meeting with Mainline and knocked their socks off," Wynn added. She squeezed my knee. "Don't worry. The guys are already working with them. You aren't competing."

"They picking you up?" Tate asked. I detected no shrewdness in his gaze, only plain curiosity.

"I haven't heard. But I haven't been at work all week." Except Monday, when a phone call from Gianna had prompted me to call Mae.

"You'll get it," Wynn said confidently. "They're not in the business of making bad decisions, and Foster House is a good decision."

"They'd have to rely on me to grow to meet their needs." I could put my plans on paper all I wanted, but people were unpredictable, and the economy could take

"You can do it, and you showed them you can," she said as if that solved it.

Her words circled around me, closing in like a warm hug. I wasn't used to bald confidence in me, plain and out there for everyone to see. Even Darin hadn't been that showy, like he'd feared obvious affirmation would make me run. Not Wynn.

"I learned from the best." My hand slipped down her back to rest on her hip, and she wiggled that round ass against me.

"I can't believe Dad didn't tell us he helped you." Tate shook his head.

"Dad was like that," Tenor said. "We were playing checkers, and he was playing chess."

"We didn't fuck around when we thought Myles could replicate everything we were doing and grow bigger than us." Teller studied me. "But you haven't come out with a bourbon product."

"Didn't need to. There are fewer flavored whiskeys dominating sales. I saw an opening and went for it."

I got more evaluating glances from everyone but Wynn.

"He said Copper Summit already does bourbon right, so there was no need to compete." Wynn rolled her eyes toward me. "But he'll never tell you himself."

A smile played over my lips. My petite, sassy champion.

Autumn hopped down from her stool and went around the bar. She dug out a jar of Luxardo cherry liqueur. She added a stream to her bourbon-and-Sprite mix and stirred it around. "You guys remember when

He wanted a local small-batch line to sell at farmers' markets. The whole place smelled like spiked apples for months."

"So many apples," Wynn groaned.

Junie giggled. "None of us wanted to drink it after feeling like we bathed in it every day."

Summer's fond smile had a faraway quality to it. "Then when we did, we couldn't taste a damn bit of apple."

"It gets lost in the profile of the grain," I couldn't help but explain. This has been my life since my early twenties. After I had mastered whiskey, I'd started playing with other flavor profiles. "We back-mix the fruit for the flavor."

Wynn chuckled. "That's on us, not researching the how-to properly. No more fruit after that."

Tate slipped off his stool, gently setting Scarlett on her feet. She took his seat while he went around the bar. He squatted and dug in a bottom cupboard, in the far back, and withdrew a bottle full of smooth amber liquid.

When he straightened, grief rippled over his features. "Dad wanted us to split this on the night of his funeral. It's why I suggested we come to have a drink. Mama knows. Dad always said bourbon's made for sipping and to enjoy the best bottles with family." He piled several squat glasses on the counter. Each one emblazoned with the coppery mountains that were Copper Summit's logo. Splashing bourbon into each one, he continued, "This is a small batch he made for the family. One of Granddaddy's recipes that he made only

"To Dad." We all raised our glasses. He took a sip and smacked his lips. "Damn, that's good." He tipped his head back like he was sifting through which memory he wanted to share. "Dad taught me how to drive stick by making me try to go uphill. I killed the pickup ten times before we crested the damn thing. Your turn, Foster."

Surprised, I looked around, waiting for an argument, but all I saw were expectant faces. Wynn's fingers gave me an encouraging squeeze.

I wasn't one of them. But I was holding a special batch of bourbon just for Baileys, and I had memories of Darin to share. Tate's had been lighthearted, and I'd keep mine the same. I lifted my glass in a salute. "He told me to dress for the job I wanted—and that ladies love a man in a suit."

"To Dad!" Wynn shouted, and we all drank. She leaned back to murmur, "I like the cowboy look, too."

I pressed a kiss to the base of her neck. An action as natural as breathing.

One by one, everyone shared a lighthearted snapshot from their life with Darin. After the first round of toasts, my phone buzzed. I tried to ignore it, but messages continued to flood my phone.

"Excuse me." I lifted Wynn down. She gave me a questioning look that I didn't acknowledge. Only one person would light up my phone like this.

I walked into the dark entry area. They had an info desk like Foster House. More like, my distillery had an info desk like them, but as per my brand, I did it bigger and staffed the thing full-time with Braxton until he left for college.

The litany of messages meant Gianna was drunk or high or both.

GIANNA

Did you go to that bastard's funeral?

Myles.

MYLES.

You did, didn't you? I knew it.

What'd he ever do for you?

That whole family sucks.

You're not one of them. You know that, right?

You'll never be like them.

People like that use us to feel like heroes. Fuck them.

You come all this way and you don't stop in? Fuck you.

Fuck you fuck you fuck you fuck you.

You don't wanna come see me? Fine. I'll find you.

I ran a hand through my hair. Shit.
Shit.

Gianna was on a tirade, and when that happened, everyone in her vicinity would pay. She wouldn't wait for my confirmation or denial. I was close enough for her to get her hooks into. The Baileys were in mourning, and I couldn't let her intrude. I couldn't let her taint anyone

going in my life.

There was only one thing to do. The only way I dealt with her when she threatened any peace I found.

"Hey," Wynn said from close behind me.

I spun, shoving my phone into my pocket. "Hey."

Her gaze dropped to my pocket, then lifted to my messed-up hair. She lifted her brows like she was waiting for me to elaborate on who was on the other end of the phone and what had upset me. I wouldn't. She probably wondered who contacted me so late at night, but again, I wouldn't tell her. I'd never drag Wynn into the dirty past that infused my present. "Let's get back to the toasts."

Her expression morphed into disappointment. "Sure. We waited for you."

All my life, I'd tried to have better, to get treated better, to be better. I deserved it, and I refused to let that belief wobble. But when it came to the Baileys, it'd always been clear. They deserved better than me.

Wynter

Floating on a solid buzz, I crawled into bed, already undressed. Same with Myles. He climbed in behind me and was immediately over and in me. With my mouth fused to his as he rocked in and out, I didn't have to worry about keeping quiet. He brought me to an easy climax, and I shuddered in his arms as he tightened

"That was different," I whispered to him. He was still inside me, and I stayed wrapped around him. I'd never experienced such a soft, passionate climax, but there was something about it. Something that niggled at the back of my mind.

He gave me a long, deep kiss. "Everything about you is different." Carefully, he withdrew and tucked me in next to him.

I was too tired to worry about cleanup or condoms and in his warm and cozy embrace, I couldn't bring myself to move. I let my eyes drift shut. The alcohol muted the warning bell at the back of my brain. The phone call. The haunted look in his eye. The sex that felt like a goodbye.

Sleep overwhelmed me. And when I woke to the sun streaming through my blinds, with a dull ache at my temples, I knew before I opened my eyes he'd be gone. Just like I knew I wouldn't find him helping with chores or cleaning eggs. His guest room would be empty, and his car wouldn't be parked by the garage.

He'd left me again.

CHAPTER TWENTY-ONE

Wynter

"What about that guy?" Autumn sucked a straw between her lips, but her gaze was on a man by the bar.

Autumn had dragged me to Curly's Canyon Grill for dinner after a day of figuring out new marketing pitches for two small-barrel batches we were releasing this winter. A holiday special, but I was over my good cheer.

Since Autumn wouldn't give up until I pass-or-smashed the guy she was referring to, I took a look. He was about my age, which never used to be a detractor, but guess what? He wasn't fucking forty.

"I don't like blonds," I muttered into my drink.

She let out a sigh. "Why did it take me so long to realize that?"

Each week that went by, stretching into two months, more sympathy would fill her gaze. There was no moving on from a certain owner/CEO of a whiskey distillery.

I lifted a shoulder and stuffed a fry into my mouth.

to Myles. Daddy had understood that the way to Myles was through his work ethic. Mama was all heart. I'd gotten to Myles through his business, and he wouldn't let me in beyond that. What had driven him away had something to do with the mysterious phone calls, but he'd never share.

Autumn sucked from her straw until she slurped the bottom. Then she clucked her tongue. "I'm not one to say you've gotta move on. You got your heart broken, and you were really into that tall-dark-and-tortured thing, but—"

"Autumn."

She held a hand up. "Let me finish, please," she said in her firmest teacher voice. "I don't think you have to jump in bed with another man. I think you have to quit moping over the other man first, and you're not. You're not moving on. I find you hugging your childhood stuffed toy and crying—"

"Leave Bunyan out of this. And I was not crying." Not after the first month.

She gave me her *be quiet, please* teacher look this time. "And Teller says you stare off into the distance at your desk."

"I'm thinking of taglines." Shitty ones. Nothing sells top-shelf bourbon like *Have a spirit to celebrate the Holy Spirit*. Or slightly better *Deck the halls with bottles of Holiday Summit Bourbon*. I'd either lost my touch while on my hiatus to escape watching Daddy get sicker, or... Myles had fucked it all out of me. Any feminism I had inside me withered.

I started to let out an indignant gasp, then slumped. Teller was right. The alcohol wasn't speaking to me anymore. "I don't know what to do."

"Have you tried to talk to someone?" she asked gently.

I wrinkled my nose. "Mama said he went through a lot I'll never understand, and—"

"About you, Wynter," she said, exasperated. "A conversation with a professional that isn't about *him*. About you and why you are still so heartbroken."

"Because I still have hope." I blinked back tears. The confession had come without my permission. "I feel like he'll show up again. He'll tell me he's just as miserable and that he's sorry and that he needs me. Or something." I willed the tears to go away. We were tucked in a booth by the window, and I shifted my gaze to the deepening blue sky. The sun would set soon.

"What if he's moved on? What if he's happy back as the playboy CEO?"

Was she trying to make me sob? "Look, I'm pathetic, I know."

"You're not. But I worry about you."

"I just need more time. And a slogan for the holiday specials because I've got nothing."

"Maybe calling them Holiday Heartbreak would work better."

I laughed, startling myself with a snort, which only made Autumn snicker harder. I tossed my straw wrapper at her. "Heartbreak Summit isn't a bad name, but not for a Christmas release."

"How about this—'If you're going to get trashed over

I giggled. "'Montana made heartbreak.'"

"Ohmigod, that's good."

"Teller would never okay it." I let out a breath. "Hang in there with me, okay? I had such a long-term thing with Myles, mostly in my mind, that the complete end to it might take a minute."

"That makes sense. I forgot you low-key stalked him much of your life. Do you really not know about his homelife before us?"

I shook my head. "Only that he'd been in the system for a while. He never talked about his parents, or lack thereof, or why he got pulled from his childhood home. He gets these calls and texts, and he always hides them. I don't think his assistant even knows who they are."

"Do you think it's from the same person?"

I shrugged. "I don't know."

"Is it the mystery that's keeping you hooked?" She was back to using her professional tone. Concerned, trying to goad me into figuring out for myself why the hell I was sitting in the sandbox and refusing to move.

"Maybe," I said just to get her off my back. I was descending into a pit of hopelessness.

"Okay, well, knowing is half the battle. You always were a nosy one. Speaking of nosy, who was the woman who stopped by the other day?"

"Mama wouldn't tell me." The lady had been angry, throwing her hands in the air and shoving her finger in Mama's face. I'd been walking up from the pasture, getting snuffled by my emotional support horse, and I'd seen them arguing. The woman had driven a beater that rumbled like it had never been manufactured with a

ance of a man had gotten her to leave.

She'd looked haggard and gaunt and like she would keel over in a stiff breeze.

Autumn hummed. "Tate said Mama was spitting mad but told him it was nothing." She rolled her eyes. "She tried passing it off as someone who took a wrong turn and got ornery, but we don't buy it."

"We seem to have a history of parents keeping things from us."

"Truth."

In my case, it wasn't just my parents. A certain uptight man hadn't shared much with me either, and I'd followed that big red flag like a beacon.

Myles

"Morning, Mr. Foster," Braxton greeted as I strode by.

"Morning." The word was polite, but the tone was "*Fuck off.*" Nothing against Braxton. My cranky tone was starting to become permanent.

I took the stairs, bypassing the elevator like usual. I needed the extra time on the stairs these days. Time to mentally prepare myself for not seeing a gorgeous blond with a sassy mouth behind the desk.

Mrs. Crane had been back for a month, and she'd given me a wide berth since she'd reentered the office.

I was becoming a next-level asshole, but I couldn't help it. Anytime I got to a place where I wasn't

That woman had ramped up her pestering to new levels. She was becoming increasingly insulting and belligerent. I knew how broke she was. The likelihood she would make the trip to Denver to make my life hell was infinitesimal, or I'd have hired extra security for the distillery.

As if to punctuate the thought, my phone buzzed.

Only twice had it been Wynn. The morning after I left, I'd gotten a message that said she was sorry I had to leave. I hadn't replied. What could I say? Her taste was still on my tongue? My presence in her life would only poison it? I didn't know how to be a Bailey?

Then a month later I'd gotten **I miss you** from her.

I'd almost changed my number. But the thought of never receiving random messages from her was too damn scary to contemplate.

I crested the top of the stairs and marched toward my office.

Mrs. Crane glanced up from her desk. Her reading glasses were perched on the end of her nose, and she looked at me with a *don't you dare lash out at me, or you know I'll walk* expression. Half the reason I kept her around was because I didn't need ass-kissing staff. I could handle gratitude, even if it made me want to crawl out of my skin, but ass-kissing was infuriating.

No wonder Wynn and I had worked so well together.

My mood darkened.

"Mr. Foster, the project manager called."

"What the hell's wrong now?" I snapped, not at her personally, but the damn expansion was proving to be a

"Nothing's wrong. He has more questions."

So many questions. Half the time I was talking to him, I wondered if they had fabricated their website and testimonials, and I was really their first client. Maybe the whole interview process had been an elaborate con, and now I'd committed millions to rookies.

But hey, I'd landed the national distribution contract. Mainline was even working with me on numbers until Foster House could meet the quantities they wanted to see.

The contract Wynn had been instrumental in landing.

"Have him call me tomorrow." I needed to cool off. I didn't know why today was terrible.

Days like this, not having Wynn in my life hit me more acutely than others. Was she thinking of me, too?

"Will do," Mrs. Crane said. "I'll tell him tomorrow at nine."

She knew to catch me before the normal issues of the day tanked my mood further. Like a still going down. Or barrel supply issues. Or an employee found drunk on the job.

All of which had happened this week.

I shut myself in my office. I went to the window and glowered out. The peaceful view did nothing for me. Nothing helped me out of the gutter the days dove into without Wynn.

What was it about her?

I didn't buy into our connection. Yes, we had a history. I'd read her stories. That was it. As an adult, she'd been a breath of fresh air and perhaps the ego dent

stronger. But those feelings did me no good, and Gianna would dive in like a wrecking ball anyway.

Mrs. Crane knocked on the door.

"Come in." *And tell me what was so urgent you couldn't send a message.* I looked over my shoulder, expectant.

She poked her head in. Her mouth was set in a line, and her eyes were full of caution. I tensed so much the impending cramp of a Charley horse began in my back.

"Sorry, Mr. Foster. Braxton said there are two men here to see you?"

She didn't have a fucking clue who I was expecting or why. And if she didn't know, I didn't know.

The answer was no one. "They can make an appointment like everyone else."

A shadow moved behind her. Alarm spiked in her expression, and she pushed the door open. I was already standing up, worried my assistant would put herself in harm's way.

"We're not just anybody." Tate nodded to Mrs. Crane. She was blocking the door, as feared. "Sorry for the abrupt visit, ma'am, but we know what he can be like."

Teller was behind Tate, and they both had their arms folded, glaring at me. They didn't quite look like they'd come right off the ranch, but close. Flannel shirts over solid-colored T-shirts, blue jeans, and cowboy boots.

Darin's words twined through my head. *Dress for the job you want. I want to stay owner of Copper Summit, so I can wear whatever the hell I want.*

His sons must have the same mantra.

Mrs. Crane looked back and forth between us.

contest with them. "It's all right, Mrs. Crane. Thank you."

She stepped to the side but pinned them each with a stern stare as they entered. Then she put her hand on the doorknob. "Ring if you need anything—or anyone."

Meaning she'd call the cops. I had no wish for Foster House to make the news in such a scandalous fashion.

"Nice place." Tate went to the couch his sister had slept on when it stormed. I had maybe slept on it a few times since I had returned. And used the same blankets she'd used.

"Why'd you fucking leave?" Teller snapped. "With no goddamn word. Over twenty years later, and you pull the same immature bullshit?"

"It's none of your bus—"

"Now that's where you're wrong," Tate said calmly, crossing his boots at the ankle. "Wynter is having a hard time."

My abs clenched. A physical hit. She wasn't doing well? She was supposed to bounce back, realize there were better guys out there, men who liked to joke around and laugh and go out instead of work so much they had a loft connected to their office. She was supposed to find a good guy, tolerate absolutely no bullshit from him, and fall blissfully in love and have the babies I continued to convince myself I didn't want.

"She was a natural at marketing." Teller paced the office, hands on hips. "Now she sucks. Like you took all her talent with you."

"She's fucking talented," I said in her defense. She'd

Drink responsibility. Drink Foster House.

Foster House. The only bit of flavor you'll need.

Foster House. The door's always open.

I had trashed the last one. I never had an open door. Except when she'd worked here.

He gave me a flat look. "Holiday Summit. It's got the wheats."

That was pretty bad. "She wasn't serious."

"That's the thing." Teller flung his hands up and continued to pace. "I think she's at her wits' end. Her creativity is in hiding. We've been rerunning specials of her previous recipes because her stuff is..." He spun and stomped in the opposite direction.

"Uninspired," Tate finished.

"She can't rely on me to do her job." Yet I felt like a giant dick.

"I agree. But you also ditched us. And Mama."

I had. I owned it and had the hardest fucking time not regretting how I'd left. "It was for your own good."

Tate tipped his head back. "We're all adults, Myles."

So was the trouble hounding me. "It's better if I stay out of Montana."

"Way to sound cryptic, dickweed," Teller said. "Why'd you leave? We bonded and shit that night at the distillery. Since you reappeared, we gave you a chance I never would've thought you deserved."

Tate nodded.

I had to give myself a moment before responding. I'd felt the same and had thought those emotions were wishful thinking. Something I couldn't have. Then Teller says that shit.

me? I wouldn't have hurt Wynn if I didn't have to. It was better this way."

"For who? You?" Teller asked.

"If you're in trouble, we can help." Tate lifted a shoulder when I shot him an incredulous look. "I didn't know you and Dad had that connection. I didn't know how much you respected him—and the way you respect Mama? Means a lot. Wynn doesn't date doofuses."

"If she does, she gives herself bangs after the breakup," Teller added.

Her bangs went almost to her chin. How fast did hair grow? When had some jackass broken her heart? "Does she have bangs now?"

"Surprisingly, no, but then Autumn might've hidden the scissors."

I hadn't hurt her enough to make her cut her hair. Not that it'd detract from her looks at all. I couldn't give fewer fucks about a girl's hairstyle, but I liked having something to hang on to when—

Wrong time to think about sex with Wynn. She didn't have bangs.

Because the hurt you caused went deeper, asshole.

I needed to get off the Wynn topic. A difficult task with her brothers here. "Did you two drive?"

Tate stood and stretched. "We flew. Tested out that private jet co-op Wynn told us about. There's a lot of money coming in and out of Montana, so it was easy to find one."

"This is our free test flight." Teller stopped by the door to my office. "We have to leave soon. Gonna give us a personal tour of the place?"

built. But taking these guys through everything? Being open about what practices I'd learned from Copper Summit and how I'd adapted them to Foster House? That would be a special honor.

I could've done the same with Wynn, but I hadn't known. The thrill inside me died. She'd have to find her inspiration in someone else. Meanwhile, I'd live without it.

CHAPTER TWENTY-TWO

Myles

It had been a month since Tate and Teller's visit, and I wasn't in any better of a mood, but I'd evened out to a predictably shitty attitude I could moderately control.

I stood at the window, staring out for far too long every day. As long as I was lost in the scenery, I could let my mind roam. This was the only time I let myself wonder. About her.

Had she gotten over me yet? Was she making the stellar cocktails she was known for again? Had she gotten her marketing spirit back?

I turned just as a message popped up on my screen from Mrs. Crane. **The marketing department sent some research samples for you.**

It better be marketing materials. If they were running new cocktails past me, I might throw my laptop across the room. There was nothing that didn't remind me of her.

marketing department, but I also wanted final say on who we advertised with. My promo manager didn't always know what I knew about people in the industry. She didn't have as good a feel for who would be a mistake to interview with and who wouldn't.

I clicked on the first link. Our limited-time holiday whiskeys were getting stocked on shelves. We were booking promos for the next calendar year already, and she was especially working on St. Patrick's Day. Green beer didn't have to be the only drink people had that night.

A podcast started. Whiskey enthusiasts who traveled the country, touring and tasting at various distilleries, and then discussing the place and the product. I had given my marketing team approval to be featured as guests on podcasts. Not me. Never me.

I listened to part of the episode at double speed, then poked around their website, checked out upcoming guests, and listened to highlights of old episodes. On a notepad, I jotted down the name of the podcast under my approved column.

The next one I pulled up was a YouTube channel. I went through the same routine. New podcasts and channels didn't pop up often, but if one did, or gained in popularity, my team was on it.

I jotted down a few more shows I approved of.

The next link had a note with it. **We were invited as a featured guest.** I clicked the link to a YouTube video, and a face popped up on the screen. My world skittered to a halt, and I stared, letting the webcast play in regular time. Wynn.

something that made her laugh, but I didn't hear a damn word. I was intent on her reply.

"All of us know every aspect of the distillery, Matthew, from the cleaning to the distilling to the marketing." She was smiling, but her eyes flashed. No one else would realize she was irritated. Matthew, the cocksucker, must've made some sexist assumption.

"But you don't like getting your hands dirty?" This from the other guy. What was the jackass's name?

She laughed, a fake, hollow sound. Again, no one would be able to tell but me. "If you knew my daddy, you'd know how funny that question is, Pete."

"Speaking of your dad," Matthew said, turning a little more serious. "I'm sorry to hear about his passing."

"Thank you," she answered, her expression galvanizing, like she'd promised herself she wouldn't cry.

"Can you tell us the history of Copper Summit? Your grandfather started the distillery?"

"Making moonshine goes back a lot farther in the family, but my great-granddaddy started to sell it, and then he mastered making bourbon, and the Baileys never looked back."

Pete held up a hand, speaking into his headset. "Now, it's no secret you and your sisters are adopted. We read interviews where your father talked about family and the importance of giving back to the world. You grew up with several foster siblings, too, correct?"

She nodded, rolling her lips in. I leaned closer to the screen.

"Your brothers and sisters are all in the family business in some way?" Pete asked.

they like."

Pete nodded. "How about those foster kids? Are they involved at all?"

Her jaw tightened for half a heartbeat. Again, I was likely the only one who'd catch it, an expert in all things Wynter Kerrigan. That jaw clench was for me. "No. Many of the kids were only with us anywhere from days to a couple years at the most."

"And in the cases of the kids who were with you for a couple years, no interest?" Matthew's question rang with sincerity. He wasn't probing to be nosy, he was curious, as most people would be. My shoulders grew tight. Had he made the connection? Would it matter if he had?

"Well, yes, but to what extent, we don't always know, and their privacy was and has always been important to the family."

"Gotcha. Not every foster kid grows up to build a whiskey empire, right?" Pete's laugh was obnoxious and oblivious.

Wynn's placating smile was as empty as her laugh. She moved the topic toward everyone's roles in the business.

I listened, avid, hanging on the moments she laughed and a real smile peeked through. When the episode wrapped up, I hit play again.

And again.

And again.

After the fourth round, I scrubbed my face and pushed away from the desk. I didn't have a response ready for the marketing team. I hadn't gotten through all

What would it take to have her in my life?

A dangerous thought. An impossible one. If I didn't have Gianna, I had Colorado. This building. My brand. My products. The empire I was well on the way to constructing. Foster House would be as big of a name as Jack Daniel's and twice as philanthropic. No one would know, but I would. I would know how wrong everyone had been about me and where I came from. I would know I was not a piece of shit. That my presence in this world meant something. And that my money could go toward decent, productive people.

I closed my computer and went to stand in front of the window. I really should be setting a timer for this shit.

My phone rang. The hairs on the back of my neck stood up.

Gianna was escalating. She was on the end of the line, probably ready to cuss me out again for being worthless and a regret.

The ringing stopped. Started again.

With an angry huff, I spun away from the window and grabbed the phone off my desk. Gianna's number. As expected.

"What now?" I answered.

"I guess that answers my question," a man said.

This was new. Gianna had never mentioned other men in her life. She never gave me details, no doubt because they would make me less likely to aid her. So why was a man speaking to me from her phone number? My body went cold. "Who are you?"

"Gianna's son."

damn thing. Gianna was cunning and controlling, and she'd wield whatever information she had to gain an ounce of control, but usually for drugs. My stomach roiled. This guy wasn't her son. Was he?

"You know I'm telling the truth, but don't worry. You continue on with your happy life pretending we don't exist."

"We?" Cold leeched farther into my veins. "Gianna never mentioned kids."

"Don't act surprised," he said, his voice devoid of humor. "My brother and I are content to stay out of your life. But I have to tell you first that she's gone. Overdose."

"She's dead?" The words *overdose* rang in my head. Gianna. Gone. Sometime during her incessant pestering, I had come to think of her as immortal. If a woman like her hadn't perished from the way she lived by now, nothing could destroy her. She was the one who ruined everything.

I wasn't prepared to never have her on the other end of the line tormenting me. I wasn't prepared for the empty hole she'd left in my life. I wasn't prepared to accept that after all she'd done to me, I might actually mourn her.

"Yes, Myles. Our mother is dead."

Wynter

. . .

muffled the vibrating of my phone, but when I shoved them off and blinked at the screen, I saw a list of missed calls, all from one number.

Myles?

I sat up. He was calling me. After months of wishing to see his name flash on my screen, I was frozen. The phone buzzed again. I squinted at the time. It was one fifteen in the morning.

Confused, elated, and afraid I was dreaming, I answered. "Hello?"

"She's dead, Wynn," he slurred. "Fucking dead."

Dread filled my veins. Had tough Mrs. Crane passed away? Or, and this was coldhearted, had the thought of finding a new assistant who could put up with him driven him to drink? "Myles, are you okay?"

"She's dead." He let out a caustic laugh. "I never thought she'd die. I didn't even hope for it. But she's dead, and god help me, I'm happy and sad and—I have fucking brothers I didn't know about."

Frowning, I swung my legs over the edge of the bed. He wasn't making sense and that wasn't Myles. "I'm sorry—who passed away?"

"My mother."

Oh. *Oh no.* Poor Myles. I didn't know a thing about his mother. I had chalked his silence about her up to a premature death either before he'd been removed from his childhood home or shortly after. But she'd been alive until now? How close had they been? "I'm so sorry."

"Don't be. She was an awful person who kept trying to get drug money from me."

"And she kept the fact that I have two brothers from me. *Bitch*."

The recognizable sound of ice tinkling in a glass caught my ear. "Myles, are you drunk?" I knew the answer, but how open was he willing to be?

"Yep," he said, popping the p. "I'm fucking wasted. Apple doesn't fall far from the tree."

"You're not like that."

"I hurt you."

A drunk Myles was still too aware to lie to. "Yes, you did."

"She'd have made your life hell."

"You don't know that."

A heavy sigh gusted across the line. "Yes, I do, Wynter Kerrigan. I know exactly how she fucks with people in my life."

He didn't elaborate. "And your brothers?"

"Want nothing to do with me. I don't even know their names." More ice tinkling. "I don't know how old they are. We have to have different dads, I know that."

Had his dad passed? But talking about his father wouldn't help him in this state, so I stuck to what he'd called about. "Can you meet them? When's the funeral?"

"She shouldn't get a funeral. There'll be no one at her graveside anyway unless they're looking for money or drugs."

"Where did she live?"

"Bozeman," he mumbled.

No wonder he'd been uptight and looking over his shoulder when we'd gone shopping and out to eat. Hurt resonated inside me. He hadn't shared his paranoia with

"No. I can't come back. And I can't be with you. God, it's fucked up that I called."

"Why—"

"I'm a mess. You have a beautiful life, and you're too fucking good for me. Trust me. I grew up thinking I deserved better, but when it comes to you, you deserve so much better than me."

"Myles—"

"I'm sorry I called." The line went dead.

I let out an indignant gasp. Of all the...I let out a growl, then shoved my hair out of my face. A drunk and grieving Myles was alone, hopefully in his loft and away from the stairs, and he thought he didn't deserve me.

What a stubborn fucking man.

So what would I do about it?

CHAPTER TWENTY-THREE

Myles

The pounding in my head woke me as much as the savory smells teasing my nose. My stomach cramped while at the same time begging for real sustenance after the assault on it last night.

The events leading up to my first drink yesterday piled into my head. The phone call. Gianna. Brothers. Telling Mrs. Crane to shut down the office through the weekend. I'd wanted to be left the fuck alone to process the double shocks I'd received yesterday.

Then hitting my personal bar. I'd meant to stop after one drink. I detested getting drunk. I hated the lack of control, the unbridled thoughts I was too inebriated to stop. I'd rather be an uptight prick than a sad drunk.

I pried my eyes open. I was flat on my back, on my bed. That part wasn't unusual. I was fully dressed in my slacks and button-up shirt. Thankfully I wasn't a tie guy, or I would've strangled myself in my sleep.

while making no promises not to heave up any food I put in it.

"You're finally awake."

I was fucking dreaming. There was no way I was hearing Wynn's voice in my loft.

I tipped my head up enough to look around the place. She was sitting in a high-back chair she'd scooted closer to the bed. Her silky hair was thrown in a crooked ponytail and she wore a Copper Summit hoodie and jeans. Fucking gorgeous, dark circles under her eyes and all.

A bag from a soup-and-sandwich shop sat on the nightstand, along with a bottle of water and some headache meds.

I deserved a fucking migraine. "What are you doing here?" I croaked.

I was going to roll up to sit, but I stuck to rolling to my side when the room started spinning.

"I caught a flight after you hung up on me." She gave me a knowing smirk. "I knew you wouldn't answer if I tried calling back."

Ah, hell. "I called you?"

There was the flash of hurt I always caused her. "You don't remember?"

I didn't bother shaking my head. I heaved to a seated position and gripped the edges of the mattress. What had I told her? Had I confessed to how empty I was inside? Had I revealed that I was fucking scared because without Gianna telling me I was the only thing she regretted, what did I have to prove? "I'm sorry I bothered you."

"Otherwise that damn pride of yours would've left you to suffer on your own."

I prodded my aching temples. "So I called you, and you flew here? Did you use the private jet your brothers did?"

She stopped what she was doing and stared at the wall. My plain wall with an abstract art piece that was better suited to a generic hotel chain than someone's living space. "My brothers were here?"

Shit. "A month ago."

"Aren't you full of surprises." She took out a bowl of soup and peeled the lid off. A few drops of liquid sloshed out from the extra force in her movement. Noodles and carrots poked out of the broth. Chicken noodle soup.

"They were worried about you."

"They're always worried about me and my sisters. I'm surprised they thought you would be."

"Wynn."

She held a spoon up. "We're not getting into it now. You look like hell, no offense."

I pushed a hand through my hair, making my headache stronger. I had called her. She'd realized I was drunk and in a bad place, and now she was here. "You didn't have to come." I took the spoon to stay on her good side. I wanted the soup as much as I didn't want it.

"If you don't see that's not the point, then I'm not defending my decision." She took out a second soup and two wrapped sandwiches. Mine would be stacked with roast beef and veggies and hers would be turkey and cheese and avocado. She handed me my food and sat back in the chair with hers. "I had no idea you'd shut the

I cradled my soup, not bothering to hide my inspection of her. Despite her comfy wear, she looked as tired as I felt, minus the hangover.

My call must've been in the middle of the night, when I'd been several drinks into feeling sorry for myself. "What time is it?"

"After two."

She'd caught an early enough flight to land, order food, and get here. How long had she been waiting for me to wake up? "You shouldn't have come."

"You sure about that?" Her usually warm stare was direct and unforgiving.

No. I wasn't sure. I liked having her here. I'd rather welcome her better than this, but this was all I could summon. I kept eating.

The food went down better than expected. I started on the sandwich next. She'd gotten exactly what I wanted. We ate in silence. I downed the entire bottle of water. The dizziness hadn't entirely abated, but I no longer felt like I'd been slammed into the wall by a full barrel.

Her presence was soothing. If I had awoken alone, I might've lurched into my office and poured another drink. But with Wynn sitting across from me, my mind was clearer. My thoughts weren't as fuzzy and tumultuous.

I crinkled my sandwich bag and gathered all our garbage. The smell of stale alcohol clung to me, fatigue with it. I hadn't gotten quality sleep. It was the middle of the day, and I could go back to bed. But I wasn't

"I'm going to shower." I stood, making sure I wouldn't faceplant before I took a step. "Get some rest, Wynn."

She only watched me disappear into the bathroom. Part of me hoped she'd join me, but the most coherent part of my brain knew I'd be useless. I could grunt out a quick fuck, but neither Wynn nor I wanted that.

She deserved better. I faintly recalled saying those words. Had they been on the phone with her?

I let the spray pummel my body, keeping my head safely away from the pounding after I washed my hair. When I was done, I dried off and wrapped a towel around myself. I hadn't brought in a pair of shorts. I wasn't used to not being able to walk around naked in my home.

I hadn't changed the codes. I'd never thought Wynn would care enough to use them.

Perhaps I'd hoped she'd use them one day. But not for this.

When I exited the bathroom, clean and with my teeth brushed, I stopped. The blinds had been partially closed to shadow the room. In my bed, the side I didn't use had a sleeping Wynn tucked in. She was on her side, her back toward the middle of the bed. Her sweater and jeans were neatly folded on the nightstand. The shirt that was visible above the blankets looked like an old Foster House shirt, a faded blue from fifteen years' worth of laundering. My shirt.

The view was so damn right. Wynn in my bed, wearing my clothing.

I didn't have the energy to fight the rightness of the

not taking her into my arms but satisfied at being within arm's reach, sleep claimed me.

Wynter

A wall of steel was behind me, and a hand was pressed against my belly. I let out a happy moan. I could wake up like this more often, a possessive arm around me and the smell of amber-laced sage surrounding me.

Wait. My eyes flew open. I wasn't in my bed. I wasn't even in Montana.

And the heat source behind me was Myles. Finally. I wished I could've woken up to him under different circumstances, but I was grateful he hadn't run me out as soon as he'd seen me in his place.

"Let me hold you," he murmured into the nape of my neck.

Tension drained out of me. "How long did we sleep?" I wanted to roll into him, but also, my hair probably looked like a rat's nest. The flavor of chicken noodle soup was still in my mouth.

"A few hours." His voice was a raspy rumble, and he stroked his thumb in little circles on the skin of my belly. He slid his hand lower.

A whimper escaped. It'd been so long since he'd touched me last. I craved him. But this wasn't the right time. "Myles."

"Wynn—do you need this?"

"What about you?"

"Making you come makes me feel good."

How could I argue with that? With his strong arm around me and his fingers close to giving the best pleasure I'd ever known, I couldn't refuse him. I slid my legs apart to give him better access.

A sexy, deep growl came from him. He slid his other arm under me until I was fully in his hold. He was kissing my shoulder and the back of my neck.

"You know what seeing you in my bed does to me?" His fingertip hit my clit. I was already wet for him, had been as soon as I'd realized he was the one holding me.

"Tell me." After waking up alone to find him gone, I had to hear it.

"You make me want things I shouldn't have." He pushed his finger through my pussy and thrust inside me. His thumb landed on my clit. Pleasure was growing inside, coiling tighter. "I'll never quit wanting you." He stroked in and out of me with his finger while steadily brushing over my clit. "I'll never quit wanting to spend my time between your legs."

My moan was needy. The way I was clamped to his chest, unable to move unless I was making room for him to get me off, did it for me. I went from asleep to ready to climax in record time. "Myles, please."

I wouldn't be able to hold myself together for long. Three months was an eternity.

"Come for me."

I shattered on command. Writhing in his hold, bucking my hips, trying to grasp every last bit of pleasure he was willing to give.

satisfied.

"I need to be inside you, Wynn." He lifted my top leg, propping it on his knee. The broad tip of his cock slipped through my pussy. "Just a few strokes with nothing between us?"

He was asking permission. He could've done anything. I wouldn't have put up a thread of resistance. "Yes."

I knew what we were risking. He did, too, or he wouldn't have asked. But if he was like me, he craved a deeper connection. No barriers. Just us.

He pushed inside, slowly filling me, not taking his time but also not frantically thrusting. He seated himself all the way, then placed a hot, wet, open-mouthed kiss on my shoulder. "Fuck, you feel good. Fucking perfect."

Feathering his hand back around, he was on my clit again. I undulated, and he didn't move. He remained that way as he propelled me to another orgasm.

I was doing all the moving, but I was able to feel the tremors in his arms as he held himself still. The trembling of his body, doing all it took to keep from losing control as I bucked wildly on him.

"Myles! Yes!" I slammed into the peak and let the ecstasy wash me away.

He thrust once, twice, then pulled out. Hot jets of cum hit my back right above my ass. We were too close for his cock not to get pinned between us.

"Fuck, Wynn," he grunted as he came.

I held on to his arm, loving how I drove him crazy. Loving these brief moments when there was nothing

Hating that the next moment, I would be alone again, even lying next to him.

Myles

We'd had wakeup sex. We'd had shower sex. With a goddamn condom this time. What had I been thinking? I didn't risk pregnancy, but I had woken up so damn grateful she hadn't fled from my bed like I had from hers. She'd been warm, compliant, and all mine.

I wanted someone to be mine.

Foster House was enough. I'd been content with this place for almost twenty years.

Have you, though?

I'd been ignoring that thought all night.

Since we'd napped so late in the day, we weren't going to bed anytime soon. I'd called Cooper to bring more food. Empty Thai containers were in the garbage with leftovers in the fridge. We hadn't talked about anything of substance beyond the food and the weather—cold with snow flurries. Wynn was curled up in the opposite corner of the couch as me, her feet tucked under my thigh. Cozy. Familiar. Somehow more intimate than having her wrapped around me in the shower like after we'd woken from our nap.

She'd fielded some calls and messages from her family. "I told Mama your mom died and that I came out here to be with you, and she got the others to back off."

"Not much at all. Do you get drunk often?"

That wasn't what she was asking. I must've told her something about my mom. "No. I've seen what addiction can do to people and those around them. I got drunk once before, and I hated every moment." I'd had too much to drink out of spite. Then I'd gotten into a fight in the bar and had to call Darin. My life had turned on a dime after that.

"Was your mom an alcoholic?"

"Gianna drank, but it wasn't her drug of choice."

"Gianna?"

"Gianna Florentina Cardellini Foster. Daughter of proud Italian immigrants who passed away in a Portland apartment fire when she was young. Her grandfather had come over after her parents, but he was from a different generation. The kind that kicks granddaughters out when they get pregnant at fifteen."

"Did you ever meet him?"

I shook my head. "Gianna never took me to meet him, and he died when I was young. My grandmother died in Italy." Telling this was like reciting someone else's story, one I'd heard but never uttered myself. "My father's parents were broke as hell, but they took her in, made them get married as soon as they turned eighteen." I stared at the black TV screen. "I remember a picture hanging up. Gianna was in an evening gown, and Devon, my dad, was in an ill-fitting tux. I was in shorts and a T-shirt, only like two. What should've been a prom photo was their wedding picture."

"You don't have that picture?"

"Nope. She said his parents were greedy bastards and

biggest asshole she'd ever met. But to Gianna, no one was a good person. She had something against everyone."

"So Gianna and Devon were on their own." She shook her head, sympathy floating through her eyes. "What happened to your dad?"

"He developed an autoimmune disease, and they, uh, just couldn't afford..." I had to clear my throat. There was a lot of my childhood I didn't think about, but none more so than my dad. "I was six, and he just got so weak. The pain was awful toward the end, and he got pain meds. And when he passed, I was eight. Gianna got the meds and a payout from the life insurance policy he'd taken out at work. Then she changed."

Wynn scooted closer, folding her legs under her and facing me. "Coming into money so young, after what she'd been through, and with no support system? That was too much for her to handle, wasn't it?"

I snorted. Leave it to Wynn to see Gianna as the victim. She had been at one time. But I couldn't afford to see her like that. My past was too depressing as it was. "*Being a mother* was too much for her to handle." I put my hand on her knee. She rested her hand on top of mine. The contact grounded me. "By the time I was ten, I was left alone for entire weekends. No supervision, and she never bought food. By then, she'd gotten into harder drugs. The money was gone, and she was starting to do whatever it took to get more, usually hooking up with men to use them for as long as she could." Were any of them the fathers of my brothers? Or did Gianna have

Wynn winced. "That's awful."

I nodded. "Yep. I was taken away when I was eleven, and I was so damn angry. I'd been taking care of myself for so long. Why did I have to suddenly listen to someone else?"

"Some of those homes weren't better than what you left?"

"Only a few were truly bad, like the one I was in before I came to your house. The rest I ruined—with Gianna's help." I let out a long breath and laid my head back on the couch. "She would put ideas in my head during our visits. Even when the visits were supervised, there were still ways to fuck with my head. Sometimes she'd call or find me at school. I'd tell no one. It was me and my mom against the world, and foster homes don't really get trained adequately for kids like me. Then when I was fifteen, she tried to convince me to steal from the family I was with. I didn't. I was sick of her taking what I had. I was tired of giving it. Figured no one else should have to."

"You started to see that she wasn't living for you but for herself?"

Wasn't that the truth. "So she got close to the kid a year older than me. He had his own anger at life and was dabbling in drugs. Gianna wouldn't have known where to find him if it hadn't been for me."

"Oh no." Her wide eyes brimmed with anxiety. "She didn't."

"The only time she was generous in her life was giving him drugs."

Her soft gasp tore at my heart. "Did he—"

my resentment toward him. "But he said I gave the shit to him."

"They believed him?"

"Didn't matter. They couldn't prove it. After that, they placed me farther from Bozeman—until eventually I ended up with the Baileys." I rubbed her knee. "I could tell right away I didn't want to fuck that up, but I almost did."

"What changed your mind?"

I tipped my head forward to meet her gaze. "A little girl made me feel useful."

Her lips parted. I had to look away.

"I kept my distance as much as I was allowed from Gianna. She behaved, too. I think she realized I had my limits. But the less I shared with her, the closer I got to aging out and becoming legally emancipated from the system, the more scared she got. She started making veiled threats...about you guys."

Her eyes flared again. "No."

"She did it again when she figured out I was at your dad's funeral."

"You left because of her?"

"I would've left anyway."

"Myles." She crawled onto my lap. I folded my arms around her, and she rested her head on my shoulder. "Are you going to her funeral?"

"God, no." I didn't know if there'd even be a funeral. "My brother, whatever the hell his name is, wasn't very forthcoming. I think he's under the impression I knew about him." I let out a dry laugh. "As if he doesn't know what she's like at all." I swallowed. "What she was like."

She sat up to face me. "It's okay, you know. Your feelings are going to be complicated."

I got lost in the warm depths of her eyes. "How can you be so understanding?"

"Having to figure out how to love and be furious with one set of parents while trying to love and accept another set of parents makes a girl need therapy. My birth parents were good people, but I was a scared and confused kid, and I was so furious with them. Angry at them for things they probably couldn't help. Upset that they hadn't had cows like the Baileys or a house like the Baileys, and that they hadn't had to deal with foster homes and adoptions. Mostly my feelings stemmed from how they'd had the audacity to die and leave me and my sisters orphans." The corner of her mouth kicked up. "A tangle of feelings like that can mess anyone up, but I've had years to process. Mama made a lot of runs to the counselors in town. They helped in so many ways. Never could crack our fear of storms, though."

I wasn't surprised all her sisters had issues with storms after what they'd been through. "She doesn't deserve me at the funeral."

"And your brothers?"

"I don't know anything about them."

She placed her hands on my shoulders. "I guess the real question is...how much do you want to know about them?"

CHAPTER TWENTY-FOUR

Myles

We took my car to Montana. I drove, and Wynn navigated around the snowed-in routes through Wyoming.

Coasting down the long driveway to the big house I'd left three months ago before the break filled me with anxiety. The snow dotting the brown landscape only proved how long it'd been since I'd left. Only the trees stayed green, and the higher the mountains crested, the more snow capped them.

I was back on Bailey land. Tate and Teller had visited me that one time, and then they'd gone, and I had assumed I wouldn't see them again. I had convinced myself I would be fine without seeing Wynn again. But she was stubborn, and it turned out, so was I.

Tomorrow, I'd meet my brothers. Wynn thought she was coming along, but I had no idea what we'd be walking into. I didn't want her to witness how Gianna

—I paid for them.

I'd gotten their names. Our mother had named us Myles, Lane, and Cruz. Some inside driving-themed joke only she'd been in on.

Lane was the one who'd called. He hadn't picked up when I'd rung Mom's phone back. Or when I'd messaged him to talk.

Finally I'd texted him.

> Do you really believe our mother when she said I knew about you?

Eventually, he'd replied.

> Fair point.

Then he'd sent the day and time he and Cruz were meeting with the funeral home director. There'd be no funeral, no viewing, no reception, just arrangements to put her in the ground. Then I could figure out how to live without her harassment.

Mae came outside, a wide smile on her face and relief radiating from her. She'd thrown her long, puffy black winter coat on but hadn't zipped it. I got out and went straight for the apology. Unlike my mom, I knew when I was wrong, and I wouldn't be afraid to admit it. "I'm sorry, Mae. For the way I left." A cloud of condensation left my mouth as I spoke.

Her arms were out wide. "I'm sure there was a reason."

I was encompassed in her warm embrace. My hold

a functional, healthy way.

The guilt that usually welled up until I wanted to push away stayed at a low simmer. Gianna hadn't been more than her addiction for a long time, but it was hard to shake the loyalty of a son.

"I'm sure you can figure out the reason why," I said as I pulled away. Cold snaked in around me with the wind. My jacket was in the car.

Wynn slid a hand across my back as she passed. She had her winter coat draped over her other arm, and the backpack that held the only clothing she'd packed over her shoulder. "I'm going to make us a bite to eat."

"Let's go in." I gestured for Mae to follow Wynn. Mae looked like she wanted to talk to me, but I wasn't willing to keep her out in the cold for privacy. Wynn knew enough. "I'll grab my bag."

Mae looked over her shoulder, then back at me. "She was here," she said quietly.

Gianna? Ice trickled into my veins. "She came to the house?"

She couldn't have harassed the Baileys without me knowing.

I'd have known. Right?

Fuck. My skin went from ice to hot and prickly. I'd left, and she'd harassed the Baileys anyway? Goddammit. My issues shouldn't spill over on anyone. "How bad was she?"

Shame spiraled in my gut. Her behavior shouldn't reflect on me, but I took responsibility for it. My absence was supposed to save others from it.

It hadn't. All it had done was dilute her effects *on me*.

The sympathy that filled her gaze told me enough. "She was agitated. Angry. So, so angry. Desperate."

That described Gianna most days. The difference was that she could usually mask it. She couldn't manipulate if she revealed what she'd become, and if she hadn't been keeping her mask in place, then she'd been deteriorating. As I'd suspected.

The loss squeezing my lungs sent confusing signals to my brain.

Mae closed the distance between us and squeezed my arm. "It's okay, you know. What you're feeling. You're not just mourning the addict who made a mess of your life, you're going to grieve for the mom she was when you were young. The life you two could've—should've—had. She's going to leave a hole, no matter what."

My grief bloomed. So fucking true, and I hated it. But to hear someone else understand, just like Wynn had? I could get through the pain easier. "Thanks, Mae. It's hard to get used to."

"I'm glad you let Wynter know what was going on."

"I shouldn't have called her." That earned me a hard look from Mae, but I had one more major question. "Did you know I have brothers?"

Her brows popped so high it was a wonder she didn't reel backward. "No. Brothers? How many?"

She hadn't known. Part of me had been fearing betrayal, but the concern was a moot point. "Two. That I know of. She got them to think I was ignoring their existence."

"I wish I was surprised." Her breath puffed out.

"Go inside, Mae. You're getting cold."

was grinning by the time I got to my car. Yet when I caught my reflection in the window, a resentful, disappointed reflection of my mother stared back at me.

She'd never leave me. And I'd have to make sure her lingering effect on this world didn't hurt people I loved, especially Wynn. The only way to keep her out of harm's way was to isolate myself.

Wynter

"He left without me!" I yelled into the phone. I'd told that headstrong jackass I would have to run to the distillery in the morning and catch up with a few emails I'd abandoned when I'd gone to Denver. And when I'd returned to the house, he'd left. I'd headed straight to the guest room to double-check that yep, the simple black suitcase he'd packed was gone before I'd called Summer.

Fury and hurt tumbled inside me. What would it take? What did I have to do to get that man to let me in?

"Are you sure he's in Bozeman?" she asked.

"That's where Lane and Cruz are." I'd filled her in on Gianna and the brothers.

"Maybe he's grabbing a few groceries?"

"The man's ghosted me four times now."

She tsked. "Then you should leave him in the dust. Change the locks while he's gone."

didn't know if he'd come back, so I'd have to find him. "Which funeral home do you think he's meeting them at?"

"You keep chasing after him, he's going to keep taking you for granted. Let him go, Wynter. If he's willing to do what he has to, to be with you, he will."

"It's not a pride thing. He's hurting."

"And he keeps hurting you." She wasn't going to waver.

"I guess you'll have to trust me."

"I'll be there with crappy wine and excellent bourbon when he breaks your heart. Enjoy your bangs."

I growled. "Just because you're the oldest doesn't mean you know anything." Yes, I was being childish.

"Keep telling yourself that. Mountain View Funeral Home. They have the best prices and a decent reputation. A popular choice if money's an issue."

"Thank you." I didn't feel grateful. Her earlier words had hit a target my brain couldn't ignore.

Four times. Three if I didn't count when we were kids, but I shouldn't ignore those red flags. I should stop and think about chasing after a damaged man who'd made little effort to pursue me.

But he took care of me during storms.

Fair trade?

Wasn't starting to feel like it.

I darted out of the house and ran right into Teller.

"Whoa, where's the barn fire?"

I scowled at him. "It'd be in the barn."

"Which one? The pole barn? The calving barn? The—"

Didn't that question hit me in the gut. Myles had gone out to help with chores, like the dutiful guest he could be. Tate hadn't acted surprised, just put him to work. "He went to Bozeman." I tried to step around him without landing in the snow.

He blocked me, nimble for a big, imposing oaf. "Without you?"

"Teller, not you, too."

"Not me, too? More than one person is trying to talk sense into you?"

"You don't know what he's been—"

"Guess what? It doesn't matter. He's old enough and smart enough to know how to treat someone. Leaning on the excuse of his upbringing or that his mama was psycho doesn't matter."

"She was an addict."

"Doesn't matter, Wynter. If some guy kept breaking Autumn's heart and making her cry, would you encourage her to go back to him?"

I opened my mouth. Shut it. I'd want to gut the man. I'd be calling Summer behind Autumn's back to plan a way to shred three of his tires instead of four so insurance wouldn't cover the damage. He'd find the trees in his yard toilet-papered—and his car, his mailbox, and his entire house. We'd come up with so many half-brained ideas that were scary yet tempting enough to carry out. And if Junie was home? We'd all get tossed into jail.

But what if Autumn felt as strongly for this hypothetical guy as I did for Myles?

Then I'd wonder why she didn't have more self-respect.

with his brooding glare. Then he'd hired me, and I'd been toast.

I was indeed toast. Burned and crispy and hurting. But I couldn't ignore how I felt about him. "What if I'm in love with him?"

Teller scratched the back of his neck. The tip of his nose was red, and so were the apples of his cheeks. His Carhartt hat covered his mahogany hair and the tips of his ears. "I'd say you have to ask yourself if you want to chase him until you end up living in Foster House. Will you spend your time hoping he never moves without you? Do you want to be afraid you're going to randomly find him gone?"

Hot tears filled my eyes. I sniffled.

Teller grabbed my shoulders and stooped to meet my gaze. "I doubt he'll agree with me, but he's thought of himself for most of his life. It's going to take a cold blast in the face to make him see how selfish he's being. And if he can't wake up and see what he's got right in front of him, then do you really want to be the girl always trying to keep a guy's attention?" He patted my shoulders and then moved around me to go inside the house.

I jingled the keys in my fingers. The cold metal against my chilled fingers would make my skin lose sensation. I concentrated on the feeling, clinging to the encroaching numbness. My head grew clearer the colder and more uncomfortable I got.

Did I want to be the girl always trying to keep a guy's attention?

This morning, I'd been highly paranoid. At work, I'd rushed through my emails, approved marketing strate-

I'd told myself I didn't want to keep Myles waiting. That he had unfinished, important, deeply personal business he was waiting on me for.

But I'd been scared. The distance between us this morning hadn't been his distraction, or his trepidation, or that he was half in his head about work he hadn't expected to miss.

He'd purposely held himself away from me, knowing he was going to ghost me.

I jingled my keys again. I could go back into the warm house, wait to see if he returned, and if he didn't, I'd get on with my life. Or I could try to find him in Bozeman. And on the drive there, figure out what to say when I saw him.

CHAPTER TWENTY-FIVE

Myles

The funeral home looked like it could be an insurance office building, all angles and glass walls. A residential area sprawled on one side of the place and a church and an actual insurance office were on the other side. Where was the mountain view?

A lanky young man was standing outside the funeral home, surrounded by a cloud of smoke. He was adding to the cloud, squinting and crooking his mouth as he exhaled.

His shaggy hair could use a trim—or a hacksaw—and his scruff should just go. I parked and got out. He took a drag and eyed me. A guy always on the defense. I used to have the same look. I probably still did.

"Lane?" I asked.

The man's eyes narrowed. He took another slow puff from his smoke and studied me. I continued walking toward him. If he didn't want to answer, I'd go inside and

blood relative or not.

"Cruz," he said when I almost walked past him, getting a chilly lungful of cigarette smoke.

I stopped and looked him over. Christ, was he even eighteen? "You and Lane want to hold our happy reunion after we deal with paperwork bullshit?"

He shrugged like he didn't care either way. "Speaking of paperwork bullshit..." He took another pull, then tossed the butt on the ground and let it smolder against the cold concrete. "You got Venmo or something to pay for this?"

Once I'd gotten the info on where and when, I had expected to fork over all the cash needed to take care of Gianna's remains. But if that was all my brothers tried to fleece out of me, I'd be surprised.

A small tendril of sympathy cinched around my chest, weak and fragile but still there. If this kid was over twenty, I'd be shocked. Lane couldn't be that much older. Had they had more contact with Gianna? Had they been closer to her? Had they been smothered by the python of her manipulation?

I had assumed I would have to pay to be out of their lives, but I hadn't considered wanting to stay instead. How did they feel? "Where's Lane?"

Cruz kicked his almost-burned-out cigarette off the sidewalk and into the snow-packed lawn with his heavy black boot. How magnanimous of him. He jutted his chin toward the door.

I walked in with him, his fresh-ashtray smell surrounding both of us. He went around the corner to an office that said *Director,* but he didn't go inside.

The deep, hostile voice had to be Lane. I'd heard Gianna use the same phrase.

"I understand that you're upset," someone responded. An older man, probably the director or some other poor schmuck used to dealing with broke-ass family members. Family members who were embarrassed and pissed they'd been left with the bills of a defunct mother who'd smoked or injected or drank all of their money.

When I appeared in the office door, Lane looked over. He resembled Cruz with the longish dark hair and dark scruff. He had brown eyes like his brother. Same dad? Some guy who'd funded Gianna's habits for more than a few years?

Instead of dressing like he fronted a grunge band, he wore jeans with holes and a ratty sweater.

"About fucking time." Lane pushed out of his chair. He gave me an appraising look from head to toe, his mouth curling when it reached my loafers. I had dressed the same as I would for the office. The only difference was the long, black wool coat and cream scarf.

I returned the inspection. Lane didn't appear much older than Cruz, but his eyes said otherwise. How often had Lane put himself between Gianna and Cruz? How much had he hid what our mother was really like so Cruz didn't have to experience what we had?

I switched my gaze to the pleasant man behind the desk. He'd be about Darin's age, which for some reason, made me instantly calm. I'd be a dick to hate the guy on sight with his wire-rimmed glasses, thinning gray and blond hair, and cream-colored sweater over a dress shirt.

He glanced impassively between all of us, but relief filled his face when he met my gaze.

He rose and extended his hand. "Hello. John Silvan. Nice to meet you."

I shook his hand. Firm, cool grip and a bit of surprise. But he had to have a backbone to still be tolerating Lane's attitude. "Myles Foster. Whatever you need, I'll take care of it."

The relief magnified. "Have a seat. You're, uh..." He glanced from Lane to Cruz.

"Brothers," I finished as I draped my coat, folded, over the back of an office chair, and sat. I left out that this was my first time meeting them. Fuck, I looked like I could be their father. Did we have the same last name?

"Right. Your brothers are welcome to stay."

My estimation of John went up. He could've booted them, and I wouldn't have argued. By the time I was their age, I had learned how pointless outbursts were. Except for the night I got drunk, which would've been pointless if it hadn't been for Darin.

Lane scoffed, but he stayed seated. Cruz leaned against the door.

John ran through the paperwork for the cremation, where the remains could be interned since none of us wanted to cart Gianna around or have her toxic ashes on a mantel. When he got to the cremation casket, I tapped one of the top-line options.

Lane sat forward. "Why are you wasting money on her?"

"I'm not," I said calmly, but my estimation of him rose. It wasn't greed in his tone, like he'd expected me to

funeral home's generosity."

Cruz snorted and shook his head. He hadn't moved from the door. Was he invested in Gianna's aftercare, or curious about me?

John's silver brows lifted. "Oh, it's unnecessary, but your generosity is appreciated. For an urn, would you like...." He opened another pamphlet. I went for another higher-rated option.

"You're getting that urn?" Lane shook his head. The urn was fancy, too nice to be stuck in a dark space for eternity, but I didn't care.

"All right." John shuffled papers. "That's all taken care of. Lane said a private ceremony was unnecessary, but I recommend—"

"He was right."

John gave one nod and moved on. "For the final resting spot, we can do a burial or a columbarium. You can also—"

"Burial." The weight of Lane's and Cruz's attention was on me. I wasn't going to explain in front of John my driving need to have a place to go to curse her out or just sit and pretend that maybe I'd had a normal life, if only for a little while. I wouldn't discuss what I felt with my brothers either. If they didn't have the same thoughts, I'd only be left the fool. The older, wiser, yet more attached brother. If they did have the same emotions clogging their chests, I doubted they wanted to talk about it either.

I took care of the expense immediately to keep John from stressing about an awkward conversation.

How weird was it to hear her name come out of someone's mouth so respectfully. There were no hushed tones because *you know what she's like.* As if talking about her would damage me further or summon the beast herself.

"Thanks," I said gruffly. "You have my number."

He'd made sure to get that first thing. I rose and got into my jacket. My brothers shuffled out before me.

Lane shoved his hands in his front pockets and meandered toward the door. "What now?"

An irritated *how about a thank-you?* nearly left me. Then I'd officially be the crotchety old man. "How 'bout we go somewhere to talk?"

Cruz fell into step beside me. "Do you really live in a mansion?"

Lane rolled his eyes at his brother, but he watched me like he was intent on the answer.

"No. I have a loft where I work. A mansion is a waste of money."

"Which you got a lot of," Cruz said, half a question, half a statement.

Yes. "I do all right." I stopped to face both of them before we headed out the door. "And only because of the generosity of one family who was pivotal to me not being an epic fuckup. Maybe I'd have done okay without them, I don't know, but I'm grateful as fuck I didn't have to find out."

"And your point is?" Lane came off flippant, but his gaze was shrewd.

"No free handouts. You want to talk and get to know me? I'd like that. Finding out I had family was a big

"But I'm not interested in fielding calls and messages for money to pay for houses and cars."

"That would be an apartment," Lane said smoothly. "And I now have her car."

"You got a job to keep them both up?"

The muscles flexed at the corners of his jaw. He was almost as tall as me. Cruz was slightly taller, always looking down his nose at someone if he wasn't slouched against a wall having a smoke.

"I work."

I slid my gaze toward Cruz.

He shrugged. "I'm between jobs at the moment."

Lane's jaw was granite. Yeah, he'd spent his life covering for his brother and protecting him. He'd taken on a role that should've been mine. Fucking Gianna.

"How long has that moment been?" I shook my head. "Are you out of school?"

His dark brows drew together. "I'm nineteen, asshole."

"And you?" I asked Lane.

"Twenty-two."

"I was right, then. Just as I got out of the system and away from her, she had more kids." I normally wouldn't have confirmed my suspicions out loud but I needed these two to know what our mother was like. That they should question a lot of damn things she'd told them over the years.

Lane huffed out a breath. "Fuck."

Cruz shrugged. "I'm just a happy accident."

Lane shot him a glare. "You were her trying to baby trap our dad when he got sick of her shit."

"She switched it to Foster when our dad walked out."

"Is he alive?"

One dip of his head and an unreadable look in his eye. "Prison."

Probably better for the guys, then.

I caught movement at the doorway of John's office. "Where's a good place to talk?"

"Our apartment smells like the worst incense known to man," Lane answered. "There's a restaurant at the end of the street."

"I'll meet you there."

Cruz blew out of the building before us. He slowed with a "Nice."

Lane gave a low hum of appreciation. Both were moving at a glacial pace. Irritated, I curved around them.

And then my gaze landed on what had their focus.

Wynn. Her white winter coat was zipped to her chin and a pink stocking hat sat on her head, but her light hair spread out over the material of the jacket. She had her hands shoved in her coat pockets, and her long legs were in thick gray leggings. The soft brown boots on her feet only completed the sexy-snow-bunny look. Her dark eyes reflected the windows of the funeral home behind us as she studied my brothers.

"What are you doing here?" I had meant to keep her from all this, from the attitude I'd known my brothers must have. Wynn wasn't to be exposed to the nastiness of Gianna's life when I went to the rental office to quit the lease. Lane would have to foot the bill himself. No free handouts.

Lane must've sensed the tension between me and Wynn. He only smirked and dragged Cruz to a white Chevy Malibu with a busted front bumper. Gianna hadn't mentioned that.

I crossed the parking lot. She was parked next to me, our cars next to each other like we were a team, only I'd left her behind. I understood she was angry, but she shouldn't have come. This wasn't her business.

"Wynn—"

She held up a fluffy Scandinavian-patterned mittened hand. "I came here for one reason and one reason only."

The old Malibu's engine started, and a loud growl filled the air. Christ, that car was a piece of shit. Her gaze darted to the left. Lane was pulling out. He openly stared as he drove by us. The passenger window was open with a cloud of smoke drifting out.

Cruz grinned like a jackass, and then they were gone.

When I turned to look back at Wynn, she stepped forward, grabbed the lapels of my coat and rose to her tiptoes. The coolness of her lips turned molten instantly. I might not want her here, but I'd always want her kiss.

I pulled her close and delved into her mouth, tasting the minty gum she must've chewed on the way to Bozeman.

She wrapped up the kiss almost regretfully and pulled away. "I wanted to show you what a proper goodbye looked like."

⸙

Wynn

He had no right to be as handsome as he was, his face carved as distinctly as the mountains that surrounded this town. The charcoal-gray wool coat hung open, and the scarf was loose around his neck.

His mouth was in a line. Stubbornness? Frustrated that I had found him? I hated to intrude on his time in Bozeman, but there was no moment like now. Not for me. I couldn't wait around for him, and unfortunately, this was the only place I'd thought he might be. If I hadn't caught him here, I'd have had to go to Denver to prove my point.

"I know the way I left—"

I flattened my hand on his chest, grateful my glove was too thick for his body heat to seep in. I had to stay strong. "The way you *keep* leaving. The way you don't talk to me. The way you hold yourself away from everyone who cares about you. It's more than I'm willing to take."

He frowned, but his gaze sharpened. "What are you saying?"

I blew out a breath and suppressed a shiver. The cold had sunk into my bones long ago and blasting the heat all the way to Bozeman hadn't helped. "I'm saying I came here only to say goodbye. I refuse to let you ditch me again, and I'm not waiting around for you. I'm saying I'm done, Myles. I'm saying I understand that I was the only one invested in us." I let out a humorless laugh. "Or the possibility of an us, I guess. Since, honestly, you never gave me an indication we could ever be more. Or that you wanted to be more."

"I wanted..." His brow was furrowed.

couldn't bring himself to open up. He wasn't reassuring me I was wrong.

Because there was no us. Never had been. Tears burned the backs of my eyes. I couldn't cry in front of him. A girl had to have her pride. I'd already stalked him and gotten a job at his company. Then I'd flown to him within a few hours of his drunk dial. I stank of desperation, and that wasn't the woman I wanted to be.

He might be the guy I wanted, but he wasn't the partner I deserved. Just like he'd said.

"You have what you always wanted." I took my hand off him, a deliberate move. Calm. Reasoned. So unlike the storm inside me. "It's only today I realized it. I can't put my wishes in your head." My throat constricted. "In your heart."

His scowl deepened. "Wynn..."

"I hope..." I had hoped for so many things. A little girl's fantasies about a tortured kid who'd only dreamed of being left alone when he grew up. "I hope you don't let your need to isolate yourself affect any relationship you can build with your brothers." I took one last look at his glacial blue eyes, the cut of his jaw, and the neatly combed lines in his hair. "Goodbye, Myles."

His confused and lost look snapped to anger. "What the fuck, Wynter?"

I would cling to his slip. Calling me Wynter instead of Wynn. Almost like he saw the real me and not just the temporary executive assistant he could fuck to make himself feel better.

I went around my car to the driver's door. "Goodbye."

"No, Myles, I'm done." I faced him and let the sadness snowball into righteous rage. We could've been so damn good together. We could've figured out the distance—hell, I would've moved. For him.

No more. I would break ground on my new house in the spring, and by fall, I would have my own place to go with my good job at Copper Summit. I would create a beautiful life for myself. Just like both sets of my parents wanted.

"I deserve better." My voice shook. Now I was warm. I let the fury sweep through me. What we could've had was right there. He'd left it behind, time after time after time. "I deserve to be wooed. I deserve flowers and nice dinners and real conversation." I lifted my chin. "I deserve to be trusted. I deserve to be treasured. I deserve so much more than the scraps you gave me. The scraps you tossed my way because you knew I'd follow the scent like a mouse heading toward a trap. Only there was no trap, just an empty cage and a selfish man."

He recoiled. "Selfish? I never asked for you to get involved in my life." He didn't crowd me, but he moved so he wasn't standing directly behind my car. "I wasn't the one who made the first move."

"Trust me," I said bitterly. "I'm fully aware. Rest assured, you no longer have to worry about me."

"Goddamn it, Wynn. I didn't—"

"Let's skip the list of everything we did and didn't do." I opened my door. "If it's an apology you want, then I'm sorry. I'm sorry I was at the Baileys' when you were there. I'm sorry I assumed too much into how you read to me. I'm sorry I applied for that job, and I'm sorry I hope everything goes well with your brothers."

I got into my car. He didn't move.

He stayed in that one inconvenient spot as I backed out and drove away.

Hot tears streaked down my face. My hands were trembling. Should I pull to the side of the road? What if he followed me?

But one check of the rearview mirror showed no familiar black car behind me. He wasn't following me.

I caught my red-rimmed eyes in the mirror. "Stupid girl. It's time to move on."

CHAPTER TWENTY-SIX

Myles

Cruz flicked the edge of his menu with his finger. The sounds of tinkling glasses and silverware on plates resonated around us. We'd been seated at a table between two empty booths. I studied my own menu, not seeing a damn thing except for Cruz and Lane exchanging questioning glances.

I'd communicated in little more than grunts since I'd walked in. The older server had even given me a censuring look when I ordered a water, the one word sounding more like *fuck off*. Wynn's kiss tingled across my lips, taunting me.

I wanted to show you what a proper goodbye looked like.

...a selfish man.

What the hell had I been selfish about? I left all my foster homes with nothing more than what I brought, except for the Baileys'—and the car had been given to

But my talk with Mae came to mind. When she'd told me that Gianna had found them, it'd been anticlimactic despite my fears, despite the fact that I had avoided everything about my childhood I was fond of for nothing. Because I hadn't avoided them all to protect them.

I'd done it for myself.

Selfish. That was how Wynn saw my behavior.

Cruz pushed his menu to the edge of the table. "Did your bae not give you a little—"

"Think hard before you finish that sentence," I snarled. They didn't know her.

And whose fault was that?

"Bruh." Cruz held his hands up. "Oh god, you're being a real dick. You go from buying the biggest and best at the funeral home to ordering water and glaring at the world. Something happened—or didn't happen, since she was a tight ten out of ten."

I glowered at my youngest brother. Something had happened. She'd fucking broken up with me.

We weren't even fucking together.

Weren't you?

Had I been as into anyone in the last year? Two years? Ten?

Christ, my entire life?

"Since we're talking about her." Lane smirked when I switched my glare to him. "How old is she anyway?"

I curled my upper lip. She was closer to his goddamn age than mine.

I narrowed my eyes, the urge to bring death and destruction onto this old diner sweeping through me. "She's too good for all of us."

He lifted a shoulder. "I can be a pretty nice guy."

"You want me to evict you?"

The way Lane sobered was unexpected. "We're just playing. Isn't that what brothers do?" he asked bitterly.

Yeah. And I knew that because of Tate, Teller, and Tenor. Goddamn it. I couldn't relax, but I could remember these guys hadn't fucked up with Wynn. I had.

What was there to fuck up? I hadn't even gone on a real date with her. She got me. We had sex—when we were in the same zip code. I thought about her every second of the day.

Fuck.

I pushed a hand through my hair. "Yes, she broke up with me." I blew out a breath. "We weren't even really together."

Lane let out a whistle under his breath. "And that's why I'm not a relationship guy." He was eighteen years younger than me, yet he was spouting the same mantra I had my entire life. When he was forty, how goddamn depressing would that be? Because that was me. An idiot who thought shunning relationships was the only way to deal with life.

"She must've thought you two were together if she broke up with you." Cruz took a long drink of his piping hot coffee.

The server had poured me some when I'd given her

from smoking like his, but I relished the pain. "It's complicated."

"You two were fucking, she got attached, but you have mommy issues and won't commit?" Lane unwrapped the napkin from around his silverware.

I blinked at him. What the hell?

His chuckle was dry. Cruz grinned and leaned on the back two legs of his chair.

Since they thought they were so smart, I added a fact that'd throw them. "Her family fostered me."

The legs of Cruz's chair thunked down. "Bruh, you were sleeping with your foster sister?"

The couple two booths over glanced at us.

"Be quiet," I hissed.

Cruz only grinned bigger. "Did you?"

"She's twelve years younger than me. *No*. She worked for me last summer, and I..." What the hell was I telling them for? But I couldn't stop. "...didn't recognize her."

"Looking at dat ass," Cruz said, and Lane snickered.

"You couldn't even see it." She hadn't turned around for them to see it. Though she'd been bundled up and so damn cute and sexy in her winter gear.

Lane lifted a shoulder. "Didn't have to."

The server stopped by, and the guys ordered a shit-load of food. They didn't ask if I was paying. I assumed I was—and they probably did, too. When she left, they turned back to me.

I'd said too much. "Enough about Wynter."

"It's cool," Lane said. "We're all left with baggage. I guess ditching a hot girl who really cares about you is yours."

ran down my spine. I hated explaining myself, yet that was all I was doing for these two.

Cruz held up a finger. "About that. How does a kid who grew up with a mom who abused every substance she could get make and sell liquor?"

"I prefer to call it spirits."

Lane tapped the table. "And Mom preferred to call her pills treats."

More explaining. "Gianna kept her worst habits away from me. She preferred to be gone and pretend she didn't have a home. Or a kid." Their interest was focused on me, and I continued, unused to having the other party know exactly what I was talking about. "I was put in the system when Gianna was arrested, and I was found alone. I'd been alone for a week. I was eleven."

"Only a week?" Lane tipped his head from side to side. "I guess Mom waited until we were teens before she ditched us longer than a weekend."

"How long was the longest?"

They exchanged a look, and Lane answered. "Six weeks? I finally got ahold of her and said we needed groceries, or I was going right to the police station to tell them she gave us drugs."

"Did she try to sell to your friends?"

They both snorted.

"What friends?" Cruz asked.

I could imagine how it went. Dirty, hungry, scared. They'd likely been walking, hormonal assholes with grungy clothes and greasy hair. Who'd want anything to do with them? But they hadn't been yanked from the house. Gianna had learned by then. I'd paid the rent and

"I don't see our *generous* mother giving up any of her stash," Lane said sarcastically.

"For control, she would."

They both nodded, accepting the answer.

"She told us you were jealous of us," Lane said. "Because we worked harder to stay with her."

Wasn't that some shit. "She never said a word."

"I wondered about that," Lane said. "You would've taken us?"

"I was barely more than a kid when you were born." I pointed to Lane, then to Cruz. "I was probably in jail for getting into a bar fight when you were born. But later? After Foster House was established? Yeah, I would've made sure you two were taken care of."

A knowing look entered Cruz's eyes. "Not by you, though."

"And that's why your foster sister dumped you," Lane added sarcastically.

Fuck these two. "I wasn't—I wouldn't—" I helped others, but I did it with my money. I formed an umbrella company to dole out scholarships. I hired adults who'd been through some of what I had. I threw jobs and money at them, and once in a while, we had a talk. Short. Superficial. I got what information I needed to know, and then I gave them money.

After that, I went to my tower in the sky. Alone. The next day, I woke up to make more money.

Was this the life I wanted? "Shit."

"Stings, don't it?" Lane stared out the window to his right.

common."

Wynter

The distillery bar was lively tonight. I was not. I was serving drinks, and I was drinking drinks. Strong ones. Not wine. My boy troubles required more than wine. Only a day had passed since I'd told Myles goodbye. The longest day of my life. I took a shot of bourbon knowing darn well Daddy wouldn't approve. Bourbon was for sipping, but not tonight.

Autumn had been called in to be my backup. Teller had said *replacement*, actually, but I wasn't going home to cry. I'd given up on someone important, and the road rash on my heart hadn't healed.

"What's this one?" a good-looking guy asked. I didn't know him from Bourbon Canyon, which meant he wasn't from Bourbon Canyon.

His stylishly long blond hair was swept to the side. He had a chin that would make an NHL player jealous and shoulders just as wide. Maybe he was a hockey player. I'd never liked sports guys. Not broody enough.

But he'd sat directly in front of me and tried to make conversation every time I wasn't serving a drink.

"Summit Sex." I tossed my hair. Oh god. Was I flirting? My inhibitions were down, and I wasn't interested, but my pride needed the nourishment. My empty

No one had measured up. No one.

Not even Myles.

"Summit Sex? I imagine that's pretty popular around here."

The scent of amber-laced sage reached me before Myles slid onto a stool next to the man. "She's taken, jackass."

The cute guy reared back. "Excuse me?"

"You were joking about how sex in the mountains must be popular over here. And then you were going to segue into somehow having sex with her in the mountains or in the back seat of your pretentious car. Or is it a truck? But she's tipsy, and you're an asshole for trying to get with her."

"What the—"

"I'm sorry for the cranky man's attitude." I wasn't drunk enough not to know I had to rescue this before Myles's big rude mouth made the disagreement physical. "Listen, drinks are on Copper Summit tonight. We can even toss in a free bottle of Wynter Summit." I wasn't above needling Mr. Foster. "Any size you want. Just let my sister know while I deal with this top-shelf asshole right here."

The stranger's smile turned smug. He knew Myles was in more trouble with me than he would've ever been. He pushed away. "I'll take you up on that."

I smiled at him, and just because Myles's gaze was burning into me, I watched the man's admirable ass in blue jeans as he walked away.

"Jesus, Frosty. Summit Sex?"

Displeasure darkened his blue eyes. "We need to talk."

"No, we don't."

"Come on, Wynn. Just a few minutes."

I faced him and flattened my hands on the countertop. "I no longer give my time to just anyone. You can't charge into my life just because you thought about it for a day."

"I didn't need a day."

Okay, that got to me. A small part of my resolve melted. But not enough. "A day too late."

"Wynn—"

"If I give you another chance, then what? I fall harder and hurt even more if you haven't changed after *one* day?" His perfect lips dipped into a frown. Frustration welled hot inside my chest. He might be closer to getting it, but he didn't quite understand how I couldn't trust him. "You think you're hurting yourself to spare others, but you're wrong. Everyone loses, but not all of us are as good at walling off our emotions."

His eyes flared, and he straightened. He stared through me like I was a ghost.

Autumn appeared at my side and put her hand on my arm. "Is everything okay?" She wasn't looking at me. She was mean-mugging Myles.

"This man was just leaving."

"I'm not going anywhere," he replied, too annoyingly calm.

"Then I am." I wouldn't be able to work with him. I'd take a page out of his book instead. I gave Autumn a quick hug. "Thank you for covering for me."

I went through the storeroom off the side of the bar. There was an exit into the back stairwell that I could take to my office. I didn't have a couch like some obnoxious CEO, but I'd sleep it off on the floor. And when I woke, Myles would be gone again.

CHAPTER TWENTY-SEVEN

Myles

A knock on the window had me jerking awake. Pain seared through my neck as I straightened my head. My hands and feet were numb, and my breath clouded the air. How the hell had I gotten any sleep in this icebox of a car?

Last night, I'd waited by Wynn's blue hybrid SUV in the freezing weather, ready to yank her keys from her until well past the time the distillery bar closed, and she hadn't left. Slowly, the parking lot had emptied. Autumn had come out, given me a glare and a *you reap what you sow* shrug, and driven away.

You think you're hurting yourself to spare others, but you're wrong. Everyone loses, but not all of us are as good at walling off our emotions.

Wynter's words had played on a loop through my head the entire time, with regret keeping me warm.

Wynter had stayed in the distillery all damn night.

engine. I must've fallen asleep. The lack of quality sleep for the last few months was catching up to me.

I peered out my passenger window. Her SUV was gone.

"Goddammit." I swung to look out the driver's window.

Teller had his hands stuffed in the pockets of his black winter jacket, his brows raised. I rolled down the window but didn't say anything. I glared out the frosted windshield, unsure how to handle this situation. Was it the first time I'd slept in a car? No. Was it the first time I'd been caught loitering? Also, no. But it was the first time someone I knew stared at me as if he didn't recognize the disappointment in front of him.

"She's done with your shit," he said, his voice as hard as the frost on my windshield. All the good grace I'd built up with him the last time I was here was gone.

"We'll see about that."

The material of his jacket crinkled as he bent. "Look, Foster, we were all rooting for you until we realized it was our shoulders she was crying on when you fucked her over. We care about that girl. She's family. You've shown us time and again you don't want that."

I scowled at him. "I have a family."

"Then why aren't you sleeping it off in their parking lot?"

My brothers barely had clothing to their name. As soon as I'd seen the state of the apartment with its broken furniture and threadbare carpet, I'd signed the car over to them. And I wouldn't be changing the lease name after all. "I'm here for Wynter."

said tightly.

"Can you see how you let her down? Can you see that she gave you a lot of chances—none of which you had to take—and she got her heart stomped on? Can you see how you made her feel used and worthless?"

"I never used her."

He straightened and scanned the empty parking lot. "How about this? She *felt* used, and you continued to make her feel that way. Why don't you get going now? You're good at that."

The barb shouldn't have stung like it did. "I'm not going anywhere until I can talk to her."

"She doesn't want to talk—"

"I know that! Goddammit, I'm trying here. You think I know how to be in a relationship?" Embarrassment brought heat back to my hands. I hadn't meant to say that.

Teller didn't laugh at me, but his rigidity eased. "I'm pretty dense when it comes to women. I mean, I'm a year younger than you and haven't been married yet either. But I do get one thing—women usually tell you. So maybe pay attention." He lifted his chin toward the road. "Mama was making a fresh pot of coffee when I stopped in to check on her before I came here."

"Is Wynter home?"

"Maybe you'll catch her." He shrugged and walked away.

I started the car and punched it into drive. I was at Mae's house within a few minutes and parked behind a stall in the garage. Loss nailed me in the gut. Darin wouldn't be here. I'd gone to his funeral, an event so big

memories of the man.

Gianna's burial wouldn't be until spring. There'd be three of us present. Maybe. I wouldn't blame Lane or Cruz for not going. But they'd probably be drawn by the same compulsion I would be. Closure. A confused grief. More than a little anger.

Mae leaned out of the door and waved me in.

Was Wynter's car in the garage? Or had she turned and burned, afraid I'd find her?

I jogged toward the house to keep Mae from getting chilled waiting for me.

She wrapped me in a huge hug. "How was seeing your brothers?"

I wanted to ask about Wynn, but knowing Mae, this was her way of protecting her daughter from me, a delicate balancing act for two people she cared about. I wasn't used to disappointment, but Mae was the only person I wouldn't bulldoze down to get to Wynn. I wouldn't give up, but I would be mindful of her feelings.

Like I should've been with Wynn's.

"Meeting my brothers went well. Surprisingly."

She waved at my coat. "Go ahead and come in. Want some coffee?"

"Please."

"Need a special blend?" She smiled, sympathetic.

I chuckled, surprised I could find it in me to do so. "Plain coffee, thank you."

She went to the counter. I hung my coat up. Wynn's wasn't on the rack along the back wall. Only the work coat she used for chores was there. She wasn't home.

"Would you like to tell me about Lane and Cruz?" Mae set a steaming mug on the table and sat down, another in her hand.

I'd only told her their names once. Yet she tracked it all. And she'd asked if I wanted to share instead of prodding me with questions. Mae paid attention in a way I'd never learned how. So much of my life had been about my survival.

Wynn was right. I was selfish. My goals. My wants and needs. Me, and Foster House was an extension of me. I didn't know how to be anything else.

But I'd learn.

"My brothers were exactly what I expected, but they were also completely different." I told her about their dad in jail, that I thought Lane had protected Cruz from all the hard parts of their childhood, where they lived. How they lived. Their cynical attitude that had a startling quality of innocence to it, especially Cruz.

"They expect to be left to hold their own." Mae took a sip. "Do you think they use?"

I lifted a shoulder. "Not the hard stuff at least."

"Well, there's that at least. Kids who grew up like them have enough challenges."

"Lane's a mechanic, but I don't know where his money's going. Gianna probably owed people, and he's been paying them. Maybe now that Gianna's gone, he'll save some. I wouldn't be shocked if Cruz couldn't hold a job."

The corner of her mouth tilted up. "His brother handled all the consequences. Your youngest brother is probably where all the money goes now. And groceries.

"What?" I cared about Lane and Cruz on principle. I was their brother. The oldest. I had escaped a lot of what they hadn't. But they were both adults.

"I'd like to meet them—if you're okay with two parts of your life overlapping."

The thought of driving my brothers to the Bailey ranch and showing them the distillery tightened knots all over my gut. I had worked so hard to keep that life separate from everything. There were still a lot of unknowns about them.

Mae tipped her head, her amber eyes full of understanding. "They're not your mother. And I've dealt with my fair share of young men with attitudes." She patted my arm. "I trust your intuition. Whatever you decide. You know where I'll be."

My forearm flexed under her touch. I wasn't used to comforting gestures.

"I have to get back to Foster House soon," I said, not answering her about bringing my brothers here.

"Your job is important to you."

A leading statement. I took the bait. "Yes. But I'd like to talk to Wynn before I go."

Mae's gentle smile lured me in. "And that's your problem, Myles. You're rushing the process with Wynter because you're going to leave."

Ouch. She wasn't pulling her punches. I dropped my gaze to the base of my mug. A brownish Copper Summit cup, naturally, with the outline of the mountains embossed on the side.

"You want her to listen to you so you can go back to Denver and be rest assured she's there when you

"My work is—" I scrubbed my face. Foster House was all I had. "I don't think I can give it up."

She tilted her head again. "Did Wynter ask you to give it up?"

I shook my head. "Her life is here."

"If you two make it that far, it's something you'll have to discuss."

"How do I get that far?" How did I leave what I'd built? Did I want to keep it at the cost of losing Wynn?

"Keep trying. Talk to her." Mae put her hand on my arm again. "Talk." She tapped at the center of her chest with her other hand. "From here."

I had woken up in a freezing cold car and found Teller, who'd imparted some unwanted, but much needed, wisdom on me. Then he'd sent me to Mae. Wynn was who I'd wanted to see, but if I wanted to talk to her, I'd have to listen to them first.

Wynter

The writing on the card that came with the giant bouquet of flowers read **My brothers are meeting your mom at 7 tomorrow night. Please be there?**

I stared at the angled handwriting. It was Myles's half-cursive, half-block letters. He would've had to go to Lilly's Pad in town, in person, to order the bouquet of sunflowers and baby's breath and pink and white roses.

How'd he known I thought roses were the low-preferred to have my flowers customized.

Which Lilly at the flower shop would've known. We'd talked about it several times over the years when I'd ordered displays for Copper Summit meetings and events.

I snapped a picture and sent the image to my sisters.

From Myles.

HOT GIRL SUMMER
Not enough.

JUNIE
Make him earn it.

AUTUMN
Ooh, those are pretty!

Out of the three replies, it was Autumn's I went back to again and again. The flowers were pretty. I liked them. Did their arrival mean he was still in Bozeman? I doubted he was staying at the little inn in town.

I shook my head, then winced. Snoozing on the floor did not help hangover recovery. He'd slept in his car last night. I'd seen him slumbering with his head bent at an angle that would taunt him all day. I'd known he was outside. Autumn had sent me a message to tell me he was waiting by my car.

I'd gone out before dawn, dog tired but sober enough to drive, ready to hear if what he had to say would satisfy the longing in my heart. And he'd been adorably asleep. I had expected him to wake up when I drove away and

And now he'd sent flowers.

I sent another message to my sisters.

> He's bringing his brothers to meet
> Mama. He wants me there.

HOT GIRL SUMMER

I'm going to be there.

JUNIE

Someone video for me.

AUTUMN

Aw, I bet they're younger versions of
him. Two minis. Mama's going to love
them.

HOT GIRL SUMMER

Autumn, they're two grown men who
are strangers. Who are coming into our
house.

The urge rose to defend these brothers I'd only
briefly seen was strong.

> I don't think they're bad guys.

HOT GIRL SUMMER

Weren't they raised by the mom who
lost him?

JUNIE

Never mind, I'm going to ask Teller to
video the meeting.

AUTUMN

Do you need me to be there?

HOT GIRL SUMMER

How old are these guys anyway?

I didn't know. We hadn't been able to talk. I hadn't let him, mostly because I doubted he would have discussed his brothers with me. They looked young.

Early twenties?

Which would fit with when Myles had thought his mom would get pregnant.

I'll be there. It'll be fine.

HOT GIRL SUMMER

I'll make sure the guys are all there.

They're not thugs.

HOT GIRL SUMMER

Mama's alone now most of the day.

She'll have them doing chores before they know it.

AUTUMN

Wynter has a point.

JUNIE

Still. Record it.

Junie uploaded a video of what looked like an empty venue. She was probably rehearsing for a performance later tonight.

AUTUMN

I can't wait to see you perform!

I sighed and put my phone down. They'd moved on from my Myles dilemma. I prodded my temples. The dull thud hadn't gone away from last night. I'd guzzled water, but a morning of looking at a screen wasn't helping.

Tenor knocked on my open door. He slouched against the frame as if he knew I had nothing better to do than chat. I'd walked into work with my hair still damp, no makeup, and dressed in an outfit a level up from pajamas. Copper Summit was a casual workplace, but I was in ripped leggings and an oversized hoodie I'd swiped from Daddy's closet. Mama had let us keep whatever we wanted.

"What's this visit from the Foster brothers?" he asked and pushed up his glasses.

"Mama wants to meet them, and I guess Myles is willing to introduce them."

"I thought you gave him the boot."

"Mama didn't."

"You wanna go to the Canyon Grill tonight and miss the show?" Tenor didn't have an alpha personality like Tate and Teller, but he was no less protective. He just wasn't as smothering, which was nice.

decided yet?"

"I don't know. I'm dying to meet his brothers." And of course to see Myles again. I'd told him off but my hope was like a phoenix and continued to rise again.

"I'm curious as well."

"Are we all going to be lookie-loos?"

He chuckled. "Summer already sent out the call that she didn't want Mama alone with a bunch of strange men. I told her they could show up ready to rob her, and she'd make them wash the floors and shovel the drive first. Then she'd feed them, and they'd forget what they went there for."

I laughed. "I said something similar."

"Summer's just upset she's not in charge. We can handle her." He came in and sat across from me. "How Myles and his brothers deal with her should tell us a lot about them."

True. Summer had gone from being the oldest, the mother hen, to being squarely in the middle when we'd been taken in by the Baileys. Moments like these, the oldest child in her had a hard time relinquishing the role.

"About Myles, though." He feathered the sunflower petals between his fingers. "I don't think he's giving up."

"He isn't facing anything emotionally challenging right now. He'll leave. Eventually." It was the only thing I knew for sure about Myles Foster.

CHAPTER TWENTY-EIGHT

Myles

I coasted down the Baileys' drive. Snow dotted the roofs of the shops and barns. Chickens pecked over packed snow in their path. A whole pile of cars and pickups lined the driveway like when I'd first arrived for the funeral. Aw hell, the whole gang was here.

"Does she own all these pickups?" Cruz had his face pressed against the window. He'd been unusually subdued since we'd left city limits and rolled through Bourbon Canyon. The closer to the ranch we got, the quieter he grew.

I thought he was turning sullen, but a look of awe had only grown in his expression.

"No, dumbass," Lane answered. He'd brushed his hair off his face and wore his nicest pair of torn jeans and a red polo shirt with no stains. Cruz had asked him if he was going to work at Target.

Cruz was still in all black, but he'd also picked

he'd also hand brushed his hair off his face. I relied on Mae to see through their exterior to their efforts. That they'd put thought into their appearance gave me faith our mother hadn't irrevocably fucked them up.

"All her nosy kids are here," Lane added, a thread of anxiety in his voice.

"No smoking, all right?" Mae might've been okay with a fifteen-year-old Wynter learning the taste profiles of bourbon, but she'd charge after a lit cigarette.

"I brought my vape."

"No vaping," Lane and I said in unison.

"Bruh, I get it. I was kidding."

Was he?

I parked, and we all got out. I took them down the familiar path between the driveway pad and the kitchen door. I was used to being the one on the outside, but this time, I wasn't. I was in the middle. Not an outsider, but not a Bailey. My brothers were going to feel like ducks in the goat pen.

Mae opened the door and leaned out, a smile wide on her face. "If I hadn't already known you were related, I'd know it now." She pushed the screen door open farther. "Come on in."

I stepped in and was encompassed in a powerful hug as if I hadn't seen her just yesterday morning. Then it was Lane's turn. His stunned but wary expression trailed around the packed kitchen.

A room full of Baileys and Kerrigans watched us. I only had eyes for Wynn. She was in a fuzzy pink sweater, the same one she'd worn when I'd fired her—point taken —with her arms hugged around her. Her soft blue jeans

arms.

The feelings tumbling through me were suffocating. This woman was my world. Without her, I didn't give a shit about anything. I had a hard time even caring about Foster House.

Foster House was my everything. Had been my everything.

Wynter Kerrigan had taken its place. She'd given me another identity, one that didn't revolve around business. She'd encouraged me to stick around when her siblings wanted to run me off. She'd prompted me to contact my brothers. Without her, I kept all the important parts of life at a distance. I hid behind my company and let everyone else live their life.

I had to stay and win my girl back.

"The pork chops aren't done yet," Mae said as she released Cruz from a crushing hug. Lane was tucked behind me, his normal bravado hiding like he was.

Did they feel like two kids shoved into a room of grownups and told to perform? They were both adults, but Wynter was the closest in age to them, and she had six years on Lane.

I'd start with introductions. "Lane. Cruz. You've met Mae. As for the rest, the guys all have the last name Bailey and their first names start with a T. The girls all have the last name Kerrigan and are named for seasons." *Frosty's mine.*

"He's mostly right," Tate said, a touch of amusement in his tone. "I'm Tate, and my wife, Scarlett, is a Bailey. My son, Chance, has our baby girl in the living room and is playing video games."

I tugged on his shirt and stopped him. His interest changed into sheepishness. I almost felt bad, but we weren't here for fucking video games. "My apologies, Scarlett. I saw a headcount of four and didn't realize Junie wasn't here."

"She was named that instead of spring," Autumn explained, like the compulsion to clarify Junie's name was bred into her. "Since technically most of June is in the spring. I'm Autumn."

The others introduced themselves, leaving Wynn for last.

"I'm Wynter."

"We didn't get a chance to meet before you dumped him," Cruz said.

"Jesus," Lane muttered.

Mae was beaming like she was in the zone. Like she'd been gone from her calling and couldn't wait to wade into my brothers' lives as far as they'd let her. "Since we're all introduced, and you two still have your coats on, would you like a tour of the place?"

"Sure." Cruz was already heading for the door. Lane gave him a funny look. As little as I knew them, I could see why. Cruz wasn't the get-up-and-go type. He wasn't the get-shit-done guy. But he was the first one outside and waiting for Mae.

I let Lane go out before me. I waited for Wynn, grabbing her ranch coat off the hook and holding it up for her. When she neared, we both had to step to the side to avoid getting trampled by the throng of people going on the tour.

The last person piled out the door. Scarlett disappeared into the living room, probably to stay with Chance. I was alone with Wynn, yet torn about ditching my brothers. They were in good hands, but I'd also bribed them with Mae's dinner, the pie she said she'd make, and that they could come to my hotel and have the continental breakfast in the morning.

Food was apparently the way to their heart.

Wynn was the way to mine. "Can we talk?" I sank into the warm depths of her eyes. I'd wait a hundred more nights in the cold for her.

"Tonight's not about us." She tried to move around me.

"Tomorrow night?" I couldn't corner her. I didn't want her to feel coerced. I'd woo her. The right way. I'd earn her trust. Somehow. "I can take you out in town, or we could run to Bozeman."

"Don't you have a business to get back to?"

"I'm working remotely. Mrs. Crane is grudgingly learning how to work virtual meeting programs, but I had to give her a raise to do it." And another week of vacation a year.

Disbelief crossed her features. "You're working from Montana?"

I nodded. "I can't win you back from Denver."

"And then what?" She shook her head. "Never mind. I know the answer."

"Distance isn't an issue. I have it on good authority there are private jet co-ops."

A smile played along her lips. "I've heard about

I brushed a strand of hair behind her ear. "We were definitely a thing. The best thing."

The seriousness in her expression deepened. "I don't know how I can ever not think you just won't be there one day."

"You'll always know where I am."

She huffed and pushed around me. "That's so much better."

"Wynn, dammit. I'm sorry. I don't know how to not fuck up. I've never done a relationship." She stopped with her hand on the door. She wasn't looking at me, but I gestured around the kitchen. "I want to get this right, but I don't know how."

She finally turned those beautiful gems toward me. "All right. Tomorrow night. We'll go to Curly's. Pick me up at six. That's when their buns are the freshest."

"Six." I fought a wide grin.

"How's your neck?" she asked quietly. When I gave her a quizzical look, she shrugged. "You looked uncomfortable in your car."

"Oh, that. Rookie mistake. I should've put the seat back. I didn't plan to fall asleep."

"What do you mean rookie mistake? You sleep in your car often?"

"A lot, yeah. Back in the day." The before–Foster House days.

Her shoulders sagged. "God, you make it hard to be mad at you."

"Do I make it impossible not to kiss me?"

"Oh my god, are you flirting?" She pinched my

I leaned in, waiting for her to push me away. She didn't, so I closed the distance. Right before our lips touched, she put a hand on my chest.

"Not before our first official date. I'd hate for you to think I'm a sure thing." She walked out, and I followed, failing to suppress my chuckle.

We were packed around a table that magically grew longer with more and more people. I'd never seen it stretched so wide. Wynn was at my side. I put my hand on her knee under the table, and she didn't shift her leg away. She didn't soften either.

Lane and Cruz were adept at fitting in. They were slouched over their plates, talking with their mouths full. Lane caught himself first, then nudged Cruz. The small elbow jabs weren't the only silent communication they'd adopted. They had various looks they exchanged.

Right now, Lane was giving Cruz an *Are you fucking serious?* stare. The rest of us were pointing the same expression Mae's way.

"I could live here?" Cruz asked.

"And work," Mae said with a firm nod.

Tate sucked in a breath through his nose. "We don't need—"

"We do." Mae straightened. "I'm not as young as I used to be, and I love this place. I really do. But I don't want to be out in the cold gathering eggs every winter."

"Chance can do it in the mornings," Tate countered.

Chance's head popped up from the huckleberry

"Chance can't be expected to get here every morning when snow's on the ground." Mae adopted her stern mother tone. "Cruz is interested in ranching. It'd be good for him to learn."

Lane snorted. One of my brothers knew what they were getting into, and it wasn't Cruz.

But...the opportunity could be good for him. Excellent, even. If he didn't run after the third day waking up before dawn and working until after the sun set, he had a shot. If nicotine withdrawals didn't convince him to give up.

Tate wasn't convinced. "I don't have the time—"

"I'll teach him." Mae lifted her chin, challenging her oldest to tell her she couldn't and to do it in front of everyone.

"I can help," Tenor added, uncaring that both his brothers were glaring at him. "I can run numbers at night. I'll work with Cruz until he can be independent."

Cruz grinned, either uncaring about the tension in the room or thriving on it. "When do I start?"

"Tomorrow." Mae waved her fork at him before she stabbed into the crust of her pie. "You can stay here, and I'll take you shopping. I doubt anything you packed will stand up to ranch work."

That was Mae's way of saying his clothing sucked. She'd done the same to me. My ripped metal rock band shirts had been lost to thick sweaters and plain tees. My crappy boots had been useless when it came to mud and dirt and snow. I'd lost every scrap of clothing that'd had a swear word on it. In its place, a Bailey Ranch or Copper Summit logo.

rather she was on my lap and my hands were under her sweater, but this was closer than I'd thought I'd get when I'd woken up this morning.

"If you need anything, surely Lane can bring it." Mae smiled at Lane. "Would you like to come out on the weekends?"

Lane blinked. "I...sure?"

"Perfect. Can you start next Saturday?"

"Yes?" Lane's wide gaze swiveled to me. His eyes said he was hooked, and he didn't know how it had happened.

Tate made a disgruntled sound. "And who—"

"I can," Teller added. His features had gone from stunned and furious to too curious to help himself. He must think my brothers' training would be a shit show he didn't want to miss. "The weekends would be perfect."

My chest clogged with appreciation. The Bailey boys might not be fully on board with my brothers learning the ropes at the ranch, but they wouldn't sabotage it. Teller and Tenor would do right by Lane and Cruz as long as they tried.

I tensed my fingers over Wynn's leg. She caressed my hand again. This family didn't have to help my brothers do a damn thing. If anything, I should be swinging in to aid them, but I'd seen firsthand how much difference the Baileys could make in a person's life. I had an open loft and stills. Here they'd learn all things cattle. Horses, too. Riding lessons when the weather was nicer. Chicken lessons. They'd teach my brothers about goats and donkeys. Hell, they'd probably review how to care for

keep a hundred and fifty animals alive...

I'd always be there for them, but here they'd get exactly what I had needed as a kid. Support and mentorship in the guise of hard damn work.

Teller and Tenor had seen what I had. The awe in Lane's and Cruz's faces. The yearning for the idyllic but hardworking life the ranch represented. They were used to working hard—for survival. This way, their efforts would be directly linked to their quality of life, and my brothers sensed it. They'd eat cuts of meat they'd never been able to afford at the grocery store, much less in a restaurant.

Mae would teach them how to cook. She'd have them mending their own sweaters and socks and coats. Lane would become as familiar with a sewing needle as he was with a wrench.

"You said you're a mechanic?" Mae asked. "Oh, won't that be handy."

Goddamn. Did Lane just blush? I knew the feeling. When one of the Baileys complimented you, you knew it wasn't smoke getting blown up your ass.

"You both will definitely earn your pay," she said, beaming.

"Pay?" Cruz's brows popped. "You're going to pay me? It's not just room and board?"

Lane put his fork down, his gaze stunned.

Tate's gaze bounced between my brothers. "You thought we were only going to feed you a little and give you a small bedroom?" When Lane and Cruz nodded, Tate grunted, disbelieving. "You'll grow to love this work so much you'd do it for free—don't mean you have to."

give us your mechanic rates."

Lane blinked. "I work on cars."

"Can you weld?" Teller asked.

"Yeah?"

"You'll do fine."

"More pie?" Mae asked.

Lane and Cruz shoved their plates out.

Wynn chuckled. I was that kid before. We all were. Get seconds before the last slice was taken.

My brothers dug in. Mae talked excitedly about the skills the guys would learn. They chewed and bobbed their heads. Was it only a few days ago I'd met them? A little over a week ago I'd found out I even had brothers? And they were already getting sucked into the Bailey orbit. They would be able to stay as long as they liked. No Gianna to ruin their opportunities. If they didn't fuck it up, they'd be on the road to a good life.

This family. They'd taken me in just the same. And I'd left. Then they'd done it again...and again.

The room grew hot and drawing a breath became a struggle. "Excuse me." I picked up my napkin, silverware, and empty plate and took them to the kitchen. The weight of everyone's gazes bored into my back, but no one stopped me.

The kitchen was cooler, but the heavy weight on my chest didn't let up. I set my items down and propped my hands on the counter.

A light touch landed on my back, and Wynn's sweet lemongrass smell surrounded me. "Don't you like the idea of your brothers working the ranch?"

"I fucking love it."

"It's a lot." I was trying really hard to take this day—this whole fucking week—in stride. "It's all really great."

"And you're waiting for it to go to shit."

I dropped my head and nodded. "Things don't go this well without going to hell. And things don't go this well this fast."

My lungs were squeezing together again, until I had to shorten my breaths. Was I hyperventilating?

I didn't hyperventilate.

Inhale. Exhale.

"It's okay for things to go well."

"I know." My brain continued fucking up signals to my body.

"But you've never had it happen before."

"Not without fighting and sacrificing and giving up everything to eventually lose it."

"You did give up everything." She put her warm fingers on my chin and turned my face toward her. I drank her in. Liquid brown eyes. Satiny skin. Compassionate aura. "You left this life behind for us. You stay holed up in your tower in the mountains to hoard a treasure—"

"You make me sound like a dragon."

"—that you can dole out, and you don't think you can do that without sacrificing your personal life."

"But my brothers—"

"Have been going without their entire life. They wouldn't be lapping up Mama's attention otherwise."

"Do you think they're going to mess it up? Give Mae attitude? Tate?" Of course they'd give Tate attitude. They weren't used to a male authority in their lives.

back Tate up. If Tate comes down too hard on them, there's Mama, Teller, and Tenor to tell him to back off. Switch any of those names around. If all else fails, Summer will come home and kick some ass. She lives for being bossy."

My anxiety began to ebb. "I've never panicked like this before."

"You've never faced your feelings before."

"Shit, Wynn. Don't hold back." I gave her a wry smile.

She squeezed my arm. "Want to help me clean up? Your brothers are still guests tonight, so Mama won't make them do it."

"She might not, but I will." I put my hand on the small of her back. As we returned to the dining room, I marveled over how right this felt. And how much the feeling terrified me.

CHAPTER TWENTY-NINE

Wynter

Time was ticking by ever so slowly. I smoothed a hand over my loose hair. I had it lightly curled and draped over a shoulder. My cashmere sweater was a deep maroon that made my skin look *Pride & Prejudice* pale instead of sickbed pale. The jeans were a darker shade than what I wore normally. I'd wear my fluffy brown boots because it was still cold out.

I bobbed a leg as it was crossed over a knee. The big windows of the living room overlooked a fenced pasture that sloped down to the valley. Behind the house, Tenor was working with a dumbfounded Cruz, who'd been dragged out of bed when I suspected he normally hit the rack. And who was also going through severe nicotine withdrawals.

Teller called it Cruz's Personal Hell Week, but I'd be surprised if the adjustment only took a week. I doubted

Myles had messaged me for updates. He was working in his hotel room in Bozeman. I'd asked him about staying at the apartment with Lane, but his expression when he shook his head told me a lot about the guys' place.

My phone buzzed.

HOT GIRL SUMMER

Have you left yet?

> No, he's picking me up soon.

It was five thirty. I was ready for the date, and he'd be early. On time was late.

You're going to cave so easy.

> Am not.

I have a bet with Autumn.

> Do I want to know?

Only if you're going to help me win a hundred bucks.

> I'm not going to cave.

I could stay strong. I'd been giving myself the pep talk all night. After seeing the way he hovered around his brothers—who were not children and had clearly handled life themselves for years—was endearing. He didn't fuss over them, but he'd also been watchful, for

opened up to me. I had fallen so far for him before, and I was only tumbling deeper.

But I would not pretend like having only a part of him was good enough for me. I came from a big welcoming family and getting only a glimpse of the real Myles Foster wouldn't be enough. What he chose to share with who was his decision. I wouldn't force him, but I also wouldn't settle for less than what I wanted.

> We'll see if you have your pants on at midnight.

Want video proof?

> That can be tampered with. Autumn will be able to tell when she has lunch with you tomorrow.

My sneaky sisters. Autumn had asked to meet me at the coffee shop tomorrow. She planned to gauge how my date went.

Care to elaborate?

Nope.

I sent her a middle finger emoji. She replied with a laughing face one.

Sisters.

"Wynter?" Mama called from the kitchen. "Myles is here."

I pushed my hair off my shoulder and purposely

opened the door. Mama kept washing dishes she didn't have to with a nice dishwasher ready to use, but this way, she could keep an eye on the shop and barn.

Myles waited with the screen door propped on his shoulder. His appearance made the twirls in my stomach go haywire. His hair wasn't slicked into its usual punishing style. A chunk fell loose on his forehead. His blue eyes were hooded as always but the way they lit just a little more when I opened the door...well, *swoon*. The jeans and his thick navy-blue sweater were new and took the corporate edge off him.

I kicked a hip out. "This guy looks like he makes whiskey for a living."

The corner of his mouth quirked up. "Don't I usually?" he asked as he stepped in. He produced a brown wrapped bouquet with sunflowers and white carnations sticking out.

"You usually look like you *sell* whiskey for a living." I accepted the flowers. "Thank you."

He handed me a box of bourbon-flavored taffy that hadn't been bought at Copper Summit's gift shop. He hadn't gone for the low-hanging fruit.

"Oh, look at those." Mama took the bundle from me and went to the cupboard she kept vases in. "I'll get these in some water so you two can get going, and I'll hide the candy from the others. Wynter can tell you how well Cruz is doing."

Interest in Cruz took his attention off me, but I didn't mind. "He's been respectful?"

"Well, as much as any nineteen-year-old who's been raised by a barely-older-than-him brother in a house

He chuckled—with real humor. "I blocked out those mornings. I've been irrevocably changed, I'm afraid."

"Oh gosh, you used to fall out of bed and crawl out of your room, grumbling the whole time." She giggled, delighted. "I saw you all over again. Cruz is older and bigger than you were when you first came here, but the picture was the same. Good thing Tenor was working with him today. I don't think Tate is ready for that level of grumpiness."

Myles nodded. "Let Tenor take the edge off with some hard work." He put his arm around me but didn't start for the door. "You think he'll do good?"

Mama would hear his unspoken question like I did. *Do you think he'll stick around?* I didn't have to know specifics about Cruz's life. He didn't have many other options, and he'd flaked on the ones he had.

She folded her arms and worried her lower lip. Myles tensed around me. I put a hand on his chest. The steady beat of his heart was strong under the thick material of his knit sweater.

"I admit, I'm not used to working with older kids." To Mama, we were all still kids. "But I have to say that if he hasn't walked out yet, he'll be here in the morning, crawling out of his room."

"He has no car."

Her eyes crinkled at the corners. "Doesn't stop them. Besides, that kid likes a challenge—he's just never been pushed before. He won't leave, and he might not understand why himself, but he'll stay." She propped a hand on

"Mama!" I said, pretending to be scandalized, but she flicked a dish towel at us.

Laughing, we walked outside. Myles didn't let me out of his hold until he'd opened the door of his car. He'd left it running, and I slid into the toasty passenger seat.

He folded his long body behind the wheel and leaned on the console. "Is it too forward to ask for a kiss before the date starts?"

I was acutely aware of what we'd done in this same car over three months ago. My body tingled. One kiss could lead to no clothing again, but we were parked in the driveway, Mama was probably watching out the kitchen window, and my brothers and his were working outside.

I pressed a soft kiss to his mouth. He cupped my face and increased the pressure, but he didn't push his tongue inside. A heartbeat later, he pulled away. Restraint was engraved in his features. I wasn't the only one keeping themselves in check.

❧

Myles

Sitting with Wynn in a quiet booth in Canyon Grill, I couldn't recall why I hated dating. We talked easily. She asked about business. I told her about the Mainline contract and when the expansion on Foster House was supposed to be done.

"Is it exciting?" she asked, pulling apart a bun left-distribution."

I should be elated. Once I'd kept Foster House's doors open for a year, I had wanted to conquer the world. Move over Jack Daniel's, Jim Beam, and Crown Royal. Foster House would be the most recognizable brand of whiskey in the US. But once the contract had been signed, I'd been halfhearted about the expansion.

I had chalked my ambivalent feelings up to having all the plans made. I hadn't scrambled. There was no drawing board or brainstorming session. I'd known who I would call and hire when I needed to pick up the phone.

But all of the plans had been set in motion after I'd left Wynn's bed. I'd had no one to celebrate with. Mrs. Crane had smiled at the news, but then she'd cut out early for her grandkid's back-to-school celebration. Braxton was working part-time around his college classes. Same with Cooper, and he didn't work in the industry anyway, so his thrill would have been only for my benefit.

"I'm proud of what I accomplished," I admitted. And I was. However... "I'm not excited."

She frowned, those pretty pink lips puffing out. The chaste kiss in the car continued to linger on my mouth, a tease of her sweet flavor. I wouldn't push her tonight. She needed time, and I wanted her to trust me.

"Why not?" she asked.

"The distribution agreement was a way to prove I'd made it, but by the time it all went through, I was still a lonely man in his office, doing nothing but work."

"You never celebrated?"

"It was just another day at the office, which I prefer. You know that."

She made a noncommittal sound. "Lane's coming tomorrow?"

I nodded. "That's the plan."

"You don't think he'll follow through?"

I considered her question, keeping my gaze on my empty plate. I'd stuck with a bourbon-glazed burger and waffle fries. Food outside of my normal fare, but I was beyond my comfort zone in a lot of ways lately. "I think he'll check on Cruz, maybe make a few extra bucks if he can put his mechanic skills to use, but to learn about ranching? I don't know."

"How did they turn out so well?" She grimaced and turned sheepish. "I mean, you weren't a bad kid either. But they made it through childhood with a mom who was..."

"Unpredictable? Unreliable? Unstable?"

"All the uns."

I'd pondered their personalities myself, and I'd asked them. "Their grandma on their dad's side was around for a while. She was a single mom, and their dad fell into a bad crowd when he was closer to their age now. I guess Gianna let their grandma into their lives. I mean, she had to if she didn't want them taken away. Lane said their grandma used to have them for overnights and go to school functions and take them clothes shopping."

"She passed away?"

"A couple years ago." The death of their grandmother had coincided with the beginning of Gianna's escalation. Had she been close to the woman, too? Had she lost one

"I'm almost envious. They got to know a grandparent."

She plucked another bun out of the container. The paper crinkled. She ripped off a chunk and waited for me to continue. This being-open-with-your-feelings shit was hard to get used to. I'd rather she could reach into my mind and know what I was thinking. Anything was better than talking about it.

Yet the urge to spill all my thoughts was there. Words piled up on my tongue. I wanted to tell her. I wanted her to get to know me. The real me. The guy I was no longer familiar with.

"Gianna's grandpa wasn't alive much longer after he kicked her out. Sometimes I wonder if that's why he did it. Was he scared he couldn't care for her and a kid, and it was better to boot her out rather than see himself fail?" I could already breathe easier.

"That makes sense."

"My dad's parents...I'm sure Gianna lied about them. Makes it worse. She kept me from a loving couple who might've been there when I had no one else."

"When did they pass away?"

"I don't know. She just told me they were horrible people, and they were dead when I asked."

"Have you tried to look them up?"

I shook my head. "I don't need to see obituaries."

"It's a lot of loss," she agreed. "Didn't you have an uncle?"

"After hearing my grandparents were gone, I didn't want more bad news. Or to hear her rant about how awful he was again." I reached across the table. I had to hold her in some way. To know she was here, and I something else. "Thanks for coming out with me."

She smiled. "I like being with you. I especially like getting to know you like this."

"You liked being with the asshole CEO, too."

Her grin deepened. "He had his charm—and a really nice ass."

She wiggled in her seat, and I wanted to groan. I could take her from the restaurant, we'd drive to a remote spot, or I could even get a room in town. I'd strip her down, one article of clothing at a time. We'd have long, slow sex, followed by frantic needy sex. Reverse that. I wouldn't be able to go slow initially. The day in my loft almost two weeks ago was more like two years ago. Too fucking long.

"Myles," she whispered. "You're looking at me like that."

"Like what?" My voice was deeper than usual. Anyone who looked at me could probably tell what I was thinking.

"Like you want me for dessert."

"You're my favorite sweet." I drew in a slow, deep breath. My lust had to be contained. I wasn't messing this up. "But I'm going to be good tonight. I'll get you home by curfew. When can I see you again?"

"I'm having lunch with Autumn tomorrow."

"Tomorrow night?"

She laughed. "Myles." Her smile died. "You have to get back, don't you?"

"I'll fly back Monday for a couple of days, and then I'll return."

"Seriously?" Her disbelief should be insulting.

"I'm not hiding from life at Foster House anymore."

You're my life.

She hummed and dropped her gaze. Several seconds ticked by. "I think I had too many buns. Can you take me home?"

How had I fucked up this time? If this was the end, I didn't know what I could do to save it, to save us. I was learning who I really was. The people in my life were expanding, and I wasn't in my loft, hiding away from everyone and everything. But Wynn wanted to go home. In the end, I might have to admit that, in the most important way, I wasn't enough after all.

Wynter

The house was quiet when I entered. Headlights flashed in the window as Myles pulled away. I licked my lips like I was trying to recreate the sweet kiss at the door with him.

He knew something was bothering me—or I wouldn't have asked to get taken home immediately—but he hadn't pried. Instead, he'd given me the sweetest, more reassuring good-night kiss.

I was anything but reassured.

I took my coat off and snapped a picture of myself, holding my arm high and getting my entirely clothed body in the frame. I sent the photo to Summer and Autumn.

Ha! You owe me, Autumn.

Figured. Summer had made it sound like she'd bet I'd be under Myles right now when it was really Autumn who had.

Autumn sent a GIF of money flying around.

Traitors. Both of them.

I could use a crappy-wine night with Junie again. She was sometimes the easiest of my sisters. A little bossy, a little sweet, but so wrapped up in her own life she didn't delve so far into mine.

I toed off my boots and slumped against the door. The cool metal soaked through my sweater. I'd rather be with Myles.

Mama entered the kitchen, mug in hand. She drank decaf this late, and the mug usually had a splash or two of a Copper Summit bourbon. "Oh. I thought I heard someone come in."

She knew I was home, or she wouldn't be snooping in the kitchen. "Yeah, I called it early."

"Not going well?" She rinsed her cup out and set it on the drying rack.

"It was going great."

She glanced at me, picked her cup back up and filled it full of decaf. She grabbed another mug from the cupboard and filled that, too. Then from underneath the counter, she pulled out a bottle of Wynter Summit. Each cup got two splashes.

I could use a third.

She handed me my mug and beckoned me to follow

I took a deep drink of the spiked coffee. The warmth of the coffee paired with the burn of the alcohol calmed my nerves. Mama sipped her drink and waited for me to talk.

I took a second deep pull. My thoughts slowly unwound. "He's working from Montana, and he's doing it for me." Mama dipped her head. She wouldn't speak until I was done talking. "What if something happens to his business? He's doing this for me when he's worked for years to build Foster House. I told him I deserve better, but how selfish am I being?"

"You deserve the best. He wants to be that best."

"It shouldn't cost him, though. Right?" Anguish filled my chest. "Shouldn't we make each other better? I can't ask him to give up his passion, his life, just to be with me."

"Do you think whiskey is really his passion?" She tapped her fingers on her mug. I recognized the cadence. All my siblings and I had faced the coffee-mug interrogations.

"Yes?" He was driven. He was talented. He knew the business inside and out. "Yes," I said more confidently.

"Do you think he wants it to be his life?" More tapping.

"Yes." When she lifted a brow, I thought harder. During the months I'd worked for him, there were times I'd caught glimpses. Him with his old friend Cadillac Sam and the way they talked whiskey and business. Myles got more expressive when he was discussing spirits. When it came to bottom lines and contracts, he was focused. Diligent, but not passionate. He'd enjoyed the

"You know why your father didn't hire a manager for the ranch when the distillery does just fine? Or why he didn't fold the operation altogether?"

"Because the ranch teaches us discipline and hard work. 'You can't have an ego when you're covered in manure.'" One of Daddy Darin's many quotes. "And to keep us out of trouble." Seven kids and multiple foster kids had needed something to do.

"Yes to all that." She chuckled. "But there was another reason. He said a company would expand to take over a person's life if they let it. He knew we'd let him give all his time to Copper Summit. He knew we'd understand. But the cows? They depended on him. The horses, too. He couldn't let Copper Summit take over his life so much that he was late feeding animals that needed him. And once he left work and got dirty, well, there was no point in going back."

"The ranch gave him balance."

Triumph filled her eyes. "Exactly. Myles has never had balance. Anything that happens with Foster House is not your responsibility." She gave me a small smile. "Did you talk to him about this?"

I sighed. "No. I ran like he did. I was selfish." I'd done exactly what I'd been upset with him for.

"Two peas in a pod."

"His pod is more altruistic than mine. Should I go to him?" If I left now, I'd only be a half hour behind him. "Cruz would know what hotel he's staying at, right?"

She snickered. "I thought Cruz was going to fall asleep in his mashed potatoes. I'm not even sure he made it to the shower before he collapsed onto his bed."

"It's late." She got up and rinsed out her cup again. I was formulating what I would say in my head when she swooped back. She gave me a kiss on the head. "It's not always a bad thing to make them think about things a little longer." Then she shuffled toward the stairs on the other side of the pantry.

I downed the rest of my lukewarm coffee. Smooth bourbon washed down my throat. I pulled the flowers toward me and buried my nose in the petals. Carnations smelled so damn good. Not as nice as the man who'd given me a sweet kiss on the forehead when he dropped me off. I'd need to think about me and Myles for a little longer, too.

CHAPTER THIRTY

Myles

I'd flown back the day before yesterday. I'd expected to be busy once I landed, but Mrs. Crane had arranged times for every department to touch base with me, and then she'd taken me on a tour of what the contractors had been up to. Progress was only a week behind schedule. The place had run just fine while I was out of town.

Now I was left with an evening free, and I wasn't set to fly out until tomorrow. My car was at the airport in Bozeman, and I was stuck at Foster House, or I'd drive back tonight. I had checked with the co-op, but the plane was booked.

So I was kicked back on my couch, remembering how fucking epic it was to wake up with Wynn in my bed. I'd made myself an old fashioned—with Foster House's Original—and tried to relax.

I made it five minutes before I called Lane.

I chuckled. He reminded me of Teller when he bit my head off. "It's more efficient than staring at my phone waiting for you to fat-finger a reply."

"I have deftly talented fingers. There're a few girls you could ask."

I'd rather not hear more about Lane's sex life. "How was the weekend?"

"Worth the drive to see Cruz miserable."

I sat forward, worry zinging down my spine. "He's miserable?"

"Tired. Cold all day. Can't cock off whenever he wants. But he's still there, getting bossed around all day by someone other than me. That's good enough."

"Mae cooks better than you."

He grunted. "That's for sure."

"What about you?"

"They tried to get me to do shit, but I fixed a few things and left. Have to give it to them—they pay faster than any customer I've ever seen."

"When you going again?" Would he be going again?

He was quiet. "This weekend."

I chuckled, knowing it'd piss him off.

"What? There's some fucking good food there."

"Next thing you know, you're going to be grooming a horse."

"I don't need to groom a goddamn horse. I don't need to get one, and I don't need to feed one."

I could encourage him or point out he was scared, but I'd rather act like an asshole brother instead. "*Buuu-uck...buck-buck-buck.*"

"I'm not a chicken, jackass!"

decide to buck me the hell off."

I laughed. "Cruz is going to ride circles around you."

He grumbled. Cruz's progress might be what got him on a horse. "Whatever, it's winter anyway. Tate said they prefer the ice be all melted before they ride. What about you? Did you win the girl back yet?"

Since he'd been open with me, and since I was quickly getting used to talking to Lane about my personal life, I told him the truth. "No. She got weird on our date and cut it short early. I don't know what I did or said."

"Did you do the flowers?"

"Flowers don't win the girl."

He grunted. "She worth it?"

"Yes."

"There you have it. More flowers."

I chuckled. "I'm going to be the first to tell you that you'll need to make more of an effort than that."

"I'm not interested in forever, Myles. You don't see our mother in a relationship and think you want that for yourself."

"I saw her in a healthy relationship." Would Wynn have had a chance otherwise? "It was after my dad died that she...changed. Took his pills. Started making claims about my dad's parents."

"She have something against in-laws?"

"Right?" We both fell quiet. "I'll let you go. Don't eat all of Mae's food without doing dishes."

"I did fucking dishes. Do you think that woman would let me get away without drying? What the hell does she think a dishwasher's for?"

What if Gianna had been lying about my grandparents? Lane and Cruz's grandmother had been a godsend.

What if my grandparents weren't even dead?

I pulled up a browser and searched for Fosters in the Portland area. A ton of names came up, but thanks to Gianna's rants, I found them anyway. Ella and Nicolas Foster.

Still fucking alive.

That goddamn liar!

I let the hatred roll through me. I'd learned a long time ago not to hide from it. Stuffing the hate in a corner was akin to planting an incendiary device in my brain. Next thing I knew, I'd be drunk dialing Wynn again, and she didn't need that bullshit.

Once the emotion died down, I dialed Wynn.

"Hello?" Her sweet voice tamped the rest of the anger down.

"Gianna lied about my grandparents being dead."

"What?" Fabric rustled.

"Did I catch you at a bad time?"

"I mean, I have to tell my date to leave, but he already got me off three times, so I think I'm good."

More anger sparked bright and died quickly. A smile stretched my lips. "Only three? Chump."

She laughed. "I am curled up with a barn cat that's recovering from a fight with some unknown creature. Mama retired her and brought her inside. Little Miss doesn't have to wear the cone of shame if she's sleeping with me."

I'd love to see her snuggling with one of the thick-

"Apparently. I don't know for sure it's them."

"Did you check for obituaries?"

No. "Hold on." I did a quick search in and around the Portland area. None of the ages fit. My grandparents would be in their late seventies or eighties. "I don't see them."

"What are you going to do?"

What would I do? My grandparents had been out of my life for over thirty years. I was forty. They'd had plenty of time to contact me as an adult. "I don't know."

"You don't have to decide now."

What if they were in their eighties? How was their health? "Soon, though."

"Or never. It's okay to just let it go, too."

How did Wynn know what I needed to hear? "If I do contact them, and they want to see me, would you go with me?"

"Are you sure?"

"Yes." No. What if Gianna was right, and my grandparents were horrible people who'd only wanted the life insurance and hadn't cared about their grandkid or their widowed daughter-in-law?

When had I known my mother to be truthful? Lane and Cruz were two big damn examples of her manipulation.

"Do you remember anything about them?" she asked.

I hadn't thought of them for so long, I had to turn into an archaeologist, wiping dirt and layers of neglect off the memories. When Gianna had told me they were gone, I had thought *Of course they were*. Why wouldn't they leave, too? "I remember they seemed kind but

moved to an apartment and then to Bozeman." Both places I barely recalled.

"I guess ultimately you aren't going to know anything about them if you don't reach out. Are they still in Portland?"

"Looks like it."

"Isn't it weird—you moved about the same distance away in a different direction?"

"I did." Where I went hadn't been a conscious thought at the time, but Gianna's rants had likely been banging around in my head. I might've increased the distance between me and the city where her troubles had originated.

I glanced at the time. Portland was an hour behind. "I'm going to do it."

"Let me know how it goes." A small mew sounded from the background. "I'm not going anywhere," she calmed the kitty.

"Wynn."

"Yeah?"

"Thank you. For not going anywhere."

"You're not as fluffy as Little Miss, but you're welcome."

I was grinning when I got off the phone. I rode the wave of good vibes and dialed the number I found online. Gotta love landlines.

An older lady answered, her voice crackling. "Hello?"

"Is this Ella Foster?"

"I'm Ella. Who is this?"

"It's..." Was I really doing this? I should've thought about making the call harder, the repercussions. But my

I pulled into what was becoming my normal parking spot at the Baileys'. Wynn and I were still dating, and other than some kissing that steamed up the inside of my car, we hadn't slept together. I kept a hotel room in Bozeman so I could check in with Lane, but the reservation was getting pointless.

Lane had been in Bourbon Canyon each weekend since the first time. He liked being his own boss, but I'd also seen him helping spread the silage around.

Three weeks had gone by since I'd first called my grandparents. After explaining to Ella I was *that* Myles, she had dropped the phone. Then Nicolas had come on, demanding to know what was going on. Once they'd heard Gianna had passed away, they'd divided into separate rooms so they could each be on the line.

Most of our conversations were them asking what I'd been up to since my dad died. I told them Gianna had ended up in Bozeman, then I had landed in Bourbon Canyon. They oohed and ahhed over the Baileys, stunned that I had been living with such a respected and successful family. When I told them Foster House was mine, they hadn't heard of the place, but when I compared what I did to the Baileys, there was more awe.

Both had asked a ton of questions about Gianna— what she'd done for work, what kind of places we'd lived in, and even how she'd looked. The naturally suspicious part of my brain insisted their leading questions had an end goal, and it wasn't my welfare, but the logical part

Nicolas had been focused on Foster House during our last conversation. *You must do pretty well with the distillery.* Another comment that had wound through my mind, whispering about my grandfather's true intentions. I ignored it. I wasn't handing over my balance sheets to show him how successful I really was. Maybe the guy wanted to be proud of his grandson.

Wait'll I tell Junior that, he'd said.

Junior was Nicolas Foster Junior. My dad's older brother. He had two years on my dad, which put him in his late fifties.

I had offered to fly out to meet them, but they wanted to see Bourbon Canyon and the Bailey place. *A quick flight is all it'd take*, they had each said.

Wynn waved out the door just like her mom right as my phone rang. I wiggled my phone so she could see. She nodded and disappeared inside.

I wanted to ditch the call and go lift Wynn into my arms, but I didn't want another call to intrude on my time with her. Might as well get it done with.

My resistance sent up a red flag. I had issues with my family. Were they due to being raised by Gianna or for a legitimate reason? Their incessant calls and questions about my childhood and my state of living were complicating things.

I answered. "Foster."

"Hey, Myles," Nicolas said with what was becoming his standard greeting. "Have you gotten the go-ahead yet?"

I had told them I'd talk to Mae about a visit, but I hadn't. Nor had I told Wynn about their request. My lips

Grandma or Grandpa. I'd reached out, but I was aware he was still a stranger. Other than saying Gianna had cut off contact, they hadn't spoken about the years I had lived with them. They hadn't talked about my dad at all. "It's not a good time to travel, and getting out to the ranch can be tricky even during good weather."

I was playing the snowfall up, but my grandparents wanted to move faster than I was comfortable. Three weeks to introducing them to people I'd been histori- cally protective of? No. I wasn't ready, and I wasn't putting the Baileys in that position.

A deep voice growled in the background. Junior. A quick online search showed a guy with piercing blue eyes like my dad's and a permanent scowl. Would I look perpetually cranky like that when I was his age?

"We can fly," Nicolas said.

"Give me time," I replied evenly. "It's only been a few weeks since we opened communication."

"Myles, we're excited to have you back in our life. We tried so hard, but that mother of yours took you away from us."

Hair prickled along the back of my neck. The tone. The slightly pleading notes in his statement. The redirection of blame. I was more than familiar with this game.

"Why do you want to meet the Baileys so badly? Why Bourbon Canyon? And while we're at it, why don't you tell me why you don't want me coming to visit you?" My questions hit rapid fire, and I made sure I sounded like I wasn't continuing without answers.

"W-well, it's not fair for you to travel."

said, joining the call. "We don't want to upset you."

Junior's deep timbre could be heard but I couldn't make out his words.

"Yes, right. We just really want to meet you." Ella's soothing tone rang with false sincerity.

Fuck.

Had Gianna been truthful about them?

"Do you want to meet me or my wallet? Do you want to see the family that did so much for me, or do you want to know what the Baileys can do for you?"

"Now, Myles—"

Ella was cut off by more rustling. Then Junior's growl came over the line. "Listen, my parents have been through enough, thanks to your mother."

"I'm starting to wonder if the tales of your behavior and treatment of Gianna were the only true things she ever told me."

"That bitch mother of yours—"

"This conversation can end now if you call her that again." I'd never thought I'd defend Gianna like this, but here I was, understanding her villain story.

"She took Devon's life insurance. That should've been ours for all the help we gave them."

My sympathy was new and deserved. Gianna had been a young, widowed mother, and they'd been after the life insurance. She'd had no support. No love. No understanding. I could regret calling my Foster grandparents, but I wouldn't regret getting a deeper understanding behind my mother's addiction.

"You owe us," Junior demanded.

I laughed. In this, I could thank my mother. She'd

that way."

"My parents have no retirement, no financial support. That money should've been theirs."

"Life insurance doesn't work like that, dickwad." And I was done with them. Forever.

"We'll get it from you. From that rich fucking family who raised you, or from Foster House—you owe us, and I'm going to make sure you pay us what we deserve—plus interest."

Junior was delusional. No wonder my parents had moved out as soon as they were legally able. No wonder they'd gone to a different state. What had life been like for them under the same roof as these three narcissistic users?

"I looked them up," Junior continued. "They have some tasty daughters, and that Mae is widowed now. She in that big house all alone?"

My blood went cold, icicles piling up in my veins, thawed only by my ever-growing rage. "You stay the hell away from them, or I will ruin you."

His wicked chuckle pumped my anger harder and hotter. "They mean a lot to you."

I could leave. Forever cut myself out of the Baileys' lives so no taint from my last name could harm them. I could do what I'd always done and leave. I'd spend one more night in Wynn's arms and be gone in the morning. Junior and my grandparents wouldn't get money or satisfaction.

Or I could pay them off. Whatever dismal life insurance payout my dad had gotten wouldn't be a problem to cover.

seen firsthand how what she was given was never enough. She'd scrabbled for more and more until she'd destroyed herself. My brothers and I could've gone down with her, but we were resilient—no thanks to the people I was on the phone with.

I wasn't willing to give up Wynn for this asshat. I wasn't ditching her for someone else's greed again. Gianna had shown me leaving wouldn't work. This time, I'd make sure I was around if there was trouble. "Here's what's going to happen. You're going to leave the Baileys alone. You're going to stay far away from Montana and Colorado. I have no issues kicking your ass back to the shithole you deserve. I'm richer than you, asshole, and I don't owe you one shiny penny. I don't owe you a damn thing."

I hung up, tossed the phone on the passenger seat, and got out. The fucking thing could freeze. I didn't bother with my luggage. My chest was heaving by the time I got to the door.

Wynn was at the table, a new floral bouquet I'd had sent earlier in the middle. I had a standing order with the florist in town, along with a monthly arrangement for Mae.

Wynn rose when her gaze landed on my expression. "What's wrong?"

I didn't stop until I was in front of her. I didn't explain but captured her mouth, swiping my tongue inside. The sweet flavor of coffee danced from her tongue to mine. She wrapped her arms around me, and I tipped her backward with the force of my kiss. I plundered her mouth, and when she whimpered and molded

"My grandparents and uncle are toxic pieces of shit. My mother was right, and I'll tell you all of it, but I really need to be inside you."

Her nod was shaky. "Mama's in town, and the guys are outside working."

"Your room?" When she nodded, I swooped her off her feet. "Hang on."

We were in her room within minutes. The blinds were cracked, but no one could spy on us unless they had their nose to the glass. The light in the room was enough that I could see every damn part of her. Perfect.

I laid her on the bed and ripped my sweater off. The undershirt followed. Then my pants. She licked her bottom lip, watching me strip.

"I don't want anything between us, Wynn."

Understanding flickered in her eyes. "I'm not on—"

"I'm not talking about birth control." I was, but I meant so much more and for a guy not used to talking about feelings, I would lay my heart at her damn feet. "I want forever with you. I love you, Wynter Kerrigan. Frosty. I want the marriage. The house—your house, right here in Bourbon Canyon. The kids. I've let horrible people chase me away from the good parts of life. You're the best thing to happen to me, and I'm going nowhere without you."

I couldn't be bared anymore to her. My dick at full rise. Her fully clothed. Me spilling out my feelings. She had all the power.

Her eyes grew watery. "I love you, too. I have for a long time. But..." She propped herself on her elbows. "I

"That's exactly why you're perfect for me." She cared about me. I'd almost ruined a future with this woman. I was ready to commit. "But I don't need time. I need you. Today, tomorrow, whenever you want. I. Love. You."

She swiped her delicious tongue across her bottom lip again and dropped her gaze to my pants on the floor. "Leave the condom."

A primal surge took over my brain. "Yes, ma'am."

"Ooh, I like that. Can I order you around more?"

"I'm yours, Frosty."

She rolled up and ripped her top off. Her bra followed. Lust pounded through my veins harder with each inch of skin she bared. She peeled her leggings down her curvy legs and lay back down.

"Then get inside me." She tugged on my hand until I was crawling over her.

Blood rushed between my ears, a steady beat, every cell in my body straining to plunge into her. I held back until my muscles shook. I wasn't rushing this. We weren't just having sex. We were making a commitment. Making love. Later, we'd do rings and vows and have more sex, but this was the beginning of forever.

"I knew from the moment I saw you in the parking lot of Foster House, you'd be the end of me." I brushed a hand down her cheek. "I didn't know it'd be in the best way possible."

She widened her legs to cradle me better. I pressed a kiss to the base of her neck. A little sigh left her. A noise that was the only measure of success I needed.

She bared her neck and arched into me. "Myles."

I'd spend the rest of my life coaxing those needy

really goddamn loud."

She moaned and rolled her hips. I couldn't hold back any longer. I slicked the tip of my cock through her soaking pussy and slowly pushed inside.

"Fuck, Wynn. Every time, I can't believe how good you feel." I stopped when I was seated to the hilt.

She slid her hands through my hair, and her heels hooked into my ass cheeks. I pumped in and out of her, loving the way her body gripped me, how perfectly we fit, the way pleasure glazed her eyes with each stroke.

She brought my head down to capture her mouth. I caught every breath, each moan, and all of her whimpers.

One day, we'd make love in our own bed. Our own house. I'd build that place for her where we were first together. Her plans. My gift.

Energy raced down my spine, coiling around my balls. I wasn't going to last much longer, and from the way heat bloomed between us and the wet slap of our bodies together, neither was she.

I hitched one of her legs up to hit deeper.

"Oh god, Myles." She ignited, her mouth dropping open, and her eyelids falling shut. Her pussy clamped around me, and I detonated.

Energy coursed through me, one long blast of lightning with the power to destroy me. I released inside of her, and she hugged me close through our orgasms. When I collapsed on top of her, she clung to me, kissing my cheek, my mouth, and my neck.

Fucking perfect.

"I really love you." She stroked her hands down my

My laughter grew. "My dick loves you almost as much as I do."

She grinned. Thanks to the light streaming through the window, I saw more than her pale hair strewn around her like a crown. Or her warm brown eyes and pink lips. I caught the flash of uncertainty.

"You think I'm going to leave?"

"I'm more worried you'll feel pressured to stay. Since we didn't use protection."

"I'm not scared of having kids anymore." I kissed the corner of her mouth and gently pulled out. We were on top of the covers, nothing between us or covering us. Open. Honest. "I was scared of having kids with someone I didn't love. There was that. Terrified I might have an accident with a woman who was the type of mother to manipulate her kids. In reality, I was terrified of having a family that would have no support if something happened to me. I didn't realize the exact reason until I saw for myself how alone and scared my mother must've been."

"Oh, Myles." She rolled into me and tucked herself against my chest. "You've got such a big heart. You know that?"

"No one's ever accused me of a big heart." I rubbed her back. "I'm going to go grab my overnight bag and laptop. Then I'm going to cancel my room in Bozeman and feed you and tell you about the phone call. Then we're going to have barely audible sex all night even though Mae will know exactly what's going on."

She giggled. "Sounds like the first of many perfect nights."

CHAPTER THIRTY-ONE

Wynter

The first thing I was aware of when I woke was a hot, warm body behind me. The steel arm banded around me was the next thing I noticed. His even breathing against the back of my neck. He was curled into me, yet cradling me, like I was his lifeline in his dreams, like he was afraid he wouldn't return from his slumber without me. When I'd slept with him at his loft, he hadn't held me this tight. Somewhere deep in his mind, he'd been pushing me away. Those guards were gone now.

A week had gone by, and I still wasn't used to this, to waking up consistently with him in my bed, with him wrapped around me. In me.

His arm flexed, and I smiled. He inhaled and nuzzled behind my ear. "You're finally awake."

His deep rumble went straight through my body to my thoroughly sexed core. I'd had more sex in the last week than all together in my entire life.

bunched around my breasts thanks to his hand pushing it up.

"You should." I ground my ass against him. We were basically living together in my childhood bedroom. Mama was delighted, Myles's brothers liked having him around more, and Foster House wasn't suffering from his absence.

"You're going to keep me in trouble with your brothers." He released me only to shove his shorts down. Next, he was pushing inside me.

I slid my hand down my belly.

His groan resonated between us. "You gonna touch yourself for me, Frosty?"

"I'm going to show you how hot I can get."

He whipped the blankets off and angled himself to plow into me while watching me finger my clit.

Someone knocked on the door. He jerked so bad he pulled out and nearly fell off the bed. I started laughing and shoved my face into a pillow. He recovered and nipped my shoulder, and I only giggled harder.

"Myles," Mama called. "There's someone here for you."

He stiffened. "Who is it?"

"He says his name is Nicolas."

Oh no. I craned my head over my shoulder and at Myles. His jaw was stone, his eyes flinty.

"I'll be right there," he growled. "Don't talk to him alone."

The warm, sexy man behind me turned into a brick wall. He rolled out of bed as taut as a two-by-four and

brothers and to the distillery when I tended bar.

I scrambled for my clothing.

"Don't go out there," he warned.

"Myles." He'd told me about the conversation, but the thought that a guy would come here and threaten us had seemed absurd. Didn't he know there were three Bailey brothers and, depending on the day, two younger Foster brothers here, too? I wouldn't discount Mama and the four Kerrigan sisters either.

"Wynn, please."

I tugged a sweater over me and was immediately swamped. I'd grabbed one of Myles's, and his sage scent surrounded me. I puffed hair out of my face. "I'll at least come upstairs."

"I'd rather you and your mom stayed away from the front door."

"The front porch is full of snow." Mama claimed the main door was for decoration only. "He's probably at the back."

His stare remained flat. "Wynn."

"Fine. I'll just go upstairs and keep an eye on Mom. Do you think he's dangerous?"

"I don't know the man." He pushed out the door.

I rushed after him. Mama was at the top of the stairs, her arms folded.

"I'm sorry," Myles said as he stormed past her.

I stopped next to Mama.

"As soon as I heard Myles's tone, I called Tenor," she whispered. "Cruz is with him. They're down by the cottonwood bottoms and will be here soon." She opened

Myles

The asshole had crowded into the kitchen and was making himself a cup of coffee. Junior. He'd thought giving my grandfather's name would make me more likely to come out. In person, he had the same frumpiness as the man from the pictures I'd seen when I'd stalked his social media accounts, the bushy brown hair and the mad-at-the-world scowl.

"Who let you in?"

He smirked at me and put the coffee pot down. "A Keurig and an old-fashioned coffee pot. Living the dream in the mountains, aren't you, nephew?"

"We aren't family. Get out."

The fucker leaned against the counter and took a long drink, making a slurping noise. "Now, the thing is, Myles, my boy. We are family. Your mom didn't want to think so, and she stole from us."

"This argument is tired. It's not my job to educate you on how life insurance works."

"We gave up so much for that—"

A warning noise rumbled out of my chest. He worked his jaw and took another sip. My fists were balled, and I was ready to haul him outside and stuff him in a snowbank. Then push him off the side of a mountain with the tractor.

"Gianna," he bit out. "Groceries got more expensive.

didn't get the car I was promised for graduation. I had to get a job. All the extra went to you and her. And my brother," he sneered. "My brother, who smuggled money so he could leave."

"Nice to hear my father was a smart man. Get out."

Another casual drink. "I went without so you can live like a king. I want what's due to me after all this time."

"There is nothing."

"Your big fucking distillery." He gestured at me with his mug. "I saw the pictures. The news articles. How you purchased that building and restored it."

I took a step toward him. I had hoped things wouldn't get physical, but I had no worries about fighting this guy.

His attention landed over my shoulder, and his eyes flared wide. I stopped my approach.

"He got that money from my husband, not you, asshole," Mae said.

I glanced over my shoulder and almost choked. Mae had the silver barrel of a shotgun pointed right at my uncle. Her hold didn't waver. Shock pulsed in my blood, but I shouldn't be surprised. Mae had lived in the Montana country her entire life. She knew how to shoot. Wynn was behind her, ignoring me as much as Junior was.

"Myles asked you to get out." Mae swung the end of the shotgun toward the front door and then trained it back on Junior. "Do you need a lead filling to hear better?"

Junior set his cup down with a thump. Rage mingled with fear in his face. "I am *owed*."

His sharp inhale made me smile. He pushed off the counter and yanked down his ratty flannel like it was a suit jacket. He walked on stilted legs out the door. I banged out after him.

He turned on me, and I shoved him. He raised a fist, but I batted his arm away. Weak. Pathetic.

"I wouldn't try that again," Tate called.

Junior spun around. Tate and Teller were getting out of Tate's pickup. He'd parked next to Junior's little blue sedan. Had Junior flown and gotten a rental? Driven? I didn't care as long as he fucking *left*.

Mae exited but stayed close to the house.

An engine sounded in the distance. The Ranger skidded to a stop in the snowy gravel behind Junior's car. A power move. Junior wasn't coming or going until we allowed it. Tenor climbed out, looking as always like a big, grumpy man with narrowed eyes behind the thick old frames he wore for chores, glaring like he wanted nothing more than to pound someone's face in.

Cruz stopped to stand right next to him. The kid had packed on muscle in the weeks he'd been working, and he stood straighter. His trademark smirk was gone.

Another car was pulling in. Lane. He would have no idea what was going on. Cruz gave him one pointed look and lifted his chin toward us. Their silent communication was all they needed. Lane stopped in the middle of the drive and got out of his car, too.

The back door smacked closed and only Junior jumped. Wynn must be outside.

Teller adjusted his gloves. "We got us a trespasser."

"He entered the house without permission, too," Mae added.

Junior's gaze was jumping between all of them. I stood firm. Unmoving. I had all the support my mother hadn't.

"Lots of dangers in these mountains," Tenor said. To my surprise, the man could be just as menacing as his brothers.

"You know what I've learned since I've been here?" Cruz asked. He clasped his hands in front of himself. "These men told me that if I went out alone and injured myself, I could get into all kinds of trouble. I could get eaten by..." He rolled a shoulder. "All sorts of things."

"Whatever finds you first," Lane said. "I heard all about people getting lost in these hills. I'm a city boy myself, and you know what happened my first day? I got turned around. Confused. It's easy to get lost."

"Easy to have an accident," Tate finished.

"It's a shame." This was from Mae. "Happens every year to people who don't know better."

Junior's hands were at his sides, clenching and unclenching. They trembled. He was terrified.

"Probably should get going now," I said. "Before you have more than legal troubles to worry about."

"You're all crazy." His voice trembled as bad as his limbs. "Crazy."

"You should remember that next time you mess with one of us," Tate said. "Whatever problem you think you have with Myles, no you don't."

I smirked at Junior. One of us. If Wynn's sisters were

He took a step, eyes rolling around him. He didn't take another step until he noticed Mae had lowered the end of the shotgun to point at the ground. Cautiously, he continued to his rental. It wasn't until he was behind the wheel that Tenor moved the four-wheeler from behind him. Lane wasn't as considerate when Junior tried to leave the driveway. My uncle had to drive into the snow-packed edges and pray that he didn't get stuck.

When the car disappeared out of sight, my shoulders unknotted. How dare that asshole threaten the people I care about?

Yet...those people who I worried about had taken care of Junior. Mae by herself had handled him, more than I could've ever anticipated.

Emotion swelled in my chest. Regret for all those lost years when I hadn't had to run, when I could've stayed and trusted the Baileys to take care of themselves as well as they cared for everyone else. Admiration for the way they'd stood by me, unquestioning. Relief. Gianna's visit had probably included shouting and fist shaking, but she'd also known when to run. Junior's stop had oozed menace. He'd meant to hurt people around me. The exact scenario I'd worked hard to avoid had played out and...everything was fine.

"So, that's my uncle, everyone. He's one of the reasons my mother was fucked up. The other two reasons are my grandparents."

Cruz scratched the back of his head. "You have some crazy luck in the genetics department, bruh."

"That's another five dollars," Tenor said to him.

Cruz tipped his head back. "I've lost a hundred

"It's going to take a thousand more dollars before you quit calling everyone bruh," Tenor replied.

Lane snorted. "Huh. Your uncle is almost as personable as our dad. Can't wait 'til he gets out of prison and tries to mess with us."

"We take care of our own," Mae said. Her finger was tapping the handle of the shotgun. "Don't you kids ever think you're not one of us."

Tenor lifted his chin to Lane. "Ready to get to work finally?"

"I had to buy warmer boots." Lane went to his car. "Since you're keeping me outside all day," he grumbled.

Teller walked toward the house. "Tate can hang out here a while. I'll go back to the distillery and make sure that idiot doesn't try something there. We'll put all the locations on alert."

"Sorry." The relief from earlier was ebbing. Humiliation grew bigger, making my skin itch. "For the trouble."

Teller passed me and slapped my back. "Keeps life exciting."

Darin used to say the same thing when he dealt with problems caused by nature or his kids or other outside forces. I'd recited several of his sayings over the years and would have to add that one.

"I'm always grateful when I don't have to use this on a critter." Mae clutched the shotgun with both hands. "But I also know when I need it. Though there's power in numbers. Good thing I have so many kids." She gave me a knowing nod.

She went inside with Teller. Tate was driving away. My brothers and Tenor were already in the shop.

enough.

I crossed to her and picked her up. "You're getting cold, Frosty."

"Mm—think you can warm me up?"

"Several times. Can you keep it quiet?"

She grinned. "Probably not, but I'm willing to try."

EPILOGUE

Myles

"OH MY GOD, MYLES!" Wynn screamed so loud her voice echoed off the still bare walls of our new house.

I pumped into her while she was bent over the kitchen island. There were no blinds on the windows yet, but the only creatures looking in were the birds flying by. The sound of our skin slapping together filled the kitchen.

Her lush ass was pushing into me, desperately trying to meet each thrust, her pussy quaking around me.

"Fuck, Wynn. Come for me."

"MYLES!" After months of quiet fucking with the occasional night of loud sex at my loft when she traveled to Colorado with me, we were finally in our house. Our new place with only us. We could walk around naked—and we did. Often. She could scream and shout while she came—like she was doing now.

I let my restraint blow as hard as the rest of me. I

pleasure being with her gave me.

"Oh my god, that was so good," she groaned and sagged against the island.

I curled around her back, wrapped a hand around her, and stroked her round belly. "Soon, we're going to have to be quiet again."

Four months to be exact. I was going to be a dad.

A goddamn father.

When the nursery was getting decorated, Wynn had asked me about baby themes and colors. Memories had slowly started unfolding from a pile buried at the base of my brain. Happy times with Gianna and my dad. Faint memories. Sounds of laughter. There'd been good times.

Now that I had more understanding of what Gianna had gone through, I resented her less. And I'd had plenty of time to talk to Lane and Cruz about our mother in the months since I'd been living in Bourbon Canyon.

I pulled out of Wynn and helped her straighten. My gaze fell to her fuller breasts and the tummy I was as obsessed with as much as I was terrified of. Whenever the fear threatened to take over, all I had to do was remember the day my uncle had tried to bully his way into my money.

This baby would have so much goddamn support, he or she would grow up wondering if there was a place on earth they could get some privacy.

"I love you, Mr. Foster." She wound her arms around my neck and pressed her head against my chest.

I carefully lifted her. She was growing used to me carting her to our spacious bathroom with a six-shower-

Bailey land. But today, they would all descend on the house.

She rested her head on my shoulder. "The caterers are showing up soon."

We were getting married. Wynn didn't care if she had a baby belly during the wedding. She only cared that the weather was nice enough for everyone to attend with enough lead time for Junie to get away from her tour schedule and that the ceremony took place on the property her dad had left just for her. Right where our house was.

October was a risk, but we had plan Cs for the plan Bs just in case it was too chilly or the weather was heinous. Wynter wanted this wedding, and I'd make it happen.

I ran us through the shower and only got my roaming hands swatted once with a giggly reprimand that people were arriving soon.

The first guest to arrive was Lane. He swaggered in through the door off the kitchen—Wynn had wanted the same entry feel of her parents' house. His dark boots were gone, replaced by cowboy boots.

"Don't dress up," I said as I poured Wynn her orange juice.

"I'm going to change. The wedding isn't for eight hours." He took the glass of juice.

"That was Wynn's, fucker." The idea of being a dad was less terrifying, thanks to this inconsiderate asshole. I found myself in a part-parent, part-brother role, and increasingly part mentor. Lane had taken an interest in distilling. Not so much ranching, but he'd hung in there

moved out. He claimed it was because Mae had commented on how quiet and lonely the house would be with all the kids gone. But I suspected he'd been dying to relocate since the first time he'd visited.

Besides, Cruz still lived with Mae and was a full-time employee. The only part of her house that was empty was the fridge after he finished raiding it.

"You have plenty of juice," he said and took a big gulp. "I wouldn't have taken the last of it."

I glared at him while getting another glass. "Why are you here early, then?"

"Teller said I could start working weekends at the distillery if I wanted. I'd be like an intern or something."

"You're going to learn to make bourbon?"

"Yeah. I'll be a rancher and mechanic during the week and learn the trade on the weekends. It's not like there's a poppin' social scene in Bourbon Canyon."

"I don't know. That Fourth of July parade was lit."

He chuckled. He laughed easier and the tightness around his eyes had relaxed since I'd first met him.

I grabbed some eggs from the fridge. Wynn had informed me that next year, we would be getting our own chickens, which also meant I would be learning how to build a chicken house and chicken run. Good thing I had a ton of siblings to help.

"So you're going to learn how to make bourbon," I said. "Then you'll build a nationally recognized brand to compete with them?"

"Seems like a waste. They've done bourbon. You got the whiskey down. Besides, what would I call my company? Prison Dad?"

assistants. Mrs. Crane had offered to train them before she retired. But there was room to grow, and since the contract with Mainline had begun, we were indeed growing. "There's already a Foster House. Seems like you'd fit right in."

"Ha. Like you'd let me in your baby."

When I was having a real baby, the business baby didn't seem as centered in my life. "Why wouldn't I? You're a Foster."

He studied me. I continued making eggs for my soon-to-be wife under his scrutiny. I cracked a few more since he'd likely stay long enough to eat my portion if I didn't. His attention didn't bother me, neither did the thought of having Lane learn the ropes.

"You'd really let me work for you?"

I was growing more certain by the minute. "I've been thinking about opening a new location." I was eager to build from the ground up again and having my brother as part of the process would be a special treat. "Unless you want to go into business yourself."

He drained his juice. "The Prison Dad label is growing on me."

"Then I know a good investor."

He smirked, then did a double take. "You serious? What the fuck for?"

"Darin Bailey was the reason I could purchase an old mine and start a distillery. He gave me a life I never could've dreamed of. Seems like a tradition to keep passing on. I have a foundation and everything for it."

A cloud of sweet lemongrass wafted around me. "Is the future being conquered before the wedding?"

dishwasher. Mae had gotten to my brothers in the most unexpected ways. "Aren't you guys supposed to not see each other?"

I lifted a brow at Wynn. Her cheeks still had a post-orgasm flush. I'd seen plenty of her today.

She caressed a hand over her belly. "We've been doing things out of order."

And it'd worked out perfectly.

Wynter

I was dancing with my husband, surrounded by crackling propane firepits and partitions to block the light breeze. I'd thought I knew the man, but I'd discovered one more thing after we'd said our vows and started celebrating with our family and friends on our new house's back patio.

He didn't know how to dance.

I didn't think he'd be interested in learning, and I didn't care, so no matter what the song was, we swayed together, happy in each other's arms. Soon to be a family of three. Myles didn't have to tell me he was scared. Honestly, I was, too. His excitement despite his fear bolstered me. Mama continued to tell me my feelings were normal like she knew exactly what was going through my head.

I rested my head on Myles's shoulder. His black suit coat was soft. I'd picked out the one I wanted him to

I was in thick fuzzy slippers, having kicked off my sandals when the music had started. The hem of my sleeveless white dress brushed the floor, and I wore a white lined cape specially designed for an outdoor autumn wedding in Montana. I liked the idea of looking at our wedding photos and seeing the beginnings of a happy little family.

He brushed a hand down my back. "She has a right to be."

Another song started playing. Chance was dancing with Scarlett, and Tate was watching them, stupid happy, with Brinley on his shoulders. Mama had their new baby boy in her arms, swaying side to side. Tenor was chatting with some of the employees from the distillery. We'd kept the ceremony small and intimate. Baileys, Kerrigans, and employees of each distillery. Mrs. Crane was teaching Braxton and his partner how to waltz. Cooper had driven her down since he'd been invited, too.

The day had been perfect despite a small chance of storms. That small chance was building into a sure thing in the distance. A fitting end to our wedding.

Tenor stepped in and pushed up his glasses. "Hey, mind if I give the DJ the okay to call it? He's worried about the weather moving in."

"Call it," Myles answered. "Everyone can stay as long as they want. We can move the party into the house."

"Most everyone wants to give the happy couple their privacy. Speaking as a brother who can read your expression when you look at your new wife, I'm fine leaving sooner rather than later." He grinned and left us alone.

"Are you eye-fucking me, Mr. Foster?" I asked.

music stopped.

"It's going to storm tonight," he murmured.

"Mm, it is. You might have to read me a story."

"I've got lots of stories for you, Frosty, but these days I like to have your tits in my hands when I tell them."

I laughed, and he twirled us around. The string lights lit his eyes, adding an extra dose of happiness. "Have I told you lately how much I love you?"

"You'll never tell me too often, Mrs. Foster."

———————

Summer wants to find a love as real as Myles and Wynter's, but when she finds out her fiancé isn't it, she's in a wedding dress and about to walk down the aisle. But she can't flee her wedding and face her family, not yet, so she hides in a cabin with a recluse of a mountain man in Bourbon Runaway.

If you'd like a BONUS epilogue and to learn how Myles and Wynter come up with their baby's name, sign up for my newsletter at walkerrosebooks.com/newsletter and you'll get a link to my bonus content and a free copy of Bourbon Bachelor.

ABOUT THE AUTHOR

I live the dream in my own slice of paradise where I get to enjoy colorful sunsets from my rocking chair while I'm working. I have my very own romance hero with Mr. Rose and there's more than a few little rose buds running around. A couple aren't so little anymore! We keep things interesting with cats and a dog and the critters that roam though the yard (fingers crossed the mountain lions stay away).

walkerrosebooks.com